Caise Closed

By

Patrick McGinty

DEDICATIONS

Don Lee for his courage and grace
Barbara J. Miles for believing in me
Janmarie Dielschneider who got me started writing
Diane O'Leary for being the best fan a writer could ask for
BRM, my editor who called me on my crap and praised me when I needed it
Xena, George, Nelson and all other cats
NBAA Tax Committee: Now you know what I've been doing when I should have been working on taxes

Chapter 1   Breakfast

The sensation of something soft and warm on my right ear was annoying enough to pull me out of my sleep. I opened the one eye not buried in my pillow expecting to see nothing in the dark room. Karen's body should have hidden the clock. Instead, the blue LED numbers glowed 3:48.

Sam again targeted my right ear. From his position on the headboard, there was no defense except to retreat under the covers. Ignoring Sam I surveyed the empty side of the bed wondering why Karen was up so early. Her positioning flight to Denver did not leave until this afternoon.

I listened to the silent house. Was she sleeping in the recliner again?

While I pondered the situation, Sam took action, his fourteen pounds landing on my side. I retained my position, hoping Sam was just seeking warmth and would settle down to rest and we could both go back to sleep. Karen would return to bed if, and when she was ready.

Sam was not here to sleep. I huddled inside my bed sheets as I marveled at the bizarre behavior of cats, my blankets almost penetrated by his claws seeking solid purchase as he made the difficult U-turn. Once turned his intent became clear. He made his way up my side until he reached my shoulder. Defenseless, I watched from the corner of my eye as he extended a paw toward my cheek.

"OK", I conceded.

I rolled to the edge of the bed, spilling Sam to the floor.

Sam advanced down the hall toward his food bowl. He paused, waiting for me to catch up. He repeated this 'advance and wait' procedure several times on the way to the kitchen. Strange. He usually headed directly to the food dish and hollered to me from there.

I groped for the light switch, filled the kitchen with light and noticed the large raccoon eating from Sam's bowl. He gauged the threat I presented, then continued eating, selecting another kibble to moisten in Sam's water bowl.

Being a man of action, I took one step forward. The raccoon reared up like a bear, paws above his head, hissing. Being brave, but not stupid, I stepped back to consider my options. I could stand here hoping the raccoon would leave after his meal or I could force the issue.

The broom leaning against the wall steeled my resolve. Arming myself with this wooden sword, I surveyed the terrain in preparation for my assault.

The raccoon recognizing my superior tactics opted for retreat, dropping to all fours, breaking for the utility room. Pursuing at a safe distance, I moved to cut off any chance of his return.

Two things struck me when I looked into the utility room: there was no raccoon and the sliding glass door was open. He had entered the house through the open back door, stopping in for a midnight snack. Mystery solved.

The motion sensor light illuminated the raccoon as he made his way across the lawn. I tracked his ambling retreat toward the undeveloped brushy gulch dividing the neighborhood. He did not hurry as he entered the shadows at the edge of the light, pausing to sniff at the shapeless mass on the ground near the tomatoes. Dry grass pricked my bare feet as I ran to the white robed figure lying face down on the grass, noting how the robe splayed about, making her look like a misplaced snow angel. I fought down panic as I forced my brain to regress twenty years. You can do this. This is a medical emergency, do what you're trained to do.

I rolled the patient onto her back noting that it was my wife Karen. The weak light hindered my visual assessment of the patient. There were no obvious signs of injury; the patient was not breathing; and her pulse absent. I initiated CPR. I talked myself though the process: extend the neck to open the airway, pinch the nose, cover the mouth with my mouth, administer four quick breaths.

As the last breath escaped, I shifted position to begin cardiac compressions. Right hand atop my left, elbows locked, and rock forward to compress the chest.

I operated on autopilot, defaulting to military training from long ago. I re-assessed the situation as I administered emergency care. The situation was not good: patient in cardiac arrest, single person CPR.

A lone individual cannot perform CPR indefinitely, I needed assistance. Protocol calls for not leaving the patient once CPR is begun, but I had no choice. I finished compression fifteen and lurched to my feet, catching my toe on the garden hose and stumbling my way to the cordless phone in the kitchen. I was almost back to the patient when I heard the 911 operator answer.

"Medical Emergency" I shouted not waiting for her to finish her initial question.

2

I winched, my knee coming down a little too fast on the hard dry turf. Two breaths and 15 chest compressions later I picked up the phone for a second.

"One, six, five, eight, one Devon Circle; 40 year old female; not breathing, no pulse, single person CPR in progress."

I performed two more CPR sets before adding: "patient location is behind house."

The operator was asking more questions, questions that I couldn't hear, questions that didn't matter. I concentrated on my CPR technique: elbows locked, count each compression out loud, two breaths, elbows locked, count compressions, two breaths. Pace yourself, do not panic, they will come. Lock elbows, count, breathe, again...

"Sir, can you hear me?"

My voice was muffled as I responded, then I realized it was the paper bag over my mouth distorting my response.

"Sir, keep breathing into the bag."

Dry grass scratching my bare back told me I was lying on the lawn.

"Can you hold on to the bag?"

I located my hands and secured the bag as he watched to make sure I could handle the task. Satisfied he headed to the ambulance, returning with the gurney for Karen.

Help had come.

An EMT intercepted me as I wobbled toward the ambulance. I accepted his support and his help getting in. He positioned me on the second stretcher, out of their way. The other two EMTs worked on the patient with precise actions, minimal talk and no wasted movements. I crushed the paper bag, not needing it but not knowing where to put it. The driver closed one door and moved to my side of the ambulance. He handed me a blanket and closed the door. I sat watching the other EMTs work on the patient.

We were almost to the emergency room when they stopped CPR.

Chapter 2   Emergency

Sitting in an exam room I had lots of time to contemplate what I could have done, what I should have done. I fought to hold on to my detached 'medical professional' persona. It was too much to think of the body lying on the gurney as Karen.

What did the ER staff think about my stoic behavior? Should I be publicly grieving, like some of the patients families I met years ago? No, for me grief is a private matter. Besides, even though there was a dead patient lying on a stretcher, I could not come to terms with the fact that the body had been someone with whom I had been close.

For now, I could second-guess my actions.

Would she have lived if I had done more CPR before calling? Should I have run to the neighbor? Did my efforts cause more harm than good?

The rational response was no. They called the code before we reached the hospital. She was dead when I found her.

I sat, reinforcing my rationalizations, waiting for the administrative process to complete. The events of the last hours conformed to my long ago memories from when I was the one working the ER. The doctor confirmed Karen was still DOA while an aide issued me scrubs and a new blanket. The doctor took a few minutes away from the only other patient in the ER to confirm I suffered no ill effect from hyperventilation. Two registered nurses emerged from Karen's exam room as I returned with coffee from the nurse's station. One nurse carried the bag of Karen's effects. I used to leave the personal belongings on the tray beneath stretcher cushion. Times change, I guess.

Back in my exam room, I was not exactly sure what I should be doing, other than waiting for the paperwork. I had not looked at her since they covered her with the sheet. Pacing did not help and the coffee cup was now a hundred small pieces of plastic foam. I was finishing my second detailed examination of every item in the room when there was a light knock. Was it the nurse with the final paperwork? No, it was the Sheriff's deputy.

He entered, offering me one of the two cups of coffee in his hands. I accepted more to have something to do with my hands than because I wanted more coffee.

He introduced himself as Deputy Miller, a large man, bear-like but surprisingly soft spoken. I told my story, starting with waking up alone and finding a raccoon in the kitchen. He listened.

After consoling me again for my loss, he asked if I wanted another blanket.

"Thanks, yes I would."

He was gone for a minute, returning with a warm blanket. Even in August, the hospital scrubs I got from the ER technician were a little too light when not wearing shoes. The heat from the warm blanket was just beginning to seep through when Deputy Miller started asking questions. Was it unusual for Karen to get up at night? Had Karen suffered from illnesses? Was her behavior unusual?

He seemed to finish a line of questions, begin a new line of questions and somehow end up at the first line of questions again. Had she seen her family lately? Were there any problems at work? Did she receive unusual phone calls or correspondence? Was she active on internet social networking sites?

"How often did your wife get up in the middle of the night?"

"Every time she has the 0600 flight to Denver, she is a pilot. Pilots work weird hours. Are we going to go through this again?"

Instead, he asked a new question: "Were you and your wife getting along?"

"What? Yes, we got along. Sure, it's hard when your wife travels, but we did OK."

"Then you would be surprised to know that someone meant your wife harm?"

"Yes."

Deputy Miller rose from the visitor's chair and walked to the head of the stretcher. He lifted the sheet and drew it back enough to expose Karen's head and shoulders.

"So then you know nothing about this?"

Karen looked like a forty-year-old woman without make-up, her short hair mussed, strewn with several of blades of dry grass. Her face held a neutral expression, free from marks or flaws. The jaw and neck appeared normal, except for the red area around the Adam's apple. Leaning closer, the skin looked chapped, discolored, as if bruises would soon appear. I straightened, mouth open, no words coming out. Deputy Miller was not so restricted.

"You have the right to remain silent, anything you say can and will be used against you..."

It's funny the details you notice in a crisis. Deputy Miller had casually positioned himself between the door and me while I was looking at Karen. He moved behind me, asked for my right hand. Not waiting, he grasped my wrist. The steel of the cuff cool then tight on my wrist. He pulled my left arm back to join my right and the cuff clicked again.

Miller steered me out the exam room toward the ER lobby. "I am placing you under arrest for the murder of your wife, Karen Winslow-Caise. You have the right to remain silent, anything you say can and will be used against you..."

Why recite my Miranda Rights again, unless you wanted to do it in front of the ER staff in order to ensure witnesses to the event? The staff watched me 'the killer' and the Deputy Sheriff parade past the nurse's station, through the lobby and out the door. Hand firmly on my elbow, I tried to pick a rock-free route as he steered me to his car. The unofficial parking space was a long 50 feet from the entrance for my bare feet.

By the time we got to the car I realized how important my arms were to my balance. The Deputy understood and issued specific instructions on turning and sitting. "Watch your head when you slide onto the seat."

He steadied my balance and put a hand on top of my head, just like on TV, to make sure I did not strike the doorframe. The drive to the jail was disturbing. Not only was I was off balance, the stress on my arms was becoming uncomfortable. We proceeded the few miles to the Clark County Jail through the increasing morning traffic. He did not stop in a parking space. Instead, we drove around to the back of the building and through a garage door. Miller waited until the garage door fully closed before guiding me out of the car.

At the windowless metal door, he pushed a stainless steel button and a voice from the speaker addressed us. "Hi Dennis, come on in."

He strained against the heavy door after hearing a buzzer produce a grinding electrical sound. The door slammed and the lock clicked, confining us in a short hall that had another metal door and another stainless steel speaker at the end. Before Miller could push the button, the speaker buzzed and the lock clicked again. He heaved the door open, guiding me into a larger room with an *L* shaped equipment console in one corner and a shelf along one wall.

To the side were two small rooms, doors open. The closest room seemed to be a holding cell, based upon the stainless steel tray attached to the wall that could serve as a bench or a bed. Deputy Miller did not give me much time to observe the sights as he introduced me to the jailer.

"Hi Samantha, this is Mr. Caise, husband of the homicide this morning."

Samantha looked to me, all business. "OK Mr. Caise, let's get you into the system, last name."

"Case, C – A – I – S – E."

"First."

"Justin."

"J – U – S – T – I – N?"

"Yes."

"Middle name?"

"Thurgood, T-H-U-R-G-O-O-D"

"Do you have any aliases?"

"No."

The questions and answers continued: date of birth, social security number, address, and what tattoos, piercings or other distinguishing marks adorned my body.

Deputy Miller removed the cuffs and directed me to stand, facing the shelf.

The jailer commanded: "I am going to take your fingerprints. Let me do all the work and don't try and help me."

She grasped the palm and little finger of my right hand, twisted the hand almost vertical, pushed the last finger segment onto a black sticky inked pad, then rolled my finger from vertical to horizontal, coating half my little finger with ink.

"Just relax Mr. Caise, don't try to help me."

Telling me not to assist made it harder for me to relax.

She positioned the finger above the blank finger print card, twisted the hand almost vertical, pressed the last segment of my little finger onto the white card, and untwisted my hand, rolling the fingertip across the fingerprint card, leaving an impression of my fingerprint.

We repeated this for all fingers on the right hand, with Samantha reminding me not to help several times. She finished the thumb with a twist that required me to rotate what felt like 360 degrees and then she looked hard at the impressions.

"Nope, I smudged the ring finger. Please, just relax, let me do the work and we will get this over with."

Not used to having my extremities forced into contorted positions I found it difficult to relax and let the officer do the work. I concentrated on making my arm limp and we repeated the process.

This time the right hand and the full finger impression passed her examination. I was starting to get the hang of things and the left hand was a first time success.

"Step over here, toes on the line. Hold the placard a little higher. Good, now turn to your left, done."

The mug shots completed, Deputy Miller recited my Miranda Rights again and asked if I was willing to talk to him. I was still trying to understand what had happened and agreed to, so we entered the second room that held a small table and chairs. We sat. I wanted answers.

"Why am I under arrest?"

Miller replied, "You are married to Karen Elaine Winslow-Caise?"

"Yes, you know that, why am I under arrest?"

"Why don't you tell me what happened and I will see if I can explain why you are here."

"I told you at the hospital, I woke up about four and Karen was not in bed. When I got to the kitchen there was a raccoon eating the cat's food and I shooed him out the back door. The raccoon tripped the motion sensor light. I saw Karen lying face down in the grass. I ran out to her and did CPR until I passed out."

"You didn't call for help?"

"I did, I ran back to the house for the phone and called 911."

"I mean for the neighbors, didn't you try to wake the neighbors?"

"I might have, I don't remember, I was trying to remember how to do CPR from training I got twenty years ago. I might have called out. I don't remember."

"It probably wouldn't have mattered, Ed is eighty and almost deaf. Mrs. Jackson is not much younger. Her house is always sealed up for the air conditioning."

"I couldn't leave Karen. You never stop CPR once you start."

"Yet you stopped to go get your phone?"

"I had to, I had to get help. I couldn't do CPR all night by myself."

"That's why the EMT's found you passed out on the lawn?"

"Yes, it was taking so long for the ambulance. I was getting

8

so weak and dizzy, it was getting hard to breathe and my heart was pounding. The next thing I remembered was the EMT holding a paper bag over my mouth."

"You didn't notice anything strange about your wife?"

"Strange, what's strange about finding your wife face down on the lawn in the middle of the night? I don't think this conversation is going anywhere, I'm done."

"So is your wife Mr. Caise, one more question. Did you plan to use the garden hose to strangle her or was it just the first thing that came to mind?"

"I have nothing more to say to you. I want a lawyer."

Chapter 4   Rules

They closed the door on the meeting room and left me sitting for a couple of minutes. A new corrections officer came and removed me from the room, gave me jail clothes and escorted me to a cell.

The guard told me to stand still and moved to unlock the door to the cell.

"Hey, what about my phone call? I have a right to call an attorney!"

"Rights, you'll have rights when I decide to give you rights," the guard said in a cool and controlling manner.

He had a command voice, something I had not heard in years. It was the middle of the night almost twenty years ago. Half asleep, half-awake I realized the loud demanding man telling me to put my toes on the line was not a bad dream. About forty of us were reeling from our first exposure to Army boot camp.

The disorientation in basic training is intentional. They want you to realize as quickly as possible that you are in a different world with different rules. I was coming to the realization that jail is a completely different world, and I had better figure out the rules quickly.

Rule: the jail is a command and control environment. If you fight the system, the system will fight back devoting whatever resources necessary to suppress your protest.

Rule: system components expect and require that subordinates demonstrate the respect that their rank requires.

Rule: you can eventually get what you want if you work within the system's rules.

Conclusion: It was time to salute the uniform and ignore the man. "Officer," I uttered in the calmest voice I could manage.

"Yes."

"Would it be possible for me to call my attorney today?"

The guard let a hint of a smile escape from the corner of his mouth.

"When they are done cleaning up from breakfast, the work crews are in place and today's defendants are off to court, I might be able to get you to a phone."

"Thank you."

The heavy door settled into place with a clang and the lock clicked to engage. Then there was soft scraping noise as the peephole opened.

"You seem like a smart man, here's a dimes worth of free advice. If you do what you are told, we'll get along just fine. Buck the system and you will be amazed at how unpleasant I can make your life."

"Yes, officer."

"You should be able to make that call in an hour or so."

"Thank you," I replied as the peephole scratched shut.

I turned away from the door and surveyed my domain, all 48 square feet. I could almost touch both walls if I stretched hard with my arms, say about six feet, and the stainless bed shelf was about 18 inches short of the back wall, providing just enough space for a wash basin/drinking fountain directly across from the stainless seat less commode.

For the first time in hours, how many I was not sure, I had time to think; no doctors, no police, no dead body, just me in my cell. What did I know about my situation?

My wife was dead, worse she had been murdered, and I was the most obvious suspect. I needed a criminal attorney.

However, who do I call? Unlike our doctor or our accountant, how many of us have an ongoing relationship with an attorney? If you like your dentist, you keep going back. When you find a tax preparer you like, you return every spring.

How many of us need an attorney on a regular basis? After your will is done and you have bought your house, the only contact most of us have with attorneys is when something bad happens. I could think of only two attorneys with whom I had any type of personal relationship: one I paid $500 to review the purchase contract and title for my house, the other is a corporate attorney for Lithium Energy Resources.

What it came down to was I needed an attorney and had no idea how to choose one. When the guard handed me the phone, who would I call?

I dreaded the thought of calling an attorney at random from the phone book.

How long before I could make a call? I looked at my wristwatch and realized it was on the nightstand next to my bed. There was no clock in the cell. The last clock I could remember was in booking, about 0730. For me to be without a clock was an assault on my reality. There had been a watch on my wrist since sixth grade. Without physical confirmation time seemed to stop. Was I on the verge of panic, or was I coming to grip with it the possibility that I many never get out of here?

Chapter 5   Human Resources

Alone in my cell I could not hide from reality. There was a good chance they could convict me of murder. The more I thought of the case the sheriff could build against me the more I wanted to crawl into to the fetal position.

I could hear the prosecutor summarizing the case: Not only did he strangle his wife with a garden hose, but also he did it for money. Two months before her death, Karen Elaine Winslow-Caise took out a half million-dollar insurance policy naming her husband as beneficiary.

The fact that the policy was an almost free employee benefit would not matter to the jury. I had watched enough *Perry Mason* reruns on TV to know that the prosecutor would play the money angle for all it was worth. Add that to the argument Karen and I had at Joan and Jerry's barbeque, and I would probably vote to convict me.

The argument was an extension of an ongoing discussion. Karen liked flying the international routes and I thought it was getting too dangerous. When drug lords start slaying people in vacation spots like Cancun and kidnapping becomes a for-profit business it's too dangerous. I did not want her flying in harm's way. I know women have the right to vote and can work any job for which they're qualified, but this was not a "woman", this was my wife, and I was concerned about her safety.

Jerry made an innocent comment about the four of us getting together more often and I agreed a little too enthusiastically. As a senior pilot, Karen could bid on the domestic routes and leave the dangerous South American routes to the younger eager pilots. Karen launched into me: she had worked too hard for too long to get where she was and I knew nothing about being a pilot, she was not giving up everything just because I was afraid to take any risks. We departed as gracefully as possible as soon as possible, leaving Joan and Jerry a lasting memory.

I sat on my bed trying to remember other situations that the prosecutor might bring up when I heard the key in the lock.

The door opened and two officers entered while a third waited outside. The first officer flashed a paper and said "We have a warrant to search your body to obtain DNA and tissue samples."

"Stand, open your mouth."

The second guard wearing blue plastic gloves used a swab to rub the inside of my cheek. The other guard logged the procedure on a sheet and placed half a barcode label on the sheet and half on the bag holding the swab.

"Left hand," the gloved guard grabbed my hand firmly, removed a plastic pick from its wrapper and scraped under all my fingernails while his partner logged and bagged the results. They repeated the procedure with the right hand. I have no idea if they were as gentle as a manicurist was, but they were thorough and efficient.

When done with the nails, the first officer produced a camera and recorded the gloved guard examining my scalp, face, neck, arms and hands. They produced more swabs, which they used to rub the palms of my hands and each finger. They completed the examination by looking at the rest of my body, but thankfully did not take any additional samples. By the time they were done, I felt less like a prize bull and more like a lamb for the slaughter.

Now I had the answer as to why I had not been showered before being placed in my cell.

Again alone, I returned to the question of who to call. My contemplation ceased at the sound of the key. At the door again was Officer 'Mentor', whose real name was Jorstadd, the same guard who dispensed advice earlier and was now directing me down the hall to a large metal door. "Stand there and enter when I tell you."

Officer Mentor applied a key to the lock, swung it open and directed me to enter. There were two small glass walled offices with phones and phonebooks on the shelf. Officer Mentor directed me to the closest office locking the door behind me. From across the room he observed my actions. Pushing the phonebook aside, I dialed.

A young female voice answered: "Lithium Energy Resources, how may I direct you call?"

"Hi Steph, this is Justin Caise, is Mary Ellen Simons available?"

"Oh hi Justin, are you coming in today?"

"No, I won't be in today, that's why I need to talk to Mary Ellen."

"OK, Justin, she just walked in, see you later." Steph disconnected as Mary picked up.

"Good morning, this is Mary Ellen."

"Hi Mary Ellen."

"Justin, Clark was just looking for you, are you coming in

today?"

"Sorry Mary Ellen, but I have a big favor to ask. I need an attorney, a criminal attorney."

"Oh my, are you ok?"

"For the moment, but I need a good attorney and I was hoping Jane could make a call for me."

"What's going on Justin?"

"Karen's dead." The silence on the other end of the line was more dramatic than any gasp.

"I didn't kill her, Mary Ellen, but I am in trouble and I am in jail."

"What can I do?"

"Ask Jane for a criminal attorney referral, someone who can handle a murder case. The attorney needs to come see me at the Clark County jail."

"OK Justin, I just want you to know my prayers are with you, let me get Jane."

"Thanks."

"Mary Ellen? I have to ask, how does my problem affect me at Lithium?"

"Officially Justin, the employee manual only states that we may take into consideration a conviction when determining an employee's continued employment. Since you are only under arrest and not convicted it is not an issue, for now. It will become an issue when you have exhausted your vacation, which from what I see in the system, you still have 14 days."

"Thanks Mary Ellen."

"Justin, right now vacation time is the least important issue. Is there anything else I can do?"

"Unfortunately, no,"

I paused, considering whether I should say it. "I didn't kill Karen."

"I know Justin."

"Stay safe, here's Jane. "

Chapter 6   You Have a Right

Knowing that one person believed me was a big boost to my battered psyche. I respected Mary Ellen, she was tough but fair, and would believe me until evidence arose to prove otherwise. I could not ask for more than that.

Back in my cell, I sat on the bed, leaned back into the wall and felt like a balloon deflating. The intensity of the last eight hours had nearly consumed me emotionally and now I did not want to think. I just sat there collapsing into my bed, moving ever closer to the fetal position.

A week ago, if someone had told me I could fall sleep just hours after finding my wife dead, I would not have believed it. I must have slept as Officer Mentor was at the open door calling my name, "Caise, lunchtime! Nobody's going to bring to you if you don't get up now! Either stand on the yellow line, or go back to sleep."

I roused myself, stood on the yellow line when told, marched to the dining area when told, ate when I was told, and returned to my cell when I was told. Such were the new rules.

In my fantasy, my new lawyer was speeding to the jail five minutes after my call to Jane. In my reality, I was sitting on my bed, fully awake, straining for the sound of a key in the lock. Unfortunately, the next key sound was for dinner not my attorney. I toed the yellow line, paraded to dinner and return to my cell growing more concerned that all the good attorneys that Jane knew were too busy to see me.

Rationally, I knew that attorneys are very busy, subject to many demands, and multiple deadlines. Irrationally I wanted my attorney to drop everything and come see me, now.

It was a few thousand heartbeats after dinner when the sound of the key returned and Officer Unhappy opened my door. Officer Unhappy was a man who looked like he had used up his allotment of happiness in childhood, and nothing would ever again bring joy to his life again. He uttered one command, "Visitor."

Officer Unhappy expected me to know the rules by now. Toes on the yellow line I waited. He locked the cell door.

We proceeded down the hall through several looked doors almost to the phone room. Lining the hall were three glass walled rooms. Officer Unhappy unlocked the first room, opened the door, and locked me inside. Beyond the plastic chair was a large window. Behind the glass was a woman pointing at the phone on my wall. I

15

had met my attorney.

"Justin Caise?"

"Yes."

"My name is Anne Schwartz. I went to law school with Jane Marshall. She asked me to come visit you. How are you doing?"

"It's been a long day. It is still hard to believe it really happened. I mean I wake up in the middle of the night and find my wife dead. Then I can't believe they arrested me in the hospital. Can they do that? Don't they have to do an investigation first? Then they strip searched me and took tissue samples. Does that mean I am stuck in here until my trial? What about evidence, what proof do they have, they didn't really even ask for my side of the story. Are they looking for the real killer? What if it was some homeless guy, how would they ever find him? When am I...?"

"Calm down Mr. Caise! Listen to me."

"But what..."

"JUSTIN, SIT DOWN!"

Every emotion suppressed from this morning had returned with a vengeance. I leaned back, removed my hand from the glass and lowered myself into the chair.

"Justin, I know this is difficult. You have never been in jail before and you are in a state of shock. Now just sit there and listen to me for a minute."

"OK."

"I know you are upset and you want to tell me everything, but there is time for that later. Let me tell you what's going to happen tomorrow."

"Tomorrow morning, we will go before a judge where you will be arraigned, that is, officially charged with a crime. When that happens, I will ask for bail. My job will be to get bail set as low as possible."

"To do that here's what I need to know: What is it about you that will make the Judge feel OK about letting you loose? What ties do you have to the community?"

"I have lived in the state for almost twenty years, I moved here after I got out of the Army. I am not the social type so I don't belong to any clubs other than Toastmasters. I have a small group of friends and I get along well with my neighbors."

"Do you own your house?"

"Yes, Karen and I bought a house three years ago. I sold a small place I owned out in East Clark County. I rolled the equity into the new house closer to the airport."

"That's nice. What about family?"

"Karen was an only child. All of our parents were dead before I met her. Neither of us brought any kids into the marriage and it was the first marriage for both of us. I have a sister in Iowa who joined a cult and a brother in Wisconsin who last I heard lived on skid row, we don't talk."

"What about employment?"

"Karen is, was, a pilot for Value America Airlines, and I work for Lithium Energy Resources as a tax accountant. That's how I know Jane Marshall."

"Now Justin, briefly tell me what happened, we'll go over this in much more detail after tomorrow, but for now, I need just enough to get you out on bail."

I was calm enough now to give a concise account of today's events. Anne listened and took notes. Asked for more detail when I got to the part about Deputy Miller asking additional questions after giving me Miranda rights, but otherwise was silent.

"OK, Justin. I will see you tomorrow morning."

"You really think I can get out tomorrow?"

"No promises Justin. The court has a mind of its own and the DA will fight to keep you here, if for nothing more than to be seen as standing tough on crime. The most important thing you need to do now is not discuss this case with anyone. I mean anyone, not the guards, not the other prisoners, not your brother or sister, not anyone. You have the right to remain silent, use it. See you tomorrow."

Anne hung up, placed a file in her briefcase, and left me sitting in the small glass walled room. I did not have long to wait until Officer Unhappy returned to take me back to my cell for the night.

I woke up in a sweat with the ceiling looking the same as it did at lights out last night. The only dream I remembered involved a large raccoon dragging Karen off into the brush, and hard as I ran, I could not catch up.

I assumed it was six thirty or seven when Officer Mentor opened the cell to escort me to breakfast. Today's variety of starch options were plopped on my plastic tray. I consumed a fair amount of the cream of grain mush and a slice of white bread seasoned with oily yellow spread.

Now that I had somewhere to go, time inside my cell dragged even more.

When Officer Mentor appeared at my cell, Officer Handy accompanied him. His job was to attach a belly chain: handcuff each prisoner to the belly chain, attach leg irons, and finally attach the leg irons to a trip line that forced us to walk in short steps.

The four of us shuffled down the hall through several locked doors and finally into the courthouse next door. The elevator transported us to the third floor where we followed the blue line on the floor to a staging room attached to the courtroom. Officer Handy detached us from the trip line and seated us on a bench in front of the railing that separated the trial area from the gallery. Our escorts took up positions by the only two exits to the courtroom.

The judge entered. The bailiff brought us to our feet. We had barely settled back down on our bench when the bailiff called the first defendant's name and case number. The DA read the charging document to the court, which prompted the Judge to address a defendant. This methamphetamine dealer, possession with intent to distribute, did not look like she could come up with the $40,000 bond ordered by the judge. The guy with the swollen face probably could not come up with $7500 for his assault charge, nor would the possession with intent to distribute heroin make his $25,000 bond.

My attorney sat at the attorney's table, writing on a yellow legal pad. The assistant DA read from my charging document. All I heard was "Murder in the First Degree."

The DA paused for effect, "In light of the severity of the crime the State requests bail in the amount of $2 Million.

Anne was out of her seat, "Your Honor!"

"The District Attorney is jumping the gun, not only was my

client arrested well before completion of the preliminary investigation, he was arrested before the autopsy was even started. Now the District Attorney is seeking excessive bail for a suspect with no prior record and substantial community ties who poses no flight risk."

"Your Honor, this is an obvious case of homicide. The signs of strangulation are text book and the paramedics were unable to intubate the victim due to the severe damage to the larynx."

"As for not being a flight risk, pursuant to a subsequent warrant issued yesterday, the sheriff discovered in excess of four hundred thousand dollars cash hidden in a fake spare tire in the defendant's car. That most definitely indicates, if not proves, an intention to flee."

"Your honor this is new information, my client is not prepared to respond at this time. I reserve the right to address release at a further date."

"The defendant is to be held on $2 million bail cash or bond, remand. Next case."

Chapter 8   Anne

The sound of the judge's gavel was still bouncing off the inside of my skull as we shuffled back to jail.

A half million dollars on a tax return is just a large number. Four hundred thousand dollars in the trunk of my car was unimaginable. What would that look like? Wouldn't that fill the car trunk? Who would have put so much money in my car and why?

Back in my cell, I was still trying to make sense of the money when the key hit the lock.

"Caise, you have a visitor."

A scowling attorney met my eyes as I sat and picked up the phone.

"Mr. Caise, a little detail like four hundred thousand dollars in cash would have been of interest to me. Are there any other little details that you think I might need to know?"

"I swear Ms. Schwartz, this is the first I knew about this. I've never seen that much money."

"Any idea at all where it might have come from?"

"None, do you know in which car they found it?"

"Yes, inside the spare tire of the RX-7."

"That's Karen's car."

"She loved that car. An '84 stick with a removable sunroof. This spring she complained about having to rebuild the steering box. If you hit a curb a little too hard it throws the rack and pinion out of alignment causing the gear to wear unevenly. She said driving it was like sailing a ship in heavy seas."

"It seemed like she was always taking it to this guy at Rafael's Metro Motors. She would never let anyone else touch it, including me."

"Well, somebody touched that car. Somebody put more than 4,000 bills inside the spare tire. The RX-7 is old enough that it has a full size 14" spare tire, not a tiny donut spare. That full size spare was a good choice, four hundred thousand dollars takes up a lot of room."

"What car did you use when you went places together?"

"We always drove my Toyota."

"Are you are sure you know nothing about the money?"

"No, nothing."

"Do you have any idea where she might have gotten that much money? Could she have received an inheritance, or an insurance settlement or money from a lawsuit?"

"Karen never talked about relatives or family of any type. If she was not flying, she was home. She liked to work in the flower beds and was always planting new flowers and bushes, but she didn't have much of a green thumb."

"Focus, Justin."

"Did she have many friends, get along with the neighbors?"

"Not really, like me she was not very social. There was only one couple we would visit on a regular basis. I work with Joan Beardsley at Lithium where she is the Accounts Payable Manager. She and Jerry never had or could not have kids. When I got married, she and Jerry began inviting us over. Then Jerry convinced me to take up golf and we played when Karen was flying."

"Ed is our neighbor on the south side and he is almost eighty. He and Karen did not seem to have much in common. Ed would try to give Karen gardening advice, which she never took. Mrs. Jackson lives on the north side and doesn't like the heat, and doesn't like the cold, so she spends most of her time in her house. Her daughters live in Texas and Florida so she does not have many visitors."

"Justin, if I had the books at Lithium Energy audited, would they find any money missing?"

"If they did, it wouldn't be due to me. I work in Tax, and yes, we write some big checks, but all in accordance with our internal controls. The financial auditors rarely have any issues when they reviewed the corporate tax provision. The tax department deals with too many external agencies that complain if they don't get their money. There is just too much of a paper trail for it to be a good place from which to embezzle."

"What's your point Justin?"

"To run a good embezzlement fraud, you need at least two people on the inside and at least one on the outside. I was never willing to take a risk like that and maybe end up in--someplace like this."

"Ok, so your point is you did not steal anything from Lithium Energy and you have no idea where the money came from."

"That's right Ms. Schwartz."

"Justin, listen to me. Here is your homework assignment: remember every detail about your wife."

"OK, do you mean like her favorite color and that sort of thing?"

"I mean everything Justin. Ask the guard for some paper so you can write your attorney. At the top of every page, you must write "legal mail." If you don't do that, they can confiscate or copy anything you write."

"Also, don't say anything to anyone about your case."

"OK, why?"

"Do you remember the sign in the meeting room on the wall above the phone?"

"Not really Anne, I was not noticing the décor."

"I'll tell you: All telephone calls are recorded and listened to by bored jail staff -- Except for calls to attorneys.

"Really, they can do that?"

"Justin, you left your First Amendment rights at the door when you got here. Anything you say can and will be used against you."

"I'll remember that."

"See that you do and one more thing to think about this weekend, I'll need $50,000 in order to continue representing you in this case. That is to get started."

"I'll see you Tuesday at the bail hearing." Said Anne, hanging up the phone a little harder than necessary.

Chapter 9   Karen

What a way to start a relationship with the person who controls your destiny. Anne was obviously convinced that I was lying. How would I be able to overcome that taint?

My contemplation about my attorney gave way to thoughts about my relationship with Karen. What can one person really know about another person? I tried to assemble a word picture of Karen, but all the words that came to mind were better suited to a resume than a description of a spouse.

I was 43 when we met. A classic geek accountant type, heterosexual but never married, never very comfortable around women. My dating history seemed to consist of women who were coming out of a stormy relationship and were looking for stability after too much excitement and uncertainty. These girlfriends enjoyed my feet on the ground, strong as a rock stability until they got bored.

For my part, I was a moth to the flame. The allure of a flashy flamboyant girlfriend was an irresistible attraction. Like a good rooster, I would display my mating plumage and invariably fail to attract the hen of my dreams because another cock with brighter colors would swoop in and steal her away. I was only able to attract these women after they broke up with Mister Wrong.

Friends tried to direct me to sensible girls, some of whom I would date. These good girls quickly noticed my inability to fake sincerity and my lack of serious interest. Eventually I concluded that the only reason to get married was to have kids. So somewhere, in my thirties, I came to the realization that the emotional trauma was not worth the prize and dating dried up.

Into this emotional desert walked Karen.

Surprise, we met at the airport. I was enjoying a preflight coffee from the Coffee People stand before boarding my once a year flight to my tax conference. I was working on a Sudoku puzzle at a stand up table in front of the coffee shop. A woman in a pilot's uniform was at the next table. She was attractive with short pilot length hair. Pilots always seen to wear their hair short: is that because they are afraid that it will get stuck in the controls in an emergency? She was out of her twenties and probably losing her grip on the thirties but still, she was an attractive flame.

Rationality prevailed and I wrote her off as unattainable and returned my attention to my number puzzle. I looked up when something entered my peripheral vision.

"Excuse me, I am sorry to bother you, but my pen just died. Would it be possible to borrow yours for just a minute? I need to make some notes on my preflight paperwork."

"Oh, by all means. Use this one," I said, pulling out another pen, the nice one I only carried on special occasions.

After thanking me, she made couple of notes on some paperwork then put her flight bag on the chair and looked through it, removing another document.

She worked for a couple of minutes, referencing the document from her bag. Then she packed up.

"Thank you so much. Enjoy your trip," she said as she smiled and returned my pen.

"Happy landings," was all I could think of saying, as she grabbed her flight bag and headed down the concourse.

It was several, no more than five minutes later when I heard her phone ring. It was still on the chair where she had placed her flight bag. Evidently, she took it out when she was looking in the bag and failed to return it. I looked down both concourses seeing several pilots but not her.

The phone stopped ringing as I picked it up. It was a modest flip phone with minimal features. There was no indication of a message maybe it was an alarm.

Portland International is not a massive airport like O'Hare or JFK. Still, there were about 40 gates between the two concourses joined by the Coffee People stand. I was doubtful I could find her at one of those 40 gates. I did not know her airline, and I only had minutes before boarding my own flight.

What should I do keep it or take it to lost and found?

What would I do if I lost my phone? If I didn't think it had been stolen, I would call my phone and see who answered, then play it from there.

Time was running out for my flight. In addition, since I did not know the location of the lost and found, I decided to hang on to the phone and see what happened.

Four hours later in Minneapolis, the phone did not show that there had been any calls. I killed a couple of hours in my hotel room and then made ready for the evening's meet and greet session. One of the big Minnesota law firms laid out the goodies for the reception. It must have been a tough year since they did not have the ice sculpture full of shrimp like last year. Still the stuffed mushrooms were good and I got my fill of hors d'oeuvres and several glasses of wine.

Being the party animal I am I was in my room by 9 pm. The phone indicated that someone called, I hit the callback.

"Hello?" a female voice offered.

"Good evening, my name is Justin Caise. I believe I found your phone today in Portland. That is if you are the woman who lost it."

"Were you the man doing Sudoku this morning at Coffee People stand?"

"Yes, I loaned you my pen."

"Thank you. Forgive me, but I wanted to make sure that you were the person I thought you were and not some criminal type. A gal can't be too careful, you know."

I engaged full wit mode and responded to her crime comment. "The last time I checked I was not a criminal, though some would consider it a crime that I am a Tax Accountant."

She laughed in response and she continued, "I want to thank you for finding my phone. I do not care about the phone, it's the contacts that are hard to replace. I know I should have it backed up, but now I'll make a point to get that done."

"Oh, no problem, I am glad I can help. All that needs to be done is to work out the logistics of getting it back to you."

"Mr. Caise, do you come to Portland often? We could meet up when you pass through."

"Please, call me Justin. Actually, I live across the river in Vancouver and it's no problem for me to get to the airport."

"Why thank you. But really, that is too much for me to ask."

"I assume you fly through Portland regularly, how about if you buy me dinner, would that relieve your sense of obligation? That is, if your husband does not mind?"

It is amazing what you can remember, or believe you are remembering, when you have unlimited uninterrupted time to reminisce. Back then, her flame was bright in my moth eyes and I was more attracted to her than I had been to any other woman in a long time. Maybe it was the fact that she was more unattainable, a woman with adventurous demands on her that would separate us. I think part of it was the command presence that captains exude, the air of a person used to giving orders and having them obeyed. Had I allowed myself to become lonely grasping at any friendly hand offered?

"That's no issue, Justin. I think dinner is a great idea. My terminal leg into Portland this time is Thursday night, how about Friday evening? Did you have any place in mind?

25

We agreed to meet at a restaurant she suggested, one of those Mongolian grill restaurants where the cooks use a mushroom-shaped grill to cook the items you select. The restaurant had a neutral open family atmosphere, not too intimate, with a slight amount of entertainment provided by watching the authentic Mongolian cooks. All I remember about the meal was that Karen laughed at all my jokes and seemed to smile a lot. I asked if I could see her again and she said yes, as schedules permitted. I handed back her phone to her and she gave me a hug, then she was gone.

The bowls were overflowing: the left hand bowl was filled with broccoli, sliced carrots, green onion, water chestnuts and noodles all soaking in lime juice and curry. The right hand bowl held thin slices of lamb, beef, turkey, chicken and sturgeon swimming in a sauce of oyster, teriyaki, pineapple juice and hot oil. My forearms were slick to the elbow with sauces flowing out of the bowls adding to the puddle on the floor.

A skating rink was not as slick as the puddle surrounding me. Any movement not perfectly balanced could cause my feet to slip out from under me. All this focus on balance distracted me from my goal of getting the cooks to notice me. People around me handed off their bowls and the cooks who ran to the huge grill. Everyone was getting food cooked except me.

I could clearly see cooks amid clouds of steam as they chopped and flipped the food with large spatulas. I could do nothing but hold my sauce dripping bowls while trying to keep my balance.

One cook out of the hundreds shouted something in Mongolian and pointed. Behind me was a sign, "Please tip cooks before cooking."

A tip, how could I tip the cooks when my money was in my pocket and my hands were full? In desperation, I balanced both bowls in my left hand. My right hand searched my pocket full of oil and managed to extract a dollar for the tip bowl.

The head Mongolian cook yelled at me and pointed at the tip bowl.

"Two, you must have two," he shouted.

I slid my hand into my back pocket brimming with oil and managed to find another dollar.

"No two, you must have two, two million dollars!" shouted the judge as he slammed the gavel on the bench.

I opened my eyes to fluorescent light, a locked door, and sweat covering my body.

Question, how can an impossible dream be so terrifying? Answer, when based on the truth. The reality was I needed two million dollars in cash or I was staying right here.

Right here was on my bunk in jail on Saturday. In a few minutes, I would discover that Saturday in jail is just like every other day in jail, the high points being the meals. Unlike the other guests I had work to do. On the way back from breakfast, I asked Officer

Smiley for paper and pen so I could write my attorney. He responded with something like "I'll check" and locked me in.

Alone in my office, which sounds better than cell, I returned to the question my attorney asked: "Who was Karen Winslow?"

Part of the answer to that question was money. Our first meeting at the modestly priced restaurant seemed to set a precedent. When we went out it was rarely to an upscale establishment. Being a traditional 'man pays on a date' kind of guy, it did not bother me, and in fact, it appealed to my down to earth style. Here was a sensible gal who did not want to fritter away money.

Karen was not a party animal, and I had given up on bars many years ago. In fact, she did not want to go out much at all. She felt that going out was too much like traveling. On her time off she wanted to relax. Thinking back, her comment would end with something like "relax with you," but now it just ended in "relax."

She seemed to find her job as a pilot increasingly stressful. She was willing to discuss the operational conditions of a flight, but was very good at diverting the conversation away from non-flight activities. Her general refrain was that 12 to 16 hours on the ground does not leave much time for sightseeing and hot spots. In addition, she had been on this general route for years so she had done all the tourist trips long ago.

When she was flying, she prided herself on her skill at spending less than her allotted per diem on meals, but I was never clear about what happened to the excess meal money. Nor did I know very much about her other expenditures because we agreed, or was it Karen demanded and I conceded, to have three bank accounts: hers, the household account and mine. Finances were not a favorite topic of Karen's and she was content to let the accountant manage the household finances.

Strange, when finances did come up it seemed that Karen was traveling and needed funds for some special expense. The usual result of these long distance conversations was that I covered her contribution to some household expense and she never got around to reimbursing the house account or me. These shortfalls did not happen often enough that I became resentful, but they percolated in the back of my mind. I suppressed the bubbling doubts because, after all, we were a partnership. The accountant in me wondered how someone who made more money than I did could run short.

The few times I did inquire about her money, she stressed

that she was maximizing her 401(k) and other retirement investments so she could retire early. So she could retire. Looking back and reviewing our talks did she ever say, "So we could retire," or was it always "so she could retire?"

Was I distorting the past in order to make sense of my current situation, or was I a naive chump involved in a game more complicated than I could imagine? Were there other traits of Karen's that I was ignoring or activities that I refused to see? What I did know was that money was important to Karen and she had less than my accountant brain thought reasonable.

Drugs and alcohol are two common ways to spend a lot of money. Stories abound of loved ones not knowing that their spouse was a drug user or an alcoholic. Karen never drank to excess, at least never around me. Even in Las Vegas when we got married, she nursed the free drinks and usually ordered juice. As for coke, meth, or some other drug, I counted on the Department of Transportation drug testing to prevent those habits.

Karen was not a fan of testing. She considered it overkill and an invasion of privacy. Her airline stressed safety and their policy was a 100% annual test for all flight crews in conjunction with the FAA required 50% annual random tests for all safety sensitive personnel. Testing was administered by an FAA certified contractor with which the airline had a nationwide contract. She particularly disliked the way the contractor would grab one or all of the flight crew at the gate just before departure and take them to the test room for a sample. It was unlikely that Karen was using drugs.

Nor did Karen display any of the characteristics of drug use such as changes in behavior or neglect of appearance.

Karen was always neat and her uniform well kept. She liked the skirt uniform more than the pantsuit. Those skirt uniforms became an issue, not between Karen and me, but for Karen and Sam.

My relationship with Sam preceded my relationship with Karen by about a year. A coworker in accounting told a tale of the sweetest kitty that befriended her the week before. It was just so loving, sweet, and pregnant. Terry was unable or unwilling to locate Miss Kitty's owner and found herself in possession of four new kittens. Terry was a master of the adoption by guilt technique, but I held my ground. Just months earlier my philosopher feline Cato had fallen to kidney disease and I was taking a break from pet ownership.

Terry played the guilt trump card when she brought all four

kittens to work. Her stated mission was to distribute three of the kittens to their new owners, her real purpose more devious. Joyce, Chris and Mary Ann each grabbed one of the domestic short hair kittens. That left Sam as the last of the litter. A black head, white nose, white chin and golden eyes looked down at me from the door of the cage. From his perch on top of the cubicle wall, the last lonely kitten called for his littermates. Desperately, I searched for an excuse.

"I can't take him; I have no way to take him home."

"That's OK; you can borrow my cat carrier." I conceded to the inevitable and accepted my new charge.

Sam got his name because of a television show. The night before Terry's Sun-Tzu pet distribution campaign, I watched a history show about Samuel Adams. The show stressed that he was a propagandist and a rabble-rouser. My kitten ownership was definitely the result of propaganda by Terry, but I hoped that Sam would not be a rabble-rouser.

Subversive is probably a better description, at least in regards to Karen. In the beginning, Sam and I experienced quality male bonding. Sam loved my cat toys and guarded my bed during the day. On cool nights, Sam would lie on or near me, sharing his warmth. In addition, Sam was gracious enough to allow me to live in his house, and provide food and litter box service. Things took a turn for the worse the first time Karen came to the house.

Rather than going out, Karen was fine with getting take out Chinese and renting a movie. We had settled into the couch and started a spy thriller. I thought I heard the sound of kitty kibble crunching in the kitchen. I watched out of the corner of my eye for Sam to enter the great room en-route to the couch staging area. From there he could make the difficult choice of taking the high ground, securing a corner position on a cushion, or occupying my lap.

As Sam cleared the kitchen wall, he was looking to his right and traversing to his left toward us. I know the exact instant he saw Karen, his left foot stopped an inch from the floor as he froze. I think he was trying to figure out how to back up on three feet without putting his left front paw on the floor. After holding his pose for a second, he ran to his right in a half crouch sneak all the way to the base of his cat condominium.

Karen was unaware of Sam's presence until I called him over.

"Oh, you have a cat," she said without emotion.

"You're not allergic are you?"

"No, it is just I have never been around animals much."

"Sam's a sweetheart, you'll love him."

Sam was slowly working his way around the perimeter of the room and shortly was within jump up distance of the couch. He remained in half crouch staring at Karen from around the end of the couch. He remained on the floor for almost a minute evaluating the severity of the threat. Finally, he took a leap of faith onto the back of the couch near my head. Keeping me between him and Karen, he approached and rubbed my temple with his cheek to reassert his ownership. Then he peered around me at Karen.

Karen remained unconcerned and uninterested.

Sam jumped onto the arm of the couch then reached out to place his front paws on my thigh. She was aware of Sam but made no effort to acknowledge his presence. With Sam's four feet in a tight cluster on my left thigh, he leaned forward to sniff while somehow maintaining his balance. Karen ignored Sam, folding her arms across her chest. Sam got within an inch of her bare elbow and recoiled. He paused once, looked over his shoulder to see if I was coming with him, and then proceeded into the kitchen out the cat door into the night.

I thought nothing of the incident.

Over the courtship, Sam and Karen kept their distance. Sam would spend his time outside or on the bed whenever Karen was in the house.

The peaceful coexistence continued until Karen moved in. The decision was more of an evolution, a compilation of small steps rather than a deliberated plan, or was it? How did we conclude that Karen should move in? Who made the decision for Karen to move in? Thinking back without the filter of a live spouse it seems that money was at the center of the decision making process. Why should Karen spend money on a hotel or apartment when she could stay here?

Maybe the move would have gone smoother if all parties had been consulted? The occupation of the house did not go unnoticed by Sam.

"That god damn cat!" cut through my sleep.

"Huh, what's the matter?"

"Your cat just destroyed a twenty dollar pair of panty hose."

"The ones you had hanging on the curtain rod in the shower?"

"Yes that little monster did it on purpose."

31

"Karen, I don't believe that Sam would do that intentionally."

"He would, and he did!"

This was a losing argument so I gave up defending Sam. Instead, I retrieved the torn hose from the garbage the next morning and had two new pair in her drawer the next time she was in town.

After that, Karen bought a special laundry bag so she could wash and dry her hose without fear of an attack by Sam. However, Sam was persistent. He waited for his opportunity and struck effectively and viciously. The skirt never stood a chance.

They make springs to close screen doors. I found they worked on closet doors too.

What was it about Sam and Karen? What did he know that I didn't?

What about Sam, was he ok? What happened to him when I was arrested? Did the sheriff take him into custody when they searched my house? Who was feeding him? Was he locked outside evading coyotes and fighting for his life?

I was still worrying about Sam when the lights went out.

Chapter 11   Employee Benefits

I lay awake for a long time worrying about Sam and woke up to begin worrying again. Here I was worrying about my cat when I was facing life in prison or worse.

I turned my attention back to my letter to Ms. Schwartz. The letter was progressing slowly in part due to the fact the pencil was only three inches long and had no eraser.

Unexpectedly I heard the key in the door and Officer Smiley was soon escorting me to the visitor rooms where my attorney was waiting.

Officer Smiley had secured my pencil, but I retained my only possession, the letter for Ms. Schwartz. She pointed to the base of the window and Officer Smiley pulled out a ring of keys, unlocked a small padlock and lifted a metal cover to reveal a narrow slot wide enough for papers.

"Do you need him to sign anything," asked Smiley?

"Yes," was the muffled reply as Anne nodded her head yes.

Officer Smiley retreated to the exterior and waited, watching through the glass.

"Hello Justin."

"Hi Ms. Schwartz, I didn't expect to see you on a Sunday, but I am happy you are here."

"Well, Mary Ellen and Jane thought I should bring you these papers, which you need to review."

The large flat manila envelope held 15-20 loose pages. The top document was 'Lithium Energy Resources Employee Benefit Plans.' Why on earth, would Mary Ellen send me benefit plan information? Did she want me to remove Karen from the medical plan?

I quickly paged through the document and noted that the last few pages were forms, and then it hit me: 'Request for Withdrawal from a Cash or Deferred Arrangement Plan under Internal Revenue Code Section 401(k) and Section 72(p).'

Mary Ellen had just provided me access to about $107,000.

I never professed to qualify as a benefits plan expert. I barely passed the class in college. The Internal Revenue Code from section 401 to section 417 is incredibly complex with baffling rules, tests and exceptions. One rule is that you cannot take a penalty-free distribution before age 59 and a half.

Right now, the tax consequences from taking a premature distribution were of limited import. If I lost the trial and ended up owing a bunch of tax what would the IRS do, put me in jail?

I was running mandatory withholding calculations in my mind - was the rate still 20%? Anne's knocking on the glass caused me to suspend my calculations. She pointed to the phone hanging from its armored cord.

"Justin, you need to sign the withdrawal form so we can tap your 401(k)."

"I can't believe it. I'd completely forgotten about my 401(k). Does this mean that you will continue to represent me?"

"Yes, Jane called me and said Mary Ellen wanted to meet with me. That impressed me. There aren't many HR Managers who would take the time and make the effort to track me down on a Saturday, especially just to give me some papers she could have mailed, and in reality was not even obligated to provide."

"Justin, I burned out my ability for people to disappoint me a long time ago. That happens when you're a defense attorney. I just hope you don't disappoint them."

"I know it looks bad Ms. Schwartz, but I did not kill my wife."

"I grew up watching *Perry Mason* on TV with my dad. There was one lesson that I learned: Never lie to your attorney. I have not lied to you. I will not lie to you. Even if it makes me look bad I will tell you the facts to the best of my knowledge."

She held my gaze the whole time I was giving my speech, while I was trying to convey as much sincerity as I could muster.

Maybe a great lawyer can defend a client she believes in just as well as the client who "deserves a vigorous defense" under the rules of the bar. I believed that being human she would fight harder for a cause she believed in. The difference might only be 99.9% verse 100%, but that one tenth of one percent might be all the difference I needed.

"You need to sign the papers, Justin." Anne said as she slid a pen thought the slot.

"Is that letter for me?" she added. "Please slide your letter through the slot, and then send the pen back as soon as you are done."

I worked on the forms as Anne read my letter.

I flipped through the pages verifying that all the documents were signed, and then pushed everything back through the slot.

Anne waved to Officer Smiley. He locked the slot cover into place and retreated from the room.

"Justin, are you sure about Karen and her car?"

"Yes Ms. Schwartz, she was very fond of that car."

I let her think a minute then interjected: "The money from my 401(k) will cover your fee, but that leaves me almost two million short for the bail."

"Let's not worry about that till we get through the bail hearing on Tuesday. Do you have any questions?"

"No, I guess not."

"Keep working on your homework assignment. I'll see you Tuesday." Anne hung up and turned toward the door.

It hit me hard. I leaned and rapped my knuckles on the glass. Anne stopped, turned, and then picked up the phone.

"I know this is not within the scope of your duties as an attorney," I stuttered.

"But could you or one of your staff go to my house and check on my cat, Sam?"

The all too familiar scowl faded from Anne's face. I would not say it was a smile, but for the first time since the first bail hearing, she did not look unhappy.

"What does Sam look like?"

"Ed, my neighbor, has a key to the house. Sam is a middle-age male, neutered, short hair, about 14 pounds. He is black and white in a tuxedo pattern, white chin, a white stripe on his nose, and golden eyes."

"There are kitty treats in a plastic pouch in the cabinet closest to the refrigerator. He should be OK as long as he can get in through his cat door. There is a bag of food under microwave in the cabinet below."

"I'll stop by your house on the way home."

"Thank you, Ms. Schwartz."

"Sure thing Justin, and please call me Anne."

Chapter 13   Two Kinds of Games

I returned to my office feeling better than I had in days. Someone was going to look in on Sam and my attorney was no longer openly hostile toward me.

I asked Officer Smiley for a new pencil and some paper so I could continue my homework.

What made Karen the person she was? When I thought about that question, I was disturbed. Once I got beyond her career, how much did I understand about the person I married?

We seemed to be a match. The stereotypical boring accountant paired with an introverted pilot. Neither of us found crowd events appealing. When an activity was available at home or the mall, we chose home.

Since we did not go out much, I introduced her to the game of cribbage. She found it boring. She picked it up quickly enough but cribbage and other card games did not hold her interest. We tried Backgammon, but that was too much a game of luck. Karen said there was little skill required by the players and it was all up to the dice who would win.

Out of curiosity, I bought a five hundred piece, jigsaw puzzle. I left it on the card table about a quarter finished waiting her arrival. She would not stop and sit to work on the puzzle. However, she would pause without sitting, add several pieces then continue her journey. She added pieces each time she walked by. The next evening she was standing at the card table making fair progress. Sam's howl from the utility room alerted me to the fact that it was time for the evening race around the house. He exited the kitchen, slipping only slightly before getting traction on the carpet in the great room. He had a full head of steam as all four feet left the ground. Usually this leap ended on the cat tower or was the lead in to a second leap onto the kitty catwalk between the cat tower and the entertainment center.

This time, Sam landed on the card table only to discover that the loose pieces provided no traction. His momentum was enough to carry him into the puzzle and through the far side. Physics being the law of the land, the puzzle exploded outward and over the edge as Sam slid the length of the table skillfully converting the plummet at the edge into a controlled fall. He walked out of the debris field with his tail held high and ego intact holding a pose that said, "I meant to do that."

I roared in laughter.

Karen stomped out of the room.

Several weeks after Sam's puzzle problem, I asked Karen what kinds of games she liked to play.

She paused, her facial expression all business: "There are only two types of games, Chess and all others."

"Would you like to play?" I asked.

She asked without malice "Are you any good?"

Pumping up my macho, I responded: "I've won a few games."

The fatal wound happened on the 36th move. I conceded on the 45th.

This game was the most serious I have ever seen Karen. She was all business, intent, focused, deliberate. She moved decisively with no second thoughts.

I was lucky to get to the 36th move, she was only curious about how good I could play.

She would never initiate a game, but would play with me if I asked. Play with, is the best description of our games. I never made it past 35 moves after that first game.

When we honeymooned in Las Vegas, she had very little interest in the casino games. She seemed content to watch me play craps, but was quick to urge me to "quit while I was ahead."

The slots held no interest for her. "Why would I play a game where someone programs how much I will win?"

We did go to a couple of shows. One Karen liked was the jousting and staged fighting at the Knights of the Round Table casino. It was impressive and entertaining to watch the knights ride horses at full speed in close quarters. The fake weapons used in the choreographed battles were strong enough not to fall apart when striking a shield. They were also strong enough to impart serious pain and injury if they contacted flesh.

The day after our visit to see the knights, I was surprised and curious when Karen said she was eager to tour Boulder Dam. I drove the rental car while she tried not to appear nervous. I guess it was unnerving for a professional driver to rely on the skills of an amateur. Once we got out of the Las Vegas - Henderson metropolitan area I thought she would relax. She did relax a little, until we got off Hwy 93 and onto the dam access road. The road was both narrow and full of curves. As a bonus, the oncoming lane was full of tourists gawking at the sights. I cannot swear to it, but I thought I saw her stepping on the imaginary passenger side brake.

Upon arrival, we immediately signed up for the extended

tour. She was very engaged throughout the tour: the long descent into the dam, walking through the tunnels, seeing and hearing the huge turbines, and asking technical questions of the tour guide. It was almost as if she absorbed some of the power created by the turbines. Was she the same way when acting as captain of her aircraft? Was she as one with the aircraft, wings and engines functioning as extensions of her arms and legs? This increased my curiosity about what she was like as a pilot. I continued my observations as we walked through the dam.

My bet was Karen would have done the tour again with or without a guide. Since they did not want unescorted civilians roaming the dam, Karen and I exited with the rest. We joined other tourists walking from Nevada to Arizona and back on the dam road. She marveled at the lake on one side and the seven hundred foot drop to the river on the other. I found it amusing that a drop of a few hundred feet could impress someone used to traveling 6 miles high.

The route to the parking area led us past two 30 foot tall winged statutes by some Norwegian artist named Hansen. Karen explained that Hansen was a naturalized American citizen and had composed many of the art works at the dam. She tried to explain the symbolism. The "Winged Figures of the Republic" represented the immutable calm of intellectual resolution and the glory of science. In my mind, the engineering of the dam was impressive enough and I did not find the same level of spiritual enlightenment regarding the art. Maybe if I had been here in the beginning, to see an empty canyon and listen to Elwood Mead explain his vision of what the dam would be, I would have a better appreciation of the art. To me the "Dam" was monument enough to the 112 people who died as part of the construction.

Karen loved the eagle-like faces and the towering up-stretched wings of the statutes set upon a black base that included a built in star map. The map served a second function. It was a calendar record of the exact date of the dam dedication. To me it looked like white dots set in black stone inside a pointed circle. Karen tried to explain the astronomical markings and boasted that all the best pilots could navigate by the stars.

She prided herself on her ability to plan the best course, whether it was playing chess or planning a flight. She reminded me of a relative I met several times in my youth. She provided the same stock advice every time we met: "Justin, know where you are, where you are going, and how you're going to get there."

Karen had the same philosophy. She knew where she was going and had a plan to get there.

The more I thought about who Karen was the more I realized how little I knew. I knew about her stated plan: work, save and retire. Now it was clear she had another plan, a bigger plan. What was her whole plan and what had gone wrong?

Obviously, Karen had not planned on dying. Did someone kill her for the $400,000? Did she fall to some indigent who spotted her outside alone?

I doubted someone sexually assaulted Karen. Would not an assault leave evidence to exonerate me? I could not remember seeing anything about her appearance that night that indicated a violent struggle. Karen did not sleep walk, so what would prompt her to go outside in the middle of the night?

Was she having an affair? Karen was too much of a planner to risk a meeting at her own house when she had so many opportunities to meet at safe locations in Portland or any other city for that matter. It did seem like Karen spent more time away from home than her schedule would warrant.

Jealousy was a possibility. Did Karen break up with someone and marry me just to escape a bad relationship? I would have liked to think that Karen went outside to meet with that ex-lover one last time to tell him it was over, and he just could not take it.

On the other hand, for that matter, it could be a she. Now that I was exploring all the possibilities, I had to include this ego destroying option. Hell hath no fury like a lover scorned, somebody once said.

What are the other motives for murder other than money or jealousy?

Killing to gain power or control is a motive, at least according to Shakespeare. I found it hard to imagine that a coworker would benefit by Karen's death. She was not an executive. Nor was she influential in the company or any pilot's organization as far as I could tell. So who would advance or benefit from her death?

In the movies, people are killed because of what they know. Could Karen have known information that was so important that it would make her death worth the risk of a murder investigation? Could she have known about smuggling, bribery, or some kind of crime ring inside the airline? Maybe she was a spy. If Karen were a spy, would the government admit the truth? That was just too fantastic, but maybe Anne could check.

For now, the most logical theory was that Karen was involved in some sort of illegal activity that yielded serious money. I doubted Karen was a mule transporting drugs in her flight bag. The police and customs would not overlook such an obvious entry point. Customs may always be one step behind, but they are ever alert for new tactics. If Karen were involved in something illegal, she would not try to stay a step ahead. She would not want the police to be in the race.

What activity would make her feel she was smart enough to beat the game? What violation of law would she deem worth the risk? What loophole did she find that made breaking the law profitable? Maybe Karen discovered someone's racket and paid the price for being nosy or being too greedy for keeping quiet about it?

Chapter 14   Bail Hearing

I spent Monday writing up my notes on my wedding. It took me a long time. Not only was the stub of a pencil slowing me down, I was nervous and excited about Tuesday's bail hearing.

Officer Mentor and Officer Smiley appeared to hook me up to the other five for the courthouse shuffle. I think it was the same courtroom, but to tell the truth I was not paying that much attention the last time. I did find it interesting that there were several people in the jury box. I assumed they were attorneys based on their dress. Ms. Schwartz arrived just after I did and assumed a position in the jury box with the others.

We rose and sat according to instructions from the bailiff. The judge addressed my companions and each had bail imposed in a manner similar to the last time I was here. Whether it was design or luck of the draw, I was the last prisoner called. Anne announced that she was my council and joined the DA at the attorney's table while I stood and watched.

Anne addressed the court: "Your honor, the District Attorney has placed unreasonable bail demands on my client. The defense requests to enter a motion that bail be reduced commensurate with his strong ties to the community, lack of criminal record and lack of evidence linking him to the crime."

The assistant DA countered: "Your honor, council brings nothing new to this discussion. The defendant had in possession a large quantity of cash and an obvious intent to flee."

"Your honor, if the District Attorney has some physical evidence linking my client to the money found in his wife's car, much less to the crime I think the court would like to see this evidence. As it stands now the only evidence is that my client lived at the same address as the victim."

"Ms. Schultz, the Court is quite capable of representing itself, but your point is taken. Mr. Ballin, what evidence do you have that indicates that the defendant presents a flight risk?"

"Your honor, the fact that the defendant was found at the scene of the crime and with almost half a million dollars in his possession..."

"Your honor, the aforementioned cash was not in possession of my client."

"Ms. Schwartz, you will follow the decorum of the court."

"I am sorry your honor."

"Mr. Ballin, can you show that the cash in question was

actually in the possession of the defendant or that the defendant in fact has any connection to it?"

"Your honor, the cash was located in a car at a house owned by the defendant, where he exercised command and control over the cash."

"Your honor, certainly the DA could resolve the issue of possession by presenting fingerprint and/or DNA evidence that placed Mr. Caise in the car and with the money."

"Mr. Ballin?"

"Well your honor, the fingerprints were inconclusive."

"Mr. Ballin, you found none of the defendant's fingerprints on the money? What about DNA evidence?"

"No your honor, as I would like the court to note that it is too soon to have any lab results."

"Well then Mr. Ballin, whose fingerprints did you identify?"

"Ah, your honor, we recovered prints from the victim and at least four other unidentified individuals."

"Well then you recovered the defendant's prints from the tire or the interior of the car?"

"No, your honor."

"Did you find the defendant's prints anywhere on the car?"

"Your honor, the car had been washed and cleaned recently and..."

"So, the answer is no?"

"Yes your honor."

"Does the district attorney have any additional evidence that would dissuade the court from granting the motion of the defense?"

"No, your honor."

"The motion of the defense is granted. The defendant is to be held on $300,000 cash or bond, and ordered to surrender his passport, remand. Next case."

"Your honor, permission to approach?"

"Granted."

Ms. Schwartz and the prosecutor walked up to the judge's bench. Ms. Schwartz spoke softly out of my hearing while Mr. Ballin quietly protested. The judge responded and they exited the court as the judge repeated his next case command.

As we shuffled back to our offices, I was trying to determine if I was better off. Instead of needing two million dollars for bail I was short about three hundred thousand.

Chapter 15   Crime Scene

The joy of getting my bail reduced was gone by lunch. A jail, just like a hotel or cruise ship, has a well thought out meal plan. There are daily basics and menu items that rotate periodically. A cruise ship that turns over passengers every week can offer a different menu at every meal every day of the year by using a seven-day plan. Unfortunately the jail was not as interested in providing its guests with delightful menu variations. We were on a three-day cycle.

Back in my cell, which I was no longer calling my office, I stewed. I had given up on making my situation more palatable and I had lost interest in writing about Karen. I was here because of something she did.

Whatever she had done, it included four hundred thousand dollars. That seemed to be at least part of the motive for her death. I was convinced the money was dirty because you do not hide an honest windfall from your spouse. If the money was hers from before the marriage, we could have taken steps to keep it out of Washington's community property allocation. Why didn't she make it part of a prenuptial agreement?

I was still trying to work out reasonable answers to those questions when Officer Mentor arrived. We proceeded to the visitor area where my attorney was waiting.

"Hi Justin."

"Oh, hi Ms. Schwartz."

"I thought you would be a bit happier to see me after what I did this morning," Anne replied in a tone I had used myself. A tone of exasperation generated when a layperson does not grasp the brilliance of your technical strategy.

"Sorry, Ms. Schwartz, it was impressive to watch you shoot down the District Attorney. He looked very silly in front of the judge. It's the bail. I'm not much closer to three hundred thousand than I am to two million."

"Justin, in this state you only need to come up with ten percent, that's thirty thousand. As soon as your 401(k) distribution gets here you will be out."

"Really? That's great. I wonder how long it will take the pension administrator to process my distribution. I can hardly wait to get out of here and get home."

"Justin, it's not that simple."

"What, I'm not getting out?"

"No, you are getting out, but you are not going home, at least not for a little while."

"Huh?"

"Your house is a crime scene. The police have the right to restrict access to the crime scene until they have completed their investigation."

"That's what I was arguing about with the DA this morning. I argued that you should be allowed back in your house based on hardship and the fact that the murder happened outside and that the state has had ample time to process the crime scene. The judge is reluctant to grant you access until the technicians release the crime scene. Do you have someone you can stay with?"

Psychology 101 was a required class in college. Psychologists do experiments on animals that should warrant arrested for animal cruelty. One particularly gruesome experiment involved giving mild electric shocks to a dog to get him to jump out of one cage into another. In the second cage, the dog is shocked again, which causes him to jump back to the first cage. The horrible cycle continues until the dog gives up. All I wanted to do right now was howl. What more could go wrong?

"What, what about, what about Sam?"

"I stopped by your house. As your attorney, I can inspect the scene but cannot touch anything. The food dispenser was tipped and empty. I did not see a cat in the house."

Sam, my closest friend and advisor, was missing. If I had never gotten involved with Karen, he would be home, safely asleep on the bed. Now Sam was missing and might be coyote cuisine.

Maybe a guy who talks to his cat deserves to be in jail. Sam and I had long conversations before I met Karen and when she was flying. He talked me out of going to work for that solar energy company. Sam did not voice the words telling me not to change jobs. He did make me explain the nature of the business and the importance of government support necessary for the survival of the company. If you cannot explain a plan to your cat in a way that makes sense to both of you, then it is not a very good plan. The company ceased US operations and moved to China a year later.

Good friends like Sam are invaluable. According to a magazine article about couples, your friends know before you do whether your new relationship will last.

Sam, my best friend, tried to tell me Karen was not right. When your closest advisor pees in your new girlfriend's shoes its best to heed his advice.

Sam was now paying the price for my poor judgment.

With a growing sense of despair I asked, "What about Ed? Did you talk to him? Maybe he has Sam?"

"I don't know if this is good news. The sheriff interviewed Ed the day you were arrested. He said he woke up about the time the ambulance was leaving and the police arrived shortly thereafter. They wouldn't tell him much. They did admit that they did not have the cat and Ed did not see animal control at all that day. Ed worked in his garden most of the day and described how the sheriff and the state police searched the yard and house. There were different officers in the house and in the yard throughout the day. They took a variety of items including the garden hose. Late in the afternoon, they towed both cars and then strung up plastic "crime scene" tape.

"So I need to rent a car too?"

"Unfortunately, yes."

"Justin, Ed said that he was concerned that Sam was on the loose. He has been leaving food and water out every day, and someone is eating it. Whether it's Sam or raccoons he is not sure. He said he thought you would do the same for his cat Holly if he had to go to the hospital."

"Yes, I would. He and I were closer than he and Karen. I would listen to his fish stories about early morning trips to the river. Other times we would trade cat treats or cat toys. A couple of times a year he would pack up his cat and dog and head to the coast for several days of fishing. While he was gone I would pick up his mail and he would give me salmon steaks for my efforts."

"It is a relief knowing that Ed is keeping an eye out for Sam. But there is nothing I can do from in here. When can I get out?"

"Like I said, as soon as the check from the 401(k) administrator arrives, assuming it is a banking day. Until then keep working on your homework."

Chapter 16   Friends

Sleep was an unrealized dream the night after the bail hearing. I felt bad that I did not have more appreciation for Anne's efforts. An 85% reduction in bail is nothing to sneeze at. I lay in the dark finding little happiness in my situation while worrying about Sam, the bail and me.

I think I fell asleep just in time for breakfast, then I could not fall asleep after. Lunch and dinner did not improve the situation. My homework sat untouched, the fatigue overpowering. Mentally and physically exhausted, I stared at the ceiling until the lights went out then, stared at the dark.

Sometime later, I dreamed Karen was alive. She smiled. It was not a pleasant smile. She looked at me from inside her RX-7 surrounded by her money. She grabbed wads of cash, bringing it up to wash her face. All the while loose bills swirled inside the car until sucked out of the sunroof. She thrust her arms upward releasing the cash into the wind. She laughed at me: loud, hard, and harsh.

Karen threw more money out the sunroof laughing as the bills whipped away in the wind. The bills churned inside the RX-7 snow globe producing a greenish grey blur obscuring the interior. Money streamed out sunroof as Karen laughed harder. More money puffed out the hole followed by something larger.

"Where is he?" I screamed.

"You are such a worrier. Look at all this money."

"Where is he? What did you do to him?"

"Oh, shut up, you're just like him, a noisy, needy, lazy lump. Shut up!"

"What did you do to Sam?"

"The same thing I am going to do to you." The determined grin on her face was evil.

Karen walked toward me ripping open the package of panty hose releasing the wrapper into the wind shear above her head.

Karen walked toward me wrapping the stocking toes around her left hand.

She walked, wrapping the waist around her right hand.

She walked, stretching the hose legs tight between her hands.

She walked, I tried to move but me feet were stuck in an invisible mud.

She walked hands forward neck high, stockings stretched,

46

smiling.

I lunged to my left.

Eighteen inches is a long way to fall when landing on a concrete floor.

Was Karen evil?

Did she really hate Sam?

For his part, Sam made an effort to be friends with Karen. Contrary to what some people think, cats are very social and live in complex arrangements. Cats are just more independent and the structures are not as obvious.

Sam attempted to show he was friendly. He would show his happy face with whiskers and ears forward and his tail high. Sometimes he would greet Karen with ankle rubbing and acknowledge her existence. Looking back, I cannot say if she responded to any of these greetings.

Karen never struck or kicked Sam in my presence, although once there was loud hissing and Sam retreated from the bedroom where Karen was changing.

She was not interested when I tried to explain the complexities of cat protocol. Sam flopping down on his side in front of her was a signal he wanted to play, not a trip hazard.

After a while, Sam gave up trying and just stayed out of her way.

Was my memory making too much of Karen's relationship with Sam? Many people do not like cats for lots of reasons. Some reasons are even valid. One of Karen's reasons was cat hair on her uniforms. Another reason was the gifts that Sam brought. Usually it was field mice in the kitchen by the cat food dispenser. I argued that the snake on her pillow a special gift, not a warning. I viewed Karen's sour relationship with Sam as a minor difference that could be resolved.

A larger issue was Karen's secretive nature. The fact that she never talked about her coworkers was a growing concern. Most people spend more time awake with their coworkers than their spouse. She related nothing about her coworkers unless prompted. There should be stories, good or bad, that you relate to your partner. Was she hiding her coworkers from me, or me from her coworkers?

Looking back, I think Karen was hiding me from her coworkers. Early on after we started living together, I made the mistake of opening her mail. In the argument that followed, Karen dismissed my concerns about missed deadlines. In firm and angry tones, she reminded me that she had been flying a long time and was capable of opening her own mail. If she wanted assistance with her job or administrative affairs, she would let me know.

Maybe I took too much initiative in opening her mail, but I never read it. I was just looking for bills and such. Her reaction seemed excessive. What was she hiding? Was it because she was involved with someone at work? If she was, was there more to it than sex or was love a factor?

If she was having an affair, it no longer mattered. It was just a past event to stir emotions. What mattered now was getting out of jail and proving that I was not a murderer.

Chapter 17   Something Stupid

The pity party lasted until breakfast when I looked at my fellow guests for the first time. That is, I looked without the cloud of fear. I had been here long enough to learn that if I kept to myself the others pretty much left me alone. The jail staff liked a quiet boring clientele and took steps to segregate any troublemakers. This order and control was made easier by the fact that this was a small institution and all the guests owned sentences of a year or less. Most hardcore cases went to the state facility. There were definitely gang elements but there did not appear to be any organized units. My status was uncertain to my hosts. There was the possibility of bail or pretrial motions that might change my situation. I was in limbo and not housed with the general population where the long-term residents lived and worked. Therefore, I spent most of my time in my cell.

This morning I took a good look at those with whom I lodged. The most notable trait was the number of tattoos. Almost all of the guests had multiple images. Some of the tattoos were obviously professional and were or had been colored ink at one time. Many of the others were low quality images not in proportion, with irregular lines, likely applied with improvised instruments. There did seem to be some images that appeared more often. Spider webs and teardrops were more common among the older inmates. I was curious, but not curious enough to ask the meaning of those two themes. Nor do I remember seeing spider webs or tears on people I met on the outside.

Few people I associated with had obvious tattoos. Those that did, had happy themes like dolphins on the ankle or a rose that peeked out of a blouse, but nothing depressing like tear drops under the eye, or the one obvious MS13 gang member who spread his gang name across his face and neck.

Another difference between inside and outside was physical health. Years of alcohol use or worse had taken a visible toll on the bodies of some of my jail associates. I learned that the horrible teeth and gums on one prisoner was a condition referred to as "meth mouth." If methamphetamine can do that to your teeth, what has it done to your kidneys or your brain? Many people in here were here in part because of substance abuse, a common theme being "I was really wasted and..."

That is not to say that I did not know or work with people with substance abuse problems. The accounting profession is known for "functional alcoholics" who work all day, drink at night and maintain a career. People I knew on the outside were not uncontrolled substance abusers. They retained enough control of their problem to avoid explaining to a judge what happened when "I was really wasted."

I had not been wasted the night Karen died and had not done something stupid. I did not belong here with these people. If I wanted to stay out, when I got out, it was up to me to save myself. The sheriff was right about one thing, I knew more about Karen's death than anyone else.

Now that I had a mission, a purpose, I was the calmest I had been since the last time I fell asleep with Sam snoozing on my chest.

Chapter 18   Where to Begin

If I were hired to investigate a murder, how would I go about the task?

First, preserve the evidence. Once I had access to my house, I needed to record the scene in detail, every inch of the interior of the house and every item. The police are not stupid. They dusted for fingerprints and seized anything that they considered evidence. Nevertheless, the police believed I was the killer and only the items related to her and me were of interest. They were not looking for evidence that someone else was involved, that was the evidence I needed.

My guess was that the police concentrated on the outside of the house and found the money as part of a 'routine' extended search to cover all bases. My plan was that there was evidence that did not appear to be evidence, because it would only look significant to me acting on the knowledge that I did not kill Karen.

After the interior, I needed to record the crawl space and the attic space. Finally, I needed a record of the yard, the shed and the carport. Then, it would probably be a good idea to inventory everything that remained. Maybe the process would help me identify something that was missing, or something that should not be there.

The size of the task was beginning to dawn on me. Was I capable of duplicating the efforts of a law enforcement investigative team? No, but then that was not the goal. Their game plan would be to use the technical examination results and laboratory testing to match physical evidence to the scene and ultimately to me. My game plan, use the same evidence gathered by the sheriff to find the real killer.

What questions would I ask if I was leading the investigation? I would want to know where the prime suspect and the victim were for at least a week prior to the crime.

The answer about the prime suspect was easy. I did what I usually did. I went to work, returned home, watched TV, surfed the internet, played games on the computer, stopped at the Post Office, fed Sam, played with Sam, mowed the front lawn, watered the tomatoes and the flowers and picked up around the house.

The answer for the victim was not so easy. I never understood Karen's schedule, even though I tried to understand how airlines work.

The FAA, the airlines, and the airports work together to

determine the routes that the airline will fly. The brand name big airlines like United and Delta are what the FAA recognizes as Part 121 Scheduled Airlines. The Part 121 carriers file schedules of the routes they will fly with the FAA, guaranteeing that they will operate these flights until they file an official route change. 'On Demand Airlines' or charter operators are ruled under Part 135 and do not have a fixed schedule. A charter carrier may fly the same route every day for a month by filing daily flight plans, but they are not subject to a fixed schedule.

Karen worked for a larger scheduled airline that served the western US from Canada to Central America. Servicing these routes is an incredibly complicated dance. The airline needs to bring together the right crews with the right planes to the right airports at the right time. If that is not sufficiently complex, add crew safety limits to the mix.

Karen vainly tried to explain the FAA requirements and I tried to understand. The next time she was out flying I looked them up. Under normal conditions a pilot and copilot:

> Must rest 10 hours before they go on duty, and
>
> May be on duty, ready to fly or flying, not more than 14 hours in a 24-hour period, and
>
> May fly in command not more than 10 hours in a 24 hour period, and
>
> Must rest for 10 hours after their flight assignment.

In theory, a pilot could make 21 ten-hour flights per month. In reality, in order to fly ten hours a day the pilots would need to make four or more two-hour flights in their 14 duty hour day. Activities such as loading, unloading and fueling eat up a lot of duty time, making it difficult for a pilot to achieve 10 flight hours in a day.

Assuming a perfect scenario, that an airline exists with a schedule that allows a pilot to fly ten hours a day every day, an energetic pilot could fly over two hundred hours every month. That is until the FAA's cumulative flight time rules kick in. The FAA limits the flight time of a pilot to not more than:

> Fourteen hundred hours in a calendar year, or
>
> Five hundred hours in any one calendar quarter, or
>
> Eight hundred hours in any two consecutive calendar quarters.

Observing this rule, our young fresh faced pilot, who wants to work as much as possible, manages to schedule the maximum thirty-four hour flight cycle. That is, ten rest hours, plus fourteen duty hours, and ten rest hours every shift. Our enthusiastic pilot reaches the 500-hour limit in 71 days. FAA rules require that a pilot not be scheduled and not accept any flight that causes the pilot to exceed the flight hour limits, so our eager beaver pilot gets the next nineteen days off. Relaxed and refreshed our pilot does it again the next quarter, or not.

The FAA eight hundred hour rule kicks in the next consecutive quarter. Our eager pilot hits the eight hundred hour limit at the 43rd day, leaving our aspiring pilot on the ground for the next 47 days. Our pilot could log another 500 hours the following quarter, but that would leave only 100 hours for the rest of the year, due to the fourteen hundred hour rule.

The icing on the cake is the 24-hour rest rule. Thirteen times a calendar quarter a pilot must have 24 uninterrupted hours of rest. At first, I thought this meant one day a week, but that was not the wording in the FAA regulation. The regulation just said 13 times per quarter not once a week or four days a month. The simple task of figuring out my wife's work schedule had turned into a major project.

It was a Friday night project for another Friday night alone with Sam.

I had created the simplest scenario possible and applying the rules was mind-boggling. I finished my fourth beer while figuring out the 500/800/1400 hour rule. After I added in the 13 rest periods per quarter rule and the fifth beer, I decided taxes were a lot easier than keeping track of pilots and planes.

What it came down to was that Karen could present me just about any schedule she wanted and I would have no viable way of confirming it was real. If it was real, did she request that schedule or did the dispatcher force it upon her? Did Karen ask for her 24-hour rest periods in Houston?

I was concluding that schedulers could make, or break, an airline and make life hell for a pilot. Schedulers need to match pilots with enough hours of unused flight time for that day with the plane. It does no good to have a fresh pilot in Denver when there is an aircraft with a timed out crew in Seattle. Airlines cooperate with each other and fly each other's crews free. Crew positioning is one of the reason ticketed passengers get bumped. An incompetent scheduler wastes the flight time of crews by violating the hours of rest rules or dumping crews in the wrong city at the end of their assignment.

Inept scheduling was a regular theme of Karen's. According to Karen, they were responsible for her not spending as many of her off days here with me as I thought she should.

The week she was murdered Karen flew her terminal leg from Denver into Portland on Tuesday night. Her positioning flight to on Thursday gave her almost 40 hours off. Her current schedule was an extended loop pattern that involved Portland, Denver, Houston, and Cancun, beginning and ending in Portland. The last flight from Denver to Portland was not due to passenger demand; it was rarely close to full. The main purpose of the flight was to get the aircraft to Portland so it was in position for the Oh Six Hundred (I was now used to the 24 four-hour clock), early morning departure from Portland (PDX) to Denver (DEN). The flight continued from DEN to Houston (IAH) and IAH to Cancun (CUN). The return leg reversed the route: CUN - IAH – DEN – PDX. This route required one aircraft, two crews, eighteen duty hours, fourteen flight hours, and six layover hours.

To me it seemed she should have a regular rest day on the terminal leg into Portland. Instead, the week she died was the exception, rest days in Houston were the norm.

Another issue between Karen and me was the support she provided for other pilots. She was in demand because she was qualified to fly on several aircraft. Therefore, when they needed to rescue a stranded aircraft she would volunteer if she had the available time. Funny how all this additional flying never translated into additional money but did require her to be away.

What did she do with that extra time?

I was asleep on the couch when Karen got home about Oh Two Hundred Wednesday. She tried to be quiet coming in the house, but Sam buried his back claws in my thigh when he jumped off my lap as he fled the scene.

"Good morning Karen, how was your flight?"

"There was a little chop over the Rockies and we picked up a headwind around Boise that set us back a bit, we did not touch down until 18 minutes after."

"Well I am glad you are home."

"You know you don't have to wait up for me, you never know when I'll get in."

"It's ok, I like to talk with you after your flight. So what is going on in my sweeties' world?"

"Justin, you will be tired tomorrow, and you don't want to be cranky with your coworkers."

"My coworkers will be fine. It's you I am interested in."

"OK, the new copilot seems to be working out, ex-military,

started out in rotor wing aircraft then decided he wanted to fly commercial and went through a civil program. That's unusual. Most helicopter pilots do not transition to fixed wing. He said he did not like the idea of ferrying workers to oil platforms or fighting fires. He liked the idea of a semi-predictable work schedule. Very good with procedures and he has the checklist protocol down cold."

"The weather in Cancun was hot and wet. The hurricane season is picking up and we were late departing IAH for CUN due to thunderstorms coming into Cancun from the Gulf, I was lucky on the return leg as we got into Houston before the storms picked up for the day there. Customs was slow for some reason, maybe they were shorthanded but we barely made our departure time out of IAH to DEN. I don't know what's up with the ground crew in Denver but they screwed up the baggage off load and we had to open the belly a second time to pull some additional bags. Then there is the new fuel saving protocol from corporate that is just asinine, don't get me started."

"How about a glass of wine to help you relax?"

"No, thanks, I will be fine. I just need to let my mind settle for a bit. You go to bed. I'll join you in a little bit."

The last time I remember on the clock was 3:39.

I did not bother to wake her when I got up for work. She was still sleeping when I left.

Looking back, I saw that we were both going through the motions of a functional relationship. The rationale in my mind for not waking Karen was I knew she needed the sleep. In reality, I did not want to risk a confrontation. It was no longer worth the effort. I no longer wanted to play this game.

Chapter 19   End of the Beginning

Maybe I no longer wanted to play this game, but I did not have a choice. I felt like I did when I played chess with Karen. We both had access to the same pieces but my opponent had more experience, better strategy and better tactics.

In chess, the opening game sets the stage for all of the events to follow. Innocent seeming initial moves affect later options, setting up or denying opportunities. It is easy to view the opening as a time for optimism, a clean board with endless possibilities, and not appreciate the danger. That is especially true when you do not know a new game has started.

What had been my naïve opening moves in this game: picking up a phone, getting married, or not realizing I was a piece in someone else's game?

This Monday morning I was ready to begin the middle game: Feeling out of the opponent, searching for openings and weaknesses, and staging resources in preparation for the end game. Maybe Anne would come see me today and we could start planning our strategy.

Luck was with me. Lunchtime was approaching and Officer Mentor arrived to escort me to see my attorney. Anne signaled and Officer Mentor opened the pass through. Anne shouted for Officer Mentor to wait and slid a document through the opening with a pen.

The eighty-six thousand dollar check was not the largest I had ever seen, but it was the largest ever written to me. I endorsed the check, returned the check and pen to Anne, and Officer Mentor locked the pass through, exiting the small room to wait.

"You look a bit more cheerful today than the last time I saw you."

"I do feel better, and thanks for coming to see me. I was not expecting you to have the check yet."

Anne smiled. "Yes that was fast. I didn't know that it was common for pension administrators to send them FedEx, or for Human Resource directors to call upon delivery."

It is surprising to find out who will support you in a time of crisis. I made mental note to let Mary Ellen know how much I appreciated all that she had done.

"...your pants size?"

I realized that Anne had asked a question that made no sense. "Excuse me?"

"Justin, what size pants to you wear?"

"Uh, I have a thirty six inch waist and 32 inch inseam, why do you ask?"

"Well, unless you plan on wearing hospital scrubs, you will need some civilian clothes when you get out this afternoon."

It seemed a lifetime ago that I had crawled into an ambulance in my underwear. Ann added my shirt size and shoe size to her statistics before she left with the check and a promise to see me this afternoon.

Release from jail was the reverse of the booking process except at the end they gave me my new Wrangler jeans, white long sleeve button shit, white athletic socks and inexpensive New Balance athletic shoes. A guard escorted through three doors to meet my attorney and her friend. Anne's associate was a fifty-something fit male a couple of inches taller than I was.

"Justin, Richard Cushing, private investigator."

I said "Nice to meet you." as we shook hands.

"Do you have any more homework for me Justin?"

I handed over the writings about Karen's last day. While Anne read I enjoyed being out in the sunshine. Richard started on the first page as Anne started the second.

Anne said, "We could go to my office to talk, but that would not really accomplish any more than talking now. Richard and I agreed it would be best to go to your house and get a visual record of the house and grounds while the light is good. The crime scene technicians released the house today, just before I posted your bail."

"I recognize that this is probably the last thing you want to do the minute you get out of jail, but memories fade with every passing hour. This is our best chance to record what you know."

"Actually Anne, I think this is a great idea. I want to help in this case as much as possible without interfering with you and Richard. I will do whatever needs to be done."

After a detour through the Kentucky Fried Chicken drive through, we headed to my house. Richard stopped and parked his pickup truck just after we turned off 15th street onto Klamas Place.

Years ago, a developer converted an apple orchard. Rural living for a handful of homeowners well beyond the city limits of Vancouver built before the much more restrictive land use laws of today. In the sixties, the area was rural county about seven miles from downtown Vancouver and a further 5 miles across the Columbia River from downtown Portland. The development remained isolated until the bridge on Interstate 205 opened the area to the larger Portland population. In the 70's the suburbs from Vancouver and Portland reached out to surround my little track.

Karen liked the house because of the close proximity to Portland International Airport. As the crow flies, the house was maybe five miles from the main runway at PDX. Using roads and bridges, the route was about eight miles, or less than 15 minutes from carport to parking garage.

Richard pulled out a plastic case the size of backpack from behind the seat. Inside the case was a professional looking video camera and various accessories. Richard motioned me over and clipped on what I assume was a battery pack transmitter and a lapel microphone to my shirt.

"I want you to speak normally and describe in detail what we see. The lavalier microphone will pick up everything that you say. We will transcribe it all later and convert what you say into lists and pictures with components."

"Do not touch anything until we get done. If we find anything of interest, we do not want to add any contamination. We don't know what we will find, and I may need you to stay in a hotel tonight and bring in a forensic specialist tomorrow."

"Finally, do you need to use the washroom?"

"What?"

"If you need to go, I do not want you using the bathroom in your house before we finish."

"No, I am fine. I am sure my neighbor Ed will let us in, if I ask."

"I will add commentary and ask questions if I feel you need to expand on descriptions or details. Ready?"

"Justin, I want you to be descriptive, and include perspective of your point of view. That will help later in reviewing the video. Don't worry about saying too much. Everything is covered under attorney client privilege. If we find something, we need as evidence we will document that in the recording and take steps to preserve the chain of custody. Key to that is that you do not touch anything that we may want to submit to the court later.

"Do you have a valid driver's license?"

"Yes."

"Then I would like you to drive and narrate while I record the views."

I got behind the wheel and pulled out from the curb.

"Slowly, Justin."

I slowed to a crawl as Richard filmed out the window.

"Talk to me Justin."

"My name is Justin Caise; I live at 16851 Devon Circle. I am proceeding to my house north on Klamas Place from 15th Street."

"More."

"Um, Klamas Place is a short street that parallels 164th Avenue to the east but only for a few blocks. Devon Circle is even shorter and terminates in a cul-de-sac. Devon should be named 12th street but it was in place before the area was annexed, so they left the name unchanged when they added the surrounding developments."

"Stop here."

As I pull to the curb: "I am stopping on Klamas Place, approximately the 1300 block on top of the culvert that drains the swale that separates the houses on 15th street from Devon Place."

Richard climbed out of the truck to film the brush on both sides of the watercourse.

"Animal trails," he said as he got back in the truck.

"The trails do not look heavily traveled, not like a popular human trail."

"Justin, do you see many homeless people in the gully?"

"I've seen a few, but not often. I think they stay closer to the river, down by highway and the rail road."

"Which house is yours?"

"It's the fourth house."

"Describe it to me."

"From Klamas Place, my house is the fourth east. It is light blue with white trim and the roof runs perpendicular to Klamas Place. The peak of the shed is visible and the ridgeline of the roof runs parallel to Klamas. Vegetation obscures the lower two thirds of the house. The county owns the swale and it makes up part of the flood control network. The vegetation is overgrown because the homeowners cannot clear beyond their property lines, due to a lawsuit by an environmental group."

"I am turning right onto Devon."

"Direction?"

"We are proceeding east on Devon Circle approximately 100 yards. There are three houses between Klamas and my house."

"Stop here, we will approach on foot. I want to film the driveway empty."

I parked and we got out of the truck in front of Ed's house. Richard swung the camera to film Ed's house and space between our houses.

"This is the residence of Ed Nordstram, 16833 Devon Circle. Ed is about eighty years old and lives with a small terrier dog Angie and his cat Holly. His wife died three years ago and he spends a lot of time working on his yard and garden."

We walked east a few feet while Richard filmed the west side of my house and moved onto the front.

"What am I seeing?"

"The northwest corner of the house is the master bedroom. It is an unusual layout. Usually the main bedroom is away from the street, I guess they did not see street noise as a problem because Devon is a cul-de-sac. The small frosted window is for the bath attached to the master bedroom. The rest of the front of the house facing Devon is the living room with the large picture window. The two car driveway extends the width of the house and the back half is covered by a carport that is flush with the front of the house."

We walked past my empty driveway.

"Whose house is this?"

"This is Mrs. Jackson's house. I think her first name is Phyllis, she rarely comes out of the house and I have never been inside. She has a yard service take care of her property. The yards are not separated by a fence but there is a row of mature arborvitae shrubs that separates our back yards."

We walked past Mrs. Jackson's house and Richard filmed without comment to the end of the cul-de-sac where we reversed our route while Richard videoed the opposite side of the street. We turned into the driveway.

Years ago, I lived in an apartment complex in Portland. Each apartment had covered parking for the tenant. One morning I approached my assigned spot and encountered a strong sense that something was wrong. I physically walked into the empty parking

60

space to convince myself that my car was actually gone.

The feeling was similar as we walked toward the carport. The emptiness of the double carport pressed against my chest like a bad omen and the 'Crime Scene' plastic tape stretched across the carport presented an impenetrable barrier.

"Justin! Justin, talk to me."

"We are walking south up my driveway. The main door of the house opens onto the driveway, another unusual design feature of this house."

Richard withdrew a Buck™ knife from his pocket with his free hand and somehow flipped it open. He filmed himself cutting the crime scene tape and then folded the knife against his thigh.

"Let's continue into the back yard, while the sun is high. Talk to me."

"The carport was probably added after the house was built. It was not as a tall as the peak on the main part of the house and not low enough to fit under the eave so there was a gap in coverage between the two structures.

"Perspective?"

"The driveway runs south from the street. There is a twelve by eight foot tool shed immediately to the south of the driveway that is flush with the east edge of the drive, about three feet from the arborvitae hedge. I have to keep the hedge cut back so the shed walls can dry and not develop dry rot. The shed rests on a concrete pad poured separately from the driveway and abuts it to form a continuous slab. "

"We are at the end of the driveway concrete looking southwest into the yard. There are flowering shrubs along the west side of the yard next to the neighbor's fence, a patch of tomatoes along two thirds of the south edge of the yard. Not visible from this position is the compost pile located in the southeast corner of the yard."

"Describe for me the scene the night your wife died."

I took a deep breath and tried to picture myself presenting a tax argument to an IRS agent. "The motion sensor light above the utility room door was on. She was lying face down on the grass by the tomatoes."

"Describe the position of the body."

"I think it would help me if I walked through it."

"Wait here."

Richard filmed the ground along the back of the house and the utility room door. He then slowly walked from the back of the house the 50 feet to the tomato patch, filming the ground in detail the entire time.

"OK, put these on, and try not to touch anything."

I slipped on the blue plastic gloves, like the ones the cops wear on those TV shows.

"Walk to the back door and look for anything that does not belong."

I rarely walk along the back of the house other than to mow. If I enter the yard, it is from the utility room, the deck, or the driveway en route to the shed or the plants. The grass was green only near the flowers, the tomatoes and the compost pile. I do not water the grass in back so the only water the lawn gets is from the overspray from the flowers or the tomatoes.

The lack of a green lawn irritated Karen. My counter argument was that it made no sense to waste water on a lawn that I would then have to mow. Besides, we never entertained and she was rarely here to see it. It was the last point that irritated Karen the most, the challenge that she was not spending enough time at home.

"I am standing at the utility room door looking south-southeast. There does not appear to be anything that should not be here. The plastic netting around the tomatoes has been cut, allowing the deer to eat the tomato plants. It looks like nothing has been watered since my arrest. The ground is dry, there does not appear to be any out of the ordinary marks on the ground."

"Richard, I don't see a chalk outline for the body."

"That is only done for TV, Justin. The police don't use tape or chalk without reason. The deputies interviewed the EMTs to confirm the location of the body. Now the police video the scene using numbered index cards to identify the evidence and add as little as possible in the way of contamination."

"What did the scene look like when you stepped through the door?"

"Karen was wearing a light white silk robe that was almost full length. It was one gift from me she liked. She was on her front, head near the tomato fence with her feet pointed toward the shed. I think one knee was bent. I had to grab her upper left arm near the shoulder in order to roll her toward me and onto her back. Her right arm was under her body so she was easy to roll."

"What else?"

"I remember having to shift positions when I started CPR. She rolled on top of the hose when I turned her over. The end of

62

the hose was near the tomato patch and the length ran under her neck and left shoulder. The hose ran along her side, which I knelt on with my knee. The hose is stiff and it hurt so I pulled it out from underneath her."

"What else?"

"It was hard to see, we are a long way from the yard light and my body shadow covered her much of the time. I did not notice any injury to her neck."

"What was on the ground?"

"Nothing, all I noticed was Karen."

"How did the hose get there?"

"It is not unusual for me to leave the hose out. It is stiff and does not loop well on the hose rack above the faucet. I tend to leave it stretched out on the lawn and only coil it on the rack when I mow."

"Show me how you removed the hose from underneath your wife."

I had to think for a minute. "I remember thinking that it would hurt if I pulled the last six feet of hose and the coupling across her back."

"Justin, can you demonstrate what you did? You were kneeling beside her, what did you do?"

I knelt on the ground as I did that night. I pictured how my right knee was level with her left shoulder. I reached across her body with my left hand to raise her head while grasping the hose with my right hand, I remember that I was almost off balance and rocked back to my left. I then grabbed the hose with my left hand and pulled it from under her left shoulder as I was rising to my feet.

"Good, now go through it again and explain what you are doing."

Richard seemed satisfied with description and moved on to film the rest of the back yard. He spent a fair amount of time examining the heavy growth of brush and vegetation at the end of my lot. In spite of the environmentalist objections, I managed to keep the native foliage trimmed back with my hedge trimmer, a small chain saw and chemicals that I am sure make the green movement cringe. The latter reserved for incursions of Himalayan Blackberry. Both Ed and I had been vigilant regarding the blackberry. The portions of the swale that abutted our property were free of the thorny plant.

Richard ventured into the vegetation, filming as he descended the slope. He traveled about forty feet out to the small trees and blackberry taking panorama views before returning to my yard.

"Tell me about this part of the yard."

"We are looking at the southeast corner of my property toward the shed and compost pile. There is an open space of lawn between the compost and the tool shed. Hanging on the side of the shed is a wheelbarrow."

We walked to the shed door. "This is the west side of the shed. There is a cut lock hanging in the latch. I locked the shed the last time I mowed the lawn. Ed's weed-beater was missing from his shed about a month ago, so I had been making sure to lock my shed after mowing. My bet it was one of the neighbor kids that live on Devon."

Richard opened the door wide so we could video the contents of the shed. It was a typical shed, filled with various sporting equipment, unused building materials, yard tools and supplies, small power tools and anything else that I did not want in the house.

"Does anything appear to be missing?"

Not having a photographic memory I could consult, I had to say no. All the normal tools and equipment were hanging from the pegboard pegs, hooks and nails without any unexplained gaps or open spaces. The mower and tiller occupied their normal positions on the cement floor. We exited the shed and turned to face the house.

"Are you ready to start on the inside?"

"Yes, let's see what they have done."

"Justin, it is important that we do this systematically. After filming from the entry, I will enter the room, do a full 360 floor to ceiling panorama, you will enter and start with the wall to the right of the door. Describe all the items on or near the right side wall of the entry listing everything on that wall from the floor to the ceiling. When you are sure we have described everything on that wall we will move left to the next wall. After we have finished all the walls we will move clockwise around the items on the floor of the room not covered when we looked at the walls."

"Keep your gloves on and don't move or open anything until after I film it in its original position."

Richard and I returned to the front door and I reached into my pocket for my keys.

"Richard, I don't have my keys how do we get in?"

"Where is your hidden key?"

"I keep my spare in a fake rock under the corner of the deck next to the house."

"Let's see if the sheriff left it alone."

Fortunately, the fake rock was close to where it should have been, next to the support post. The sheriff had moved it when it was located during the search but they did not deem it evidence and the key was still inside.

I was about to grab it when Richard stopped me.

"It looks like they dusted the key for prints. Not the best of objects from which to lift a print, but they might have gotten a partial." Richard said as he dumped the key into my hand.

The door opened outward and Richard stepped forward to film the scene from the single step. He walked to the middle of the living room and filmed the whole room before inviting me in. I was expecting a scene of complete destruction as usually seen on TV. Instead, it was much more methodical and not intentionally destructive.

I did not have much to do other than describe the items. The police inspected everything. Items that could contain or conceal were open or inverted. Three framed pictures now leaned against the wall, backs exposed. Unzipped cushions from the couch joined the pictures against the wall. The empty couch now held a small pile of old popcorn and several coins proving the deputies were thorough in their search.

The rest of the house showed the same signs of systematic thorough, thoughtful procedures. They opened drawers and spread the contents for inspection. They separated the beds into components to insure nothing was between the sheets or under the mattress.

Occasionally Richard would prompt me about missing items. How many of us with or without a photographic memory could tell if something was missing from our house? Do we notice the absence of the sound of a ticking clock, or do we only notice when we look to check the time? My task of spotting the missing items was more difficult because nothing was where it was supposed to be. When all your silverware is in a pile on the counter under the silverware tray, is it all there? My assumption was that it was, or at least whatever was gone had left legitimately. The sheriff was looking for the obvious evidence and not taking random samples. Unless something was involved in her death or contributed to motive for a murder, the police would leave it alone.

We had moved from the common rooms to the office when

I first noted something missing, my computer and all storage devices. The computer was not the murder weapon. I guess they were checking for files that would incriminate me.

I expressed my dismay at being unable to identify missing items to Richard. He said he understood and that the real benefit of this exercise would come when we got 'discovery' from the prosecutor's office. Seeing what the police thought was critical evidence would help understand how they would structure their case. We continued our inventory.

I surprised myself by not noticing earlier. We were ending the inventory with the master bedroom. Karen's empty dresser had contained a relatively small wardrobe. It was really more like what someone would take on a business trip than what one would wear at home. I was unable to determine what if anything was missing. It was as we made our way to the nightstand on my side of the bed that I realized that my car keys and wallet were gone.

"Why take my wallet?"

"Credit cards mainly. The police want to check your purchase records."

"But I have no ID, no cash, and no driver license."

"Here's forty dollars. You will have to check with Anne in the morning."

Chapter 21   Etiquette

It was just getting dark when Richard left. We did not find anything that warranted bringing in a forensic specialist, so I was going to sleep in my own bed tonight.

Before Richard left we checked the phones. We could do this because I am one of a shrinking group, people who still have a landline phone and answering service on their line. I guess I was smart to have converted to phone service messaging when my last answering machine died. If I had not the Sheriff would have seized that machine too. We listened to the recorded messages, which prompted me to add two items to the missing item list. My cell phone, a pay as you go model I keep for emergencies and Karen's cell phone, which she used for airline business.

Neither Karen nor I are outgoing gregarious people, I did not expect many calls. There were not and from what we could tell there were no messages from Karen's friends. Not surprisingly, there were messages on the landline for Karen from airline dispatch. They had tried her cell phone and her home and wanted her to call in immediately. I imagined the problems caused by losing a pilot without warning at the beginning of a trip cycle. Dispatch called two more times on Friday. Then the calls stopped.

Richard suggested I give Anne a call tomorrow to see about getting my credit cards and driver's license back.

Finally, Richard helped me re-assemble the beds and then left me alone with a jumbled house. I returned a few of the items to their places as we inventoried the house. Most we recorded in place and left for placement tomorrow.

Now I stood next to our bed surveying the room. What is the proper etiquette for dealing with your dead wife's belongings? Obviously, I could not throw out anything until the case was resolved. What do you do with a pile of clothes, shoes and earrings for someone who will never use them again? Boxes suitable for storing her things were gone in the recycling. Otherwise, I would have boxed her effects and put them in the shed there and then. If I were Sam, I would pounce on and bite every piece, and then nap on the pile when I was done.

I was not a cat, so the feline option was unavailable to me, and I did not feel like napping. I stood, picked up a hanger, picked up a blouse and hung the product in the closet. Maybe not the right place to start, but it was a start. The only other appealing option was to walk down to the convenience store and buy enough beer to divert me from my quandary. If I gave into that self-destructive temptation, I might as well be back in jail. Instead, I worked my way through her clothes and effects.

Working through the items evoked memories. I caught a fingernail in a large run in one of Karen's hose, the ones that Sam liked to attack. The pristine Value America baseball cap went onto a hook in the closet. A reward issued by the airline for meeting on time performance goals that Karen never wore and hated. She had a captain's cap and that was enough, she would have preferred the extra $10. The Value America ID card lanyard issued to every employee, which she also never wore. Karen preferred to clip her ID on her uniform when she had to and carried her ID in a pocket when she could, producing it only as needed. I sat on the bed thinking while playing with the lanyard. It was about three quarters of an inch wide nylon weave incorporating the "VA" logo and held together with a safety latch. A few pounds of pressure caused the two ends to pop apart, converting the nylon necklace into a 24-inch long ribbon with a plastic clip in the middle. I was separating and rejoining the safety clasp while staring at the stack of papers left behind.

Karen loved to fly and loved to read about flying. Karen's library included 'Professional Pilot' magazine, books and government materials. One book that caught my eye was "Federal Aviation Regulations Explained" by Kent Jackson and Lori Edwards. This terse 400-page paperback included a picture of the attorney/authors, one of whom is a certified flight instructor and the other is an A&P mechanic. Supplementing the books and magazines were printouts of FAA Air Worthiness Directives and FAA Advisory Circulars such as circular 20-62D "Eligibility, Quality, and Identification of Approved Aeronautical Replacement Parts." It all seemed like dull reading to do in your spare time. Not that I did not relate, having my own reading to meet my professional education requirements. Karen used to spend most of our free time studying, but not anymore.

I ventured to the mess in the kitchen and located several large brown paper grocery bags. I filled the bags with Karen's study materials and stored them in the closet in the spare bedroom that was now an office. The clock on the microwave told me it was almost tomorrow so I decided it was time for sleep.

I was tempted to go to the utility room door for a fourth time and call for Sam to come in. Richard found it amusing that I had deviated from our inventory project several times to check for

Sam. He confessed he was a dog person, and would not tolerate a beast that would not come when called. I think deep down he empathized with me.

I turned out the lights.

It was my best dream in weeks. I was back at work. There was a large banner above my desk: "We believe you Justin."

All the correspondence in my inbox was great, like the email from the state of New Jersey. The NJ Division of Taxation heard about my plight and granted Lithium Energy an additional two-month extension of time to file the corporate tax returns.

My computer operated flawlessly with lightning speed, text and data entering my spreadsheet without error as my fingers fluttered above the keys.

Then the Company President announced a new program. Lithium was instituting a cat friendly policy. All cubicles would be equipped with kitty condos and heated cat pads so we could bring our cats to the office.

I was all excited until I remembered I no longer had a cat. Then the HR Manager said that employees could borrow a cat from the company's 401(K) plan. She already had my paperwork filled out.

I took the forms out to the cathode production plant and found the supplies manager. He reviewed my paperwork, said no problem, and directed me to the waiting room. Inside was a large cat pad, one of those foam pads with a heating element inside. There being no place to sit, I crawled onto the pad to take a nap.

I woke up from my nap as he was rubbing his cheek against my face. I reached over and scratched his head for a bit then he snuggled close as we fell asleep again.

The indirect morning light received by the master bedroom is usually enough to wake me. I was still in that phase of sleep when a dream seems real and feeling good about having Sam back when I realized I was now awake.

I did not know what would happen when I showed up at work, Sam was not lying on my chest, and I was still a murder suspect.

I reorganized my thoughts and reprioritized to the matters at hand: get back my credit cards, my driver's license and a car.

Throwing off the summer blanket, I planted my bare feet on the floor, for a second, but only a second.

It was furry, it was cold and it was dead.

Sam was back.

Chapter 22   Ed

I contemplated a 'burial at sea' ceremony in the bathroom for the mouse. Then I reconsidered; his three-inch length might not navigate the plumbing successfully on his last voyage. It was probably best to use the tried and true paper towel shroud. In theory, I could add him to the compost, but I overruled that option due to possible odor and coyote issues. Instead, I made the trek to the kitchen waste can.

Sam was at his water dispenser, probably cleansing his palate. He finished his drink and walked over to rub my legs to let me know I still belonged. I picked him up. He did not feel thin and his fur was soft and shiny. I took a long look at his face and ears and noted no new scars or battle notches in his ears. He seemed to have come through this intact.

I have heard stories about cat owners that have suffered retribution for offending their cat. Sam did not seem vindictive. Instead, he acted as if I had been away at work for a long day. He performed a lot of cheek rubbing as I held him against my chest, supporting him with my left arm while petting his back with my right hand. When Sam started purring, all was right in the world.

The reunion continued for several minutes until Sam indicated he wanted down. He plopped on the floor and commenced cat-grooming procedures, paying special attention to his toes. After his toes were clean and his face washed, he confirmed that the food dispenser still had kibbles and then headed to the back of the couch where the morning sun was proving optimal napping conditions.

I continued the cleanup of the house that I began last night. I was not sure, if the police were polite by not making more of a mess or if they were worried about contaminating the crime scene. The items that had been in the cupboards now lay out on the counter. Sealed boxed items and sealed jars were untouched, but guessing from the knife in the sink and the flour on the counter, the Sheriff had taken a long bread knife and stirred the flour and mix containers looking for hidden items.

Working my way around the kitchen, I returned what I could to storage. I tossed anything that I thought contaminated in the search then moved into the living room while paying attention to the clock.

At about seven, I moved to the master bathroom. For some reason the Sheriff decided hair and tooth brushes were valuable evidence. Last night I had to break out a new toothbrush from its package, but my shower and shaving supplies were untouched. I made myself presentable to the public and returned to the living room until it was eight o'clock.

"Law Offices."

"Good morning, this is Justin Caise, is Ms. Schwartz available."

"Oh, good morning Mr. Caise, Ms. Schwartz said that she will be back from court about eleven and she would like to meet with you."

"OK, great, I will be there."

I hung up and returned to cleaning and organizing.

The sheriff discovered and opened the fruit cocktail diversion safe. It would have been nice to have the cash I hid there for emergencies, cash for an emergency just like this. Richard had explained that the police department like everyone else was afraid of being sued. They had taken the cash into inventory so I could not claim they stole it later.

The living room was mostly intact when I asked myself if I was avoiding Ed. I had to admit that I was glad that Ed was done with work in his garden for the day when Richard and I got to the house. This was not a conversation I thought I would enjoy.

Sam opened one eye as I approached the front door.

"It's OK, I'll be back," I said and he closed the eye.

I walked over to Ed's house by an unusual route, the sidewalk. Usually I talk to Ed across the fence or enter through the gate between the two properties. This time a more formal approach seemed in order.

I walked down the drive past his pickup to the gate connecting the house to his tool shed. He too had a carport rather than a garage. I saw him purging wilted blooms from his dahlia flowerbed.

"Hello Ed!"

Ed turned away from his plants. "Hello Justin, it's good to see you are home."

"Thanks, I was beginning to wonder." The pause stretched out into its second trimester.

"I wanted to thank you for feeding Sam."

"It just seemed the right thing to do. I thought I saw him a couple of times but he would not come close, must have gotten spooked the day of all the excitement."

"About that, I wanted you to know."

"No need to explain. I don't want to be rude, but I never got along with her and Angie did not like her either. Dogs have a way of knowing. You two had only been here a few weeks and she sprayed Angie with the hose, tried to tell me that Angie got into my sprinkler."

"I am sorry for your loss, and sorry for all the trouble you are in, but I am not sorry she is gone."

"I apologize for being so blunt, but it needed to be said."

Wow, Ed was the last person I thought who would speak ill of someone.

"I have been checking the paper but there has not been a lot of news."

"I don't know a lot myself. I have a meeting with my attorney this morning to find out where we go from here. To be honest, it does not look good. Seems the more I look the more I find out I did not know about her."

"Not everyone is lucky enough to find someone like my Ilene."

It looked like Ed's eyes were going to mist up, so I sought a diversion.

"Did you see anything the night Karen died?"

Ed jerked back to the present. "No, I was just waking up when the ambulance arrived. Angie must have heard the commotion and started barking."

"Ed, did you notice anything unusual in the weeks before she died? Were there strange people at my house when I was not home?"

"She didn't have any guests that I saw. Then, she did not spend a lot of time at home. I can see both cars from the garden when they are parked under the carport. Many of the days, she would leave right after you went to work. I don't think she liked me watching her come and go."

"Ed, did you notice anything else unusual?"

"I don't know why she tried to garden. I have never seen someone with a thumb as brown as hers."

"I tried to get Karen to ask you for help, but she wouldn't listen."

"Did you talk to the neighbors Ed? Did they have anything to say about what happened that night?"

"Al Jones thought he saw a car parked on Klamas when he got up to visit the bath about three, but there was nothing there when the ambulance arrived an hour later. Everyone else pretty much slept through the whole thing. The ambulance did not use its siren near the house, so unless the lights woke them, people did not know anything happened until they looked out and saw all the police and sheriff vehicles."

"Thanks Ed. Well I need to call a cab so I can go see my attorney."

"Justin, there is no need to do that, I can give you a ride."

"Thank you Ed, but I don't want to inconvenience you."

"It's no bother. It's time to take the truck out and blow out the cobwebs anyway."

Ed cut north to Mill Plain Boulevard, instead of heading south to SR 14, aka the Lewis and Clark Highway. Effectively, Mill Plain runs the width of Vancouver and almost runs into the Clark County courthouse on its way through downtown. Ed found the six lanes of surface traffic less intimidating than the SR 14 controlled access road, and Anne's office was only two blocks from the courthouse, so I have to say Ed's method worked.

"Thanks Ed."

"Are you sure you don't want me to stick around?"

"I appreciate the offer but I need to rent a car so I can drive to work." I hoped the last part was true.

The receptionist led me back to a conference room occupied by Richard Colson and my attorney. I could not tell if Richard was working from notes or whether he already had the transcript from the tape we made yesterday. In any case, they were watching the video. It was stopped at a frame with me kneeling on the ground.

The receptionist closed the door.

"Have a seat Justin. We were just reviewing the recording that you and Richard made."

"I am guessing that it does not look good."

"Justin, I never lie to my clients. This is your case and your neck on the line and I work for you. I will do what you say we should do, but you need to know what you are up against to make those decisions."

"Washington State still has the death penalty."

Anne let me think for a minute.

"The DA is a real law and order guy who is up for re-election next year. He would like nothing better than a juicy murder trial where he can display his 'tough on crime' management style. This is a safe city. Murders don't come along that often, especially heading into an election year. He is not looking to make a deal as that does not make him look tough."

"Are you suggesting that I plead guilty to avoid the death penalty?"

"I have an obligation to ask the prosecutor about a plea deal in any case. I do not yet have discovery and will not ask for a plea offer until I have seen what they have. But when I do ask for an offer, I would be surprised if it is anything except life without parole."

Chapter 23   Out

"Is this where I give the valiant 'I am innocent' speech and shout that we are going to fight this all the way to the Supreme Court?"

I did not think I could be shocked and stunned after my time in jail. Here was my attorney giving me two options, death by lethal injection or death by boredom.

"This seems like a cruel joke. I get a few days of freedom and then I am off to jail for the rest of my life. Well, I am not ready to give up and die. If you don't want to fight this get me someone who will."

"That is not what I am saying Justin. I am just laying out the options and we are a long way from making a decision."

"Based on what we know and what happened in the video, the prosecutor is going to make the case that you strangled your wife using the garden hose. We know that your prints are on the hose in positions that make it appear that you used the hose. We know that Karen used the hose and was lying on it which means that her DNA and hair will be on the hose."

"Assuming the hose was the murder weapon, the prosecutor will make a neat case for the jury about a man wanting to end a marriage without a divorce, so he could keep all of his wife's money. By the time the prosecutor is done, the law abiding citizens of the jury will be lusting for vengeance for a cold blooded killer."

"But all the evidence is circumstantial."

"Justin, people get convicted on circumstantial evidence all the time."

"You make it sound like there is no hope."

"What is my argument Justin? Believe him, he's got an honest face?"

"Anne, you said 'if' the hose was the murder weapon."

"It's the obvious implement, so the police will start the forensic examination there. The state crime lab will be comparing the hose to the injury on her neck. They will look at the ligature marks on the neck and look for residues that link the hose to the injury."

"Ligature marks?"

"Impressions and marks made in the skin and soft tissue caused by the weapon used to strangle someone. Devices like rope leave patterns in the flesh matching the weave of the rope. Other objects, like a necklace or a pendant on a necklace, leave marks that match the object.

The hose would leave marks characteristic with the texture of the hose. What kind of hose did you have?"

"It was a cheap hose I got on sale. It was stiff, about three quarters of an inch in diameter."

"Say, that hose had almost a ribbed design, not a smooth surface. They can't take prints off that, can they?"

Richard responded, "Prints left on smooth surfaces are easily captured. Fingerprints and handprints are recoverable from most surfaces. In the case of the hose with ridges, any point where the finger contacted a surface, like the top of the ridge, would leave patterns of oil from the skin. Conversely, the skin would not contact the valley between the ridges. This would generate a striped pattern of print and blank lines giving a very good gross picture of the print but losing detail and making match points more difficult to assign. In this situation the traditional 10 point match would be difficult for individual fingers, but if they have several fingers from each hand, which is likely, the match becomes much easier to sell to the jury."

"All this is speculation," interrupted Anne. "We will have a lot of time to discuss the evidence I get discovery from the District Attorney. And, I should be getting that soon."

"How soon after we get discovery do we go to trial?"

"That is what we need to discuss today, trial tactics. If you were sitting in jail, you would have the right to go to trial within 60 days of arraignment. This rule prevents the DA from arresting people and letting them sit in jail pending trial. If the DA had a weak case, it might work to our advantage to force the DA into court before he was ready."

"Anne, are you asking me to go back to jail, just so we can force the trial to start?"

"No, that is not what I am saying. It is a tactic we have to consider but I am not advising that course of action at this time."

"So if I stay out on bail when do we go to trial?"

"Murder trials are a big deal Justin. Neither the DA nor the Judge wants to slip up on the process and trials like this easily last 6 to 8 weeks. Therefore, the judge and the court will want to schedule far enough in advance to secure a clear block of time, and the time between now and then will be needed to prepare all the pretrial motions. We are looking at next spring, at the earliest."

"So what do I do now?"

"If you still have a job, I would go to work."

"I believe I still have a job. As of right now the only way I can get to work is on the bus. I can't rent a car without a credit card or drive it without a license. How do I get my driver's license and credit cards back?"

"I spoke to the DA this morning. He said he would release the cards and license from evidence. You will need to sign for them at the Sheriff's office."

"Good. Richard, would it be possible to get a ride to the "Wrent Our Wrecks" dealer off Lombard Street in North Portland?"

Anne erupted, "No! Justin, you will rent a car in Vancouver."

"But Lithium has an employee discount program there and..."

"I don't care if they are giving away cars for free. You are not to leave the State of Washington, which means you do not cross the Columbia River and you do not go to Portland, or you will surely go directly to jail."

"Justin, you are out on bail, you are not a free man, remember that."

Chapter 24   HR

It only took two hours to get my driver's license and credit cards back.

Richard stayed with me long enough for us to realize it was not going to be an in and out card quest. I boarded a C-TRAN bus for the rental company that tries harder, which was about half way to my house. I completed the journey home in time to call Lithium and Mary Ellen to see if I still had a job.

"Hi Mary Ellen, I got out yesterday afternoon and met with my attorney today.

I was planning to come to work tomorrow. That is, if I still have a desk?"

"Clark and I have been discussing your status. Clark has raised the issue with each of the people in the tax department. Their main concern is that you might depart suddenly or have lots of time away due to court appearances, but on the whole they support you."

"My attorney will be representing me most of the time, and I will not need to be physically present. For the instances where I need to be in attendance, I should have days if not weeks of advance notice."

"She also said I should not discuss the case."

"Yes, Jane said your attorney would want you to not say anything, could you come in at nine tomorrow? Let's meet in my office."

"OK, I'll see you at nine."

I had figured that Clark would be my biggest problem, but he seemed to be OK with me returning. Now the HR Manager was hedging about me returning to work, what was that about?

Chapter 25   The Office

Lithium instituted a business casual dress code years ago, so preparing for my return to work was not a major project.

I had gone to bed happy that I was going back to work and apprehensive about facing my friends and coworkers. Since I did not have to be in until nine, I had not set my alarm.

The indirect sunlight brightened the room and I woke a bit before seven. I rolled to the edge of the bed and checked the floor. Today Sam had performed a civic service and presented me with the body of an immature starling. I silently complimented Sam on his good deed, wishing that all house cats targeted nuisance birds like starlings.

I disposed of the body in the garbage and noted that Sam was in his spot on the back of the couch catching some rays.

I performed my pre-commute preparations, topped off my travel mug with coffee, and hit the road.

As I parked the rental car, I realized this was not good. My electronic key was on my key ring, which was with the sheriff. I was thinking about how to get in the building when I saw a gal from invoicing I knew slightly. I slowed my pace to allow her to reach the door first.

"Good morning Jill, thanks."

She held the door for me as I slipped in the employee entrance. I greeted Stephanie at the reception desk and headed to Mary Ellen's office. The Tax Director, Clark Harold, was there with Mary Ellen.

All the way to work, I thought about what I would say. "Good morning I'm innocent." or "Nice day too bad someone killed my wife and framed me." I finally settled on "Good Morning," and shut my mouth.

Mary Ellen took the initiative.

"Good morning, Clark and I were just talking."

"Here's the situation," said Mary Ellen sitting stiffly with her solid poker face in place.

"The people in the Tax Department have followed your case and it has been the topic of discussion every time a new piece of information came out."

During the short pause, Mary Ellen maintained her stoic posture and Clark played with his fingers.

"The VP of Marketing and Public Relations, Johnny Chen, thinks you should be placed on administrative leave. Some of the other VPs would like it to quietly go away."

I watched Mary Ellen, looking for clues behind the stoic facade. Human Resource managers deal with emotional situations, never knowing whether the news they deliver will elicit rage or tears. Mary Ellen watched for my reaction.

"What does Sue Johnson think?"

"The CEO will support my decision. She expects me to do what's best for the company. Right now, you are a novelty. The usual comment I hear is "I don't believe Justin could have done that." My concern is that that these comments will change into "Can you believe that Justin did that?"

"From an employer's standpoint, the opinions expressed by the employees are immaterial, what is important is the time lost to all the speculation. Every time there is a blurb in the news a new round of "did he, or didn't he," will begin."

This was not going in a direction I liked. "Clark, what do you think?"

"Well, we are as not as well cross trained as I would like, there really is not anyone who has the time or the training to easily take over what you have been doing. Sally could probably muddle through the apportionment calculation, but you are the only one who really understands how to pull all the pieces together in time for the tax return."

"We could bring in a CPA from Grant Thornton™ or Moss Adams™, but that would be costly. I have contacted Accountemps for a temp but they don't have any one with enough state income tax apportionment experience to be useful."

"The staff is outwardly supportive of your plight, but there have been unguarded comments that make me believe that not everyone is comfortable with the thought of working next to someone accused of, ah, a major crime."

"I appreciate your honesty Clark."

I looked at Mary Ellen: "Justin, if you were accused of any type of financial crime I would have no choice but terminate you or place you on administrative leave."

"Clark and I determined that we might be able to make this work. IT said they could set you up with a laptop, which can access all the Lithium systems you need from your home. In addition, IT has a printer and a cell phone for you to use on company business. We decided that it would be best if Clark or I was your primary contact at Lithium and that you minimize your contacts within the company."

"Key to this is you keeping Clark informed of your progress and letting him know in advance what information will be needed so he can make arrangements to get it to you."

"What about email?"

"You will have access, but again, it would be best if we keep it to a minimum."

"I don't see that as a problem, it will take a little while to work out processes, but I don't see any major obstacles.

"I want to thank both of you for having faith in me. I know this creates problems and is inconvenient."

Mary Ellen was still in poker face mode: "One other thing Justin, in talking to the company attorneys, it was determined that your full time status would be terminated."

"Instead, if you accept, you will be rehired as a part time employee. This will give you the option of taking time off and using your earned leave or taking unpaid time off."

"You still retain all benefits as long as you work the minimum hours per week. After all this is over, you can reapply for a full time permanent position."

"But, I can still work full time. There is no need to downgrade my position."

"Justin, the alternative is unpaid administrative leave."

I would soon learn the legal term 'discovery' is defined as compulsory disclosure, as to facts or documents. Discovery requires the district attorney to show the defense, meaning me, all the evidence they may use in the prosecution of the case.

While loading supplies into my car for my home office, my new phone rang.

"Mr. Caise, this is Ms. Schwartz's paralegal. I called your office and they gave me this number."

"It's my new work cell phone."

"OK, Ms. Schwartz wanted you to stop by, the District Attorney finally provided discovery. Would you like paper copies or shall I scan and email the files."

"I like to work with paper, but if it's easier to scan I can work with emails."

"How about I do both, Mr. Caise. Ms. Schwartz likes paper too, it's no problem to copy a second set. Lots of her clients don't have computers so it's no big deal."

"Great, can I stop by in about half an hour?"

Anne happened to be at the front desk when I walked in.

"Hi, Justin, the DA finally came across with discovery. He is not being very cooperative. We should have had this a week ago."

"Now that we have it, what do I do with it?"

"Read it, study it, and know all about it. And, more importantly, figure out what's missing."

"I'll try."

"This is just the first batch. Other items will be provided as they become available and it could be weeks or months for test results to come back from the state crime lab."

"It's more than I had this morning, I'll get started."

I picked up the banker's box and headed home.

Setting up my Lithium workstation did not take long since the sheriff had thoughtfully made space by removing my desktop computer. Next, I planned my attack on the state income tax apportionment calculation for tomorrow. Finally, I turned to the project that I really wanted to begin.

My first discovery about discovery was that there was no index or table of contents. Technically the stack of papers was not loose leaf because many of the document packets were two or three pages stapled together. Maybe there was a logical meaningful order to the evidence, but I was unable to discern what it was.

Accounting is as much about record retention as summarizing financial data, many times it is as important to be able to find out the why or how of a transaction as it is to properly report the transaction. The first thing I needed to do was to number the papers consecutively, which would allow me to return the papers to their original order. Then I quickly read the entire stack.

For not knowing what to expect, it was pretty much as expected. There were statements from everyone who had contact with me that day, as were statements from neighbors and associates. The deputies and police officers all filed reports and the transcripts of radio call logs from the 911 dispatch. The house and yard were well photographed and for good measure, the police added drawings with notations regarding the position of the body, the time, date and weather.

The evidence log included items I expected and many I thought had no bearing on the case. Why the police were interested in our recent ATM transactions and bank statements, I had no idea. The importance of my car's interior contents to the level of detail that there were two left hand cotton gloves and only one right hand glove in my car escaped me.

There were few items in Karen's immaculate car other than the details of the $415,000 hidden in her spare tire. Was it important that she organized her cash stash into bundles of hundred, fifty, twenty and ten dollar bills, or that there was a total of 5500 bills?

The log continued with household items, clothing and personal items, which made little sense to me as the murder, occurred outside the house. Then there were the statements from our friends and coworkers. I guess the police were looking for comments about how I wanted to kill my wife or that Karen was living in fear.

The list of everything that would or could be entered into evidence included lab tests on samples, the emergency room doctor's report, fingerprints of me at the jail and prints lifted from objects and places around the crime scene.

Then there were the crime scene photographs: the interior of my house, the exterior or my house and Karen. Photocopies of photographs are always lower quality than the original. Looking at photos, even poor quality ones was unnerving. I worked to regain my detached medical person so I could objectively evaluate the pictures. A visible band of injured tissue about three quarters of an inch, about the width of my garden hose, extended half way around her neck.

I looked at the photos longer than I liked, but not as long as needed. I would have to revisit them, I was sure, but for now, I moved on to the police reports.

The sheriff and police reports we essentially the same but from different perspectives. I read all the reports building a picture of the scene after I left with the ambulance. Evidently, the first deputy arrived just as we were preparing to depart. I was in the back of the ambulance and did not notice the deputy's arrival.

We almost never made it to the hospital.

The emergency room of the hospital serving East County is a "Level III" trauma center. They have a 24-hour emergency room physician, but all other specialties are on call. At the time of my call, the ER doctor was involved with a patient, probably the diabetic who was there when I arrived. The ER nurse coordinated with the EMTs on the ambulance about treatment and transport of patients. The ER doctor could have called Karen DOA via telemetry and EMT observations, had he not been involved with a problem diabetic. Lawsuits being what they are, the ER nurse applied the "CYA" protocol and ordered the transport of Karen to the hospital. We were well on our way when the ER Doctor got a chance to speak with the EMTs to confirm that there was no cardiac activity, and Karen's pupils were fixed and dilated.

Based upon his brief conversation with an EMT, the first deputy secured the house and yard as a crime scene and called in Deputy Miller to start the investigation. He coordinated the taking of physical and photographic evidence.

The fingerprints on the garden hose Included latent prints of the fingers of both hands. The grip marks on the hose were enough of a smoking gun for Deputy Miller to make my arrest. I guess if I were Deputy Miller, I would arrest me too.

Chapter 27　　　Telecommuting

Since I was not facing a commute this morning I did not set the alarm. I was finding this waking up to the soft rays of the early morning sunrise a nice way to start the day. I lay in bed waking slowly to the gently increasing light. My mind wandered and I imagined myself as primitive man captive to the rising and setting sun. I pictured myself lying on the cool ground cushioned by a mat of grasses with most of the nettles removed. My sleeping mat as close to the fire as possible to ward off the chill of late Summer's clear cool nights. Pleased to wake to the rising sun and not to the sounds of a predator dragging a tribe member into the predawn darkness.

With that happy vision in mind, I was now fully awake. I performed a check of the floor to see what present was delivered by my predator in his predawn hunt. Not a thing, it must have been a slow night.

I performed my personal hygiene at a leisurely pace without shaving, knowing I was saving 20 to 25 minutes with no commute. I was ready to start work at 7:30.

Tax is a hybrid profession. The joke in the profession is that the attorneys love the law and hate the numbers, and the accountants love the numbers and hate the law. Tax is a rare area where a non-lawyer can give legal advice without being sued for practicing law without a license. Accountants can even practice before the US Tax Court without being an attorney, per Rule 200.

My task for Lithium was a simple one: determine how much of Lithium's taxable income is attributable to each state.

I was actually looking forward to this project. This was a chance to get lost in the details and forget about the upcoming trial. The task itself was not that mentally challenging. I had been though the process enough times to know the data I needed to answer the question about how much income goes where. Keeping track of the data and making sure all the parts were in place would fully occupy my mind.

How much income belongs to a state is a question that actually predates the income tax law. The early court cases that created the rules of income apportionment originated in the days of railroads and involved property taxes. As the railroads expanded their lines to move people and products between states, government saw opportunity. If a railroad laid track in their state, and carried passengers for hire in their state, then the state, or county, or city, or township, or school district assessor should be able to include the railroad property on the tax rolls and charge property tax.

Of course, the railroad argued that the only thing that could be taxed was the track, the engines and the cars did not reside in the assessor's tax jurisdiction so there was no connection to the assessor.

The states argued that if you entered the state you were subject to the laws of that state.

The railroads were getting annoyed at paying property tax on the full value of their rolling stock whenever they entered or passed through a new state. A situation similar to driving from Seattle to San Francisco and having to pay sales tax on the value of your car in Washington, Oregon and California.

Eventually the railroads and the states ended up in the Supreme Court of the United States. It is obvious that lawyers and not accountants staff the Supreme Court. Accountants would have laid out a rule that nobody would have liked but everyone would have understood. The Court came out and said 'yes' the states had a right to tax the railroads, but 'no' the states could not tax everything owned by the railroads. Finally, in a display of decisiveness, the court ruled that any method that rationally allocated the value of property, for the application of tax, would be acceptable.

The same rationale applied later to income taxes. The amount of business done in a state determines the income taxed by a state. Which raises the question: How do you measure how much business someone conducts? What is the best measure? The number of employees, equipment used, or maybe the amount of sales is the best criteria.

The states got together, well some of them, to design a model allocation method, something that everyone could use and meet the court's "rationale allocation" mandate. They promulgated many things like, how do you count employees, by the head or by payroll paid. Is rented equipment included in total property according to the amount of rent paid, the value of the equipment, or not at all? Are sales located in the state from: where the product is shipped, in the state where it is delivered, or where the contract is signed? These answers and many other issues resulted in the creation of the "three factor formula."

This group decided that a rational allocation of taxable income is determined by a three-factor formula that includes the amount of people, equipment and sales in a state divided by everything everywhere.

Other than the fact that the method was not binding on any state, it was a good plan. Virtually every state concluded 'yes it is a good method', but to make it work in "our state" with "our unique circumstances" it needs to be tweaked just a little.

That is what made my task complex and interesting. Manufacturing states felt that equipment should count for more because if you cannot make it you cannot sell it. Other states thought that most important component was the sale because if you did not sell it, you could not have any income.

In the end, every state elected to use a variation of the original three-factor formula.

My job was to compile that data needed to make that calculation for each state.

Converting my home office to my work office was a simple matter. There was ample room for my Lithium laptop where my personal PC sat before the police confiscated it for evidence. After turning on my laptop and accessing the company via a VPN login (who thinks up these acronyms?) I started pulling data. So much of what I needed to reference was in spreadsheets, or the accounting system, or digitally recorded as picture files that I did not feel cut off from the office.

In addition, there are perks to working at home, it was nice being able to grind fresh beans for each cup of coffee and the ultra-casual dress code was nice. Sam handled the disruption to his daily activities with his usual cat aplomb. About nine, after his early morning nap, he came in to see my setup and cheek rub the laptop and printer. His work done, he headed outside for his mid-morning nap, probably to stake out a semi-shady spot under the Azalea.

About three in the afternoon, I decided I had given enough time to Lithium and called it quits after logging my time and updating Clark via email. I wanted to get back into the review of the discovery, and I felt I had accomplished more for Lithium by not having the distraction of a phone and my coworkers. With a clear conscience, I turned my attention to discovery.

I read the entire stack again. Nothing seemed to stand out as important. I turned to the Value America Airlines documents. The personnel file still had her listed as Karen Winslow, even on documents well after our marriage. More disturbing was that the primary mailing address was a PO Box in Houston, Texas.

I emailed Richard Cushing asking if anyone was checking on

the PO Box in Houston noted in Karen's personnel file. Then I got on the US Postal Service web site and located the mail forwarding form, so that I could have all mail coming to the box come to me. On second, thought, I listed the forwarding address as my attorney's office. If there were something in the mail that was important, it would be best for her to touch it first.

The statements collected by the Sheriff from my coworkers were bland and generally lacking in information. The only statements that seemed damning were those from Joan and Jerry Beardsley. Joan and Jerry started their interview together. The report concluded with separate statements, indicating to me that the deputy sensed they would disclose more if they did not have mutual support. Joan and Jerry tried to put a positive spin on the argument between Karen and me at their house back in July. Nevertheless, as is the case when a professional matches wits with an amateur, the pro wins. A detailed and damning account of the fight was now in evidence.

The subpoenaed phone activity included all incoming and outgoing numbers for all calls on the phones for the last three months. It seemed like this might be important, so I entered all the phone numbers, identified by phone, and the call dates into a spreadsheet. I assigned names to known phone numbers and looked up as many as possible on the internet reverse directory listing.

I thought about calling the numbers that I identified via internet requests. If one of these numbers was the killer, did I want to alert him or her to the fact that someone was investigating Karen's call list? Instead, I summarized what I had done and forwarded it off to Richard.

Most of the phone message transcripts were from Value America Airlines dispatch trying to find Karen so she could meet her next flight. One message from my phone stuck out:

"Karen, this is Betty from dispatch. Please call in as soon as possible. I have left messages on your cell phone and your home phone. Please let us know about your status as soon as you can so we can properly staff the flight schedule."

Home phone, why was Betty calling my house and then saying she also called Karen at home?

I went to bed still thinking about that question.

Chapter 28   TGIF

Last night I fell asleep telling myself that Anne and Richard were working hard on my case. The last thing they needed was a client calling every hour asking how the case was going.

I awoke early and agitated. After giving up trying to sleep, I checked the floor for surprises and headed to the shower. I was on the laptop by six and trying to get lost in my work data. The sky had lightened considerably when Sam came in to check on me. He jumped onto the desk, inspected the laptop, let me know it was appropriate to pet him for a bit. I asked Sam what he thought about Betty's phone call. Sam rubbed my chin with his cheek then headed to the couch for his early morning nap.

I was making a cup of coffee when the landline rang.

"Justin? I wanted to talk to you about your email." I recognized Richard's voice and his waste no words manner.

"What do you know about your wife's activities in Houston?"

"Not much, Richard. She flew through there regularly as part of her route. She mentioned that she stayed there on occasion when she needed to layover or was timed out on hours."

"Justin, I contacted an affiliate in Houston when I saw the PO Box address in her personnel file. She searched the Houston utility records and found an apartment. Then she contacted the apartment manager and requested a wellness check on Karen. The apartment manager said there was no need as the police had already been there last week. Our investigator arranged to visit and sent a video of the contents of the apartment.

It was hard to tell after the police were through, but the investigator thinks someone cleaned the apartment. She saw open spaces on shelves suitable for pictures and other signs supporting that conclusion. "

"What do the police think about this? I didn't see anything about this in the discovery."

"We don't know. Anne was steamed and fired off a letter to the DA demanding the Houston Police report. The DA is playing games. He is obligated to provide information in a timely manner, but he knows he faces no real penalty until we set a trial date and the judge issues discovery delivery deadlines."

"You were a cop, what do you think this means? Will they investigate this?"

"Houston is a busy place Justin. It is not that easy to clean an apartment well enough to fool the forensic team, if they decide to devote the time and resources to the task. Then the technicians are not as brilliant and thorough as seen on TV. My bet is that they did their standard investigation protocol that catches all the major evidence. What I don't see happening is heroic, spare no cost, take all the time you need directives from management. In addition, Karen may have had a cleaner for her apartment. Who may have just happened to leave it in such a state. On the other hand, there might not be another person, and Karen just organized her effects in an unusual way. Either way, we will not know until we get the police report."

"Richard, is there anything you need me to do?"

"Just take a look at the video. Let me know if there is anything that needs additional inquiry."

"OK, I will try to get at it this afternoon. I need to do some work so I can keep my job."

"Justin, this is a marathon not a sprint. There will be a lot to do and you should definitely keep your employer happy, you will need the money."

"I know Richard, but it's a bit hard to think about taxes when I find out about things like this."

"Do your best. You should see the video file in a few minutes. It's Windows Media compatible."

I returned to my laptop and reviewed my emails, the few that there were. Clark asked that I spend some time on the Research and Development credit when I needed a break from working on the apportionment. Announcements about changes to the company benefits and modifications to the company dress code rounded out my incoming mail.

I forced my attention back to apportionment project. If I stopped to look at the video, I knew I would not be able to concentrate on taxes the rest of the day.

Chapter 29   There's No Place Like Home

Sam woke from his early afternoon nap and came into see me about two-thirty. He indicated it was time for some kitty treats by pawing at the desk drawer containing the jewels of cat cuisine. I always make Sam work for his treats by issuing them one at a time and tossing them into difficult to access locations, such as between the NordicTrack ski machine and the wall, or on top of the bookcase. The later location was a challenge for me too. While sitting at my desk I had to toss the treat such that the amplitude of the arc was great enough to clear the top while the forward velocity was insufficient to propel the treat off the backside of the bookcase. I had about a 50% success rate, so Sam got some easy treats from my misses. The last treat recovered, Sam returned to the desktop in hopes there might be a second allocation. Finding no weakness in my resolve to avoid a kitty candy overdose, he departed for one of several afternoon nap locations.

Me, I exercised my option to stop work on Lithium for the day and view the video from Richard. I pulled up his email, hesitating before opening the file. What would I see: a luxurious bachelorette pad or an economy studio?

The video started with a walk through of all the rooms. As Yogi Berra once said, it was déjà vu all over again. The police search left her apartment in a condition similar to my house. Thorough and efficient but not destructive, nothing moved unless it needed to be inspected or opened. Drawers and cupboards opened and items displayed, furniture examined and disassembled as part of a methodical search.

It was not easy for me to judge room size from the video but I would guess this was a 900 to 1000 square foot apartment. At least it looked similar to the apartment I shared in college: two bedrooms, one full bath, a half bath, a utility closet for the washer and dryer, living room and a real kitchen big enough for dining.

What I saw in the video was her home. Everything that was missing from our house in Vancouver was in Houston. On display was Karen's life.

The investigator returned to the living room and began her detailed record. She did a slow 360-degree panorama of the room. There were two windowless full walls, one partial wall separating the kitchen from the living room, and an exterior wall that extended the length of both the kitchen and the living room. The exterior wall included a large window adjacent to the dining area of the kitchen and a sliding glass door, which accessed the patio balcony running the length of the apartment.

The first windowless wall had supported four framed pictures now leaning against the wall after their inspection by the police. Open shelving occupied most of the other windowless wall. What looked like solid walnut shelving had more in common with a display case than a bookshelf. On display were all the important milestones of Karen's life.

The investigator ended her 360 rotation by exposing the framed pictures. Three were Van Gogh prints and the other was not a picture at all. The narrator informed me that what appeared to be a framed picture of a shirt was in fact a shirt. Someone had mounted a button collar short-sleeve cotton shirt in a picture frame above a photograph of a teenage Karen standing by a single engine airplane. The shirt was clean. Other than the fact that someone removed the shirttails, it was undamaged. The damage was intentional. Someone crudely cut off the tails. Obviously, this shirt was important to Karen and related to the aircraft. Maybe a prize or some type of award or the product of some ritual or ceremony, but in any case a valued memento.

Framed items occupied the display case: pictures, military patches, and awards. Nevertheless, there were several functional and novelty items on display also. The bottom shelf center was occupied by an air force helmet stenciled Winslow K. E. Flanking the helmet was a picture of Karen receiving an award on one side and a framed set of military orders on the other. Completing the row, a clock constructed from a cockpit instrument, and a pilot figurine assembled from nuts, bolts and other airplane parts.

She reserved the top shelf for her youth. On the left a framed congratulation letter signed by a congressman I did not know. The center occupied by a framed award that said General Ira C. Eaker. The right position displayed her Civil Air Patrol promotion to Lt. Colonel.

She reserved another shelf for pictures of Karen, and Karen with other people. An innocent young Karen in her Civil Air Patrol uniform, an older more serious Karen in her Air Force uniform, and pictures that included various dignitaries and mentors. Absent were pictures showing young Karen in love, or any picture ever showing her in love.

The other interesting aspect of the shelf of pictures was that that the pictures only extended about two-thirds away across the shelf. Karen was nothing if not meticulous. She would never have an unbalanced display, loading pictures to one side of the shelf was not in her nature. Karen would display a tasteful, neat and symmetrical manner. I could not imagine any cleaner retaining employment that disrupted the symmetry of the display more than once.

If Karen elected to remove some pictures, she would have reorganized the display to restore the symmetry. That begged two questions: First, who or what was in the missing pictures? Second, who would benefit from their absence?

The only other item of note in the living room was a wooden pedestal chess table with carved wooden chess pieces. Two wood chairs with unpadded arms occupied the positions behind the chessmen.

The rest of the apartment confirmed what I had come to expect from Karen: neat, organized and efficient. Karen was not big on acquiring stuff. Other than the Van Gogh prints and the framed shirt, almost everything in the apartment served a practical purpose or related to Karen's career as a pilot.

The kitchen was a bit surprising. It was better equipped than I expected. The steel pot rack mounted above the sink held six matching stainless steel copper clad cookware pots and pans. The matching large kettles had been stored in a lower cupboard and the lids stored with the sheet pans in the stove drawer.

I would have been dismayed if the stove had been more upscale than a white porcelain Kenmore gas range. In addition to the stove and full size refrigerator, there were various appliances of practical but not extravagant quality. Again, the police inventoried the refrigerator and the cupboards and for good measure stirred the rice, sugar and flour containers to check for evidence. Our investigator opened the refrigerator to video the contents. The assortment of condiments was different from mine and included what I assumed were local brands of sauces and seasonings. Otherwise it just appeared to be a moderately well stocked kitchen, which was more than what I expected from Karen based upon the amount of cooking she did in our Vancouver home.

The investigator moved down the short hall to the small bedroom. Aside from a double bed, there was a bookcase, a computer monitor and a printer on a small dark wood computer desk. Flying and government publications dominated the book collection. The unhooked computer cables evidenced the seized computer. The small closet was mostly empty and the bed mattress was bare, separate from the box springs. Finally, the small night table drawer was open and empty guarded over by the lamp and a small clock radio alarm.

Our investigator moved on the main bedroom, a windowless interior room. The police stacked the clothes unloaded from the dresser and the closet on the floor in front of several back facing framed pictures. An empty jewelry box the size of a loaf of bread sat in front of the oval mirror of the empty walnut dresser. Similar to the other bedroom, the bare mattress leaned against the wall.

I am not sure if it was significant, but there was another set of pilot luggage as well as civilian luggage pulled from the closet lying open on the floor. At least three sets of female flight uniforms lay on the floor combined with an array of civilian clothes, more than she kept in our Vancouver home.

The full bathroom was accessible from either bedroom. If there were any revelations in the cosmetic and hygiene products on display, I failed to see them. The medicine cabinet shelves were blank in spots and the contents of the drawers and under sink cabinets were laid out on the floor with all the normal items, and nothing of interest.

The investigator turned her camera to the utility room across the hall from the bedroom and abutting the kitchen. Probably because they would have caused an obstruction for the officers, the bedclothes that had been in the washer and dryer had been stuffed back in. The cleaners and soaps were on top of the machines and the ironing board was leaning against the hall wall.

The half bath accessible from the hallway was spartan and clean.

Finally, the hall coat closet was open to reveal raincoats, overcoats, boots and shoes, tossed back inside by the police so as not to create a trip hazard for them during the search.

I reviewed my notes and sat through the entire forty minutes again. There was nothing, unless the police removed it, of importance in Karen's apartment. The video really added no new information. It just confirmed what I had come to believe. There was one prominent item missing, my picture. Nowhere in Karen's home was there any indication that I existed.

It was almost five o'clock when I finished viewing the disappointing video of Karen's apartment. I put down the phone. The urge to call Richard and talk about the video faded. Nothing I saw in the apartment video that warranted interrupting his evening. Instead, I wrote him an email and copied Anne commenting on the few items I found noteworthy: the well-equipped kitchen, the lack of my picture anywhere, and the fact that all her important memorabilia was in Houston. I finished off the email with two questions to Richard. First, would the Houston police pursue the person who had been in Karen's apartment and second, had the investigator gotten any information from the other tenants.

I looked at the large stack of discovery papers crowned with the recording of my conversation with Deputy Miller when I was booked into jail. I decided I had had too much fun for one day and sat down for some mindless TV.

After the third time through the channels, I realized I had no interest in old or new movies or any old or new TV series. Since it was too early to go to bed, I might as well start my review of the research and development tax rules. There was still a good hour of sunlight left so I grabbed a beverage and my printout of the relevant Internal Revenue Code sections, the Regulations, my "Master Tax Guide" and the CCH "Practical Guide to Research and Development Tax Incentives--Federal, State, and Foreign," and headed out to the back yard. I loaded the plastic table with the reading materials and my cold malt beverage and settled down with a good book.

Section 174 and Section 41 of the Internal Revenue Code are good examples of the schizophrenic nature of Congress. One the one hand Congress wants to encourage business to invest in new products, processes and business. On the other hand, Congress does not want anyone to benefit too much. Add generally accepted accounting principles to the mix and you end up needing a 760 page book like the "Practical Guide to Research and Development Tax Incentives--Federal, State, and Foreign," to explain the rules.

In dealing with a topic like research and development, the first issue to confront is difference between accounting rules and tax rules. Businesses want to show that they are earning lots of income when talking to investors or bankers. However, when it comes time to pay their taxes, businesses want to appear destitute. Accounting rules generally want businesses to recognize expenses now rather than later. The tax rules want businesses to recognize expenses later rather than now.

So why not there just one set of rules for both accounting and tax? For the same reason that Baskin-Robbins sells thirty-one flavors, people want a flavor that meets their ice cream desires and every business wants an accounting system designed specifically for their needs.

From the start, Congress recognized that people do not like to pay taxes. Given the chance, businesses would and will structure their accounting and operations to minimize the taxes they pay. Since people are endlessly creative, Congress adopted basic broad rules to define acceptable business expenses. Then congress left it up to the IRS and the accountants to argue about what constitutes "ordinary and necessary" business expenses. I may think that Sam provides a valuable rodent remediation service and his food and vet bills are a necessary expense, but the government takes a much more restricted view of what constitutes an "ordinary and necessary" expense.

It is the same with research and development expenses. If I spend a million dollars to design and perfect a mousetrap, can I expense the million dollars? That depends. If I spend the million dollars on salaries for the engineering team, the answer is probably yes. What if I spend all the money on buildings and test equipment? The answer is no. Buildings and equipment are depreciable property. Fork out the money today, get a small deduction over several years. The IRS does not care if you built assets specifically for the research and development process, the depreciation rules still apply. What about wages paid to workers? If the worker is an engineer designing test equipment, is that salary part of the cost of the equipment or an immediate expense?

Lithium Energy Resources needed answers to these questions. The company spends large amounts every year on improving and developing new batteries to meet the demands of consumers. Which and how much of those expenditures Lithium could claim as a credit or current year tax deduction was of great interest to senior management.

This year we decided to enter a market, which we had not previously explored, aviation. Although not a large market when compared to something like consumer electronics, it had the advantage of larger profit margins and was a gateway to the military market. The market development team said if we could master the navigation of FAA standards, it would be relatively easy to meet the military specifications. The engineers were excited about what they thought was a design breakthrough that would open to door for widespread use of lithium technology in applications currently owned by old but reliable technology.

I was feeling more comfortable with research and development basics and reached for my empty glass, contemplating whether to start my review of Internal Revenue Code Section 41. Doing tax research in my back yard had its benefits. While working, I was enjoying one of those September days that make living in the world's largest temperate rain forest worth the months of clouds and rain. The sun was low on the horizon, the sky was clear, the temperature was perfect for shorts and tee shirt and it had not rained in two months so there were no mosquitoes.

Sam appeared from somewhere and performed a thoracic-lumbar stretch that almost caused his belly to touch the ground. Sam enjoyed the backstretch so much that his toes splayed wide to expose all of his claws. He yawned powerfully before jumping up onto my legs stretched between two plastic lawn chairs. I put down my glass as he moved up my thigh to stand in the preferred "pet me" position.

"Sam, what are we going to do? You saw the video."

I stroked Sam from his forehead to his tail. Sam assisted by arching his lower back into my hand with each stroke.

"What was Karen planning to do?" Sam opened his half-closed eyes to give me a look as if to say, "You knew she was up to something. Think it through."

"The apartment was not that expensive, Houston is not New York and the cost of a simple two bedroom apartment would not tax the wages of a pilot with Karen's experience. Nor was the apartment expensively furnished. The most extravagant item in the whole place was the chess table. What was she doing with her money?"

Sam reached up, placing his paws on my left collarbone. From that position, Sam rubbed his left cheek against my left jaw.

"Sam, we know she stashed a lot of her money in the spare tire of her car." Sam stopped purring to look at me and I swear he wanted to say "Duh!"

"What is it Sam, what was she doing to make all that money?" Sam turned and jumped off my leg and headed toward the house and his food bowl.

I picked up my materials and followed.

Saturday morning looked to be another beautiful day when I woke. The floor check indicated it was safe to place my bare feet on the floor. Sam seemed to be on a cold streak regarding his hunting.

In keeping with my attempt to enjoy my remaining freedom, I decided today would be a good day to trim the arborvitae in preparation for winter. I went to the closet to get a long sleeve shirt to protect my arms. The spring-powered door closed automatically upon my release when I heard the phone ring.

Richard Cushing responded to my greeting. "Morning Justin, I wanted to follow up on your email. Your comment about the kitchen helped confirm our belief that someone else knew about Karen's apartment and had been there on more than one occasion."

"As for Karen's neighbors, they were not very helpful. Karen kept to herself and her schedule had her coming and going at odd times. There were a couple of people who said that they may have seen a Hispanic male, 30 to 40 years old enter the apartment."

"When, the day of the murder?"

"No, Justin, the sightings were well before the murder. None of the tenants were able give more than a general description of the visitor to our investigator or the police."

"What about the police, what are they doing with this information?"

"Justin, the police need a little bit more than "forty year old Hispanic male" to find a suspect, especially in a city like Houston."

"Also, it looks like this guy watched crime shows. We think the apartment was wiped thoroughly for fingerprints; stripped of items linking the suspect to the apartment; and the bedclothes were washed in bleach to get rid of his DNA. There is still DNA in the apartment from hair and stuff, but we need something linking someone to Karen's apartment before we start doing DNA tests."

"So we have nothing."

"It is not good Justin. We know a little more than we did before. Now we can limit our search to half the population."

I guess that was Richard's attempt at humor. I decided it was a good sign. Maybe he believed that there was a suspect other than me.

"What did you find out about the phone numbers from the calls on Karen's cell phone?"

"Karen did not save any phone numbers under her contacts. That is very unusual. Most people are lost without their cell phone contact list."

"Most of the numbers called in the last three months were to Value America Airlines, dispatch, flight operations and maintenance numbers. The other numbers were for businesses. There were also a couple of calls from a disposable cell phone."

"Actually that does not surprise me. Karen had an excellent memory."

"That is a good question, Justin, we will explore that further."

"Did you call the numbers to find out who answered?"

"First we started with Value America Airlines. The corporate office in Denver verified the numbers as belonging to Dispatch and Flight Operations, both of which are located in Denver. They also verified that the other numbers, related to various ground support teams in Portland, Houston and Cancun."

"I called and talked to both Dispatch and Flight Operations. The dispatch group for VAA performs two functions: they design the flight schedule and they assign crews to aircraft. The schedule is a really a wish list, or a best-case scenario of when and where pilots and crews will fly. Periodically, the airline internally publishes the route schedule they will be flying in the near future. Pilots submit bids to the schedulers about which routes they want to fly. The schedules assign pilots to routes first according to their preferred bid and seniority, and then according to the needs of the airline schedule. They follow the schedule as operational conditions permit."

"The dispatchers work closely with the schedulers to match aircraft and crews to actual operations versus the theoretical schedule. When bad weather, mechanical problems, illness or other issues occur, the dispatchers may pull pilots to work as needed, as long as they comply with the FAA rules."

"Both the manager of scheduling and the manager of dispatch had similar comments about Karen: She was competent and her military training shown through. She knew her rights and responsibilities as a pilot and was professional in her dealings with dispatch, but she had no tolerance for those she felt did not know their jobs, or respect her status as a pilot and captain. They were not aware of any ongoing conflicts with other pilots, or other employees."

"Richard, that doesn't tell us much we did not know

already. Did she make any unusual scheduling requests?"

"Nothing out of the ordinary, but she did jump seat to Houston and Cancun regularly, which makes sense now that we know about the apartment."

"I also talked to Flight Ops and got pretty much the same answers. Flight Operations makes sure all the things necessary for the operation of the aircraft are in place for each flight segment: Fuel, ground support, maintenance, catering etc. Flight Ops is used to questions from pilots about the aircraft they fly. Pilots take a greater interest in the mechanical well-being of their aircraft than most car drivers, and for good reason. Karen seemed to be more involved in the mechanical aspect than most pilots. Whether that was due to her military training or her personality, it was not a trait that made anyone uncomfortable. Karen was also a bit more assertive about talking directly to the mechanics and avionics teams about systems issues. All pilots like to communicate with the maintenance teams to insure that requested repairs are fixing the problem. Karen liked to talk to the technicians directly more often than other pilots."

"That seems unusual."

"I agree, but nothing that is so far out of the norm that her manager, Dispatch, or Flight Ops thought it of note. Pilots are an interesting group of personalities.'

"In what way? The only pilot I know, knew, was Karen."

"I called a pilot friend and asked about the trophy case in her apartment and pilots in general. Pilots are a superstitious bunch."

"Really?"

"Yea, he said he knows pilots refuse to change their brand of engine oil. They are unwilling to take a chance and switch from the brand installed by the manufacturer. It's not about technical specifications or warranties, it's about superstition."

"Kind of like people carrying a good luck charm."

"My friend said he knew a pilot who called in sick every time he was assigned to fly a certain aircraft. Just because the last three numbers in the aircraft's serial number were "666." The pilot said he would not fly in the "Devil's Ship.""

"What about the things Karen kept and displayed?"

"He was impressed with the Civil Air Patrol "Eaker" award. It is not something they give out to everyone; she had to work to earn that. The regulations require that it is should be awarded by an elected federal official or a federal judge. Karen appeared to be on the fast track and he was surprised she got out of the Air Force."

"Why is that?"

"People with the discipline to get the "Eaker" award are of a temperament to do well in the military. When Karen served, the Air Force had not yet lifted many of the restrictions on aircraft that women were allowed to fly. Karen may not have liked the idea of a career of flying support aircraft."

"I can see where that might frustrate Karen."

"My friend got a kick out of the framed shirt, he had one too. It is tradition for a flight instructor to cut off the student pilot's shirttails.

"You are right, pilots are an unusual bunch."

"It dates back to the days of open cockpit aircraft. The aircraft were so noisy that flight instructors would tug on the new pilot's shirttails to give directions. When a student pilot made their first solo flight, it proved that the he no longer needed shirt tails for the instructor to grab."

"That's all very interesting, but is there anything we can use?"

"The one thing that raises the most questions is Karen's use of her free flying privileges. She spent a lot of time in both Houston and Cancun. I will contact an investigator in Cancun to see if Karen left any tracks."

"We're grasping at straws, aren't we?"

"Maybe, but it's all we have Justin. I will keep you informed if anything comes up."

I hung up the landline and returned to my bedroom to put on my yard work jeans. What is this? Looks like Sam was successful after all.

Chapter 32   Something New

For some reason Sam rated snakes as worthy of special treatment. He did not get them often and he reserved Karen's pillow for such unique trophies. Field mice, voles, and starlings landed on my side of the bed usually found by my feet if I were not alert. Snakes rated prominent display.

I reversed course back to the kitchen to get some paper towels for a funeral shroud and returned to the bed. Sam preceded me into the bedroom and jumped onto the bed. He stood victorious over his prize. That was no snake. What had appeared to be the tail of one of the indigenous garter snakes was actually a Value America Airline lanyard. Sam must have retrieved it from the closet and left it for me.

I paused to scold Sam. "Sam, why are you pulling her things out of the closet?"

Sam delivered the cat version of being shocked and indignant. He stood tail high, ears alert, eyes wide waiting for me to back down. Recognizing I was too stubborn to back down he stepped to the edge of the bed so he could rub his cheek against my thigh.

I attempted to console him. "It's OK Sam. I guarantee she is not coming back."

I scratched behind his ears to show all was forgiven. I switched to full-length head to tail petting but Sam only accepted two strokes before jumping off the bed and walking to the closed closet door. He looked, appealing for me to come over and let him in.

I dismissed Sam's actions and reached for the lanyard.

"Meerrooow" boomed from Sam's mouth.

I checked my movement, stood straight and looked that VAA ribbon lanyard. Something was not right. All of Karen's possessions were in that closet, secured behind a spring-loaded door. I knew the door spring still worked. I remembered the closet door slamming shut this morning when I left the bedroom to answer Richard's phone call. Sam had never been able to open the closet door once I had installed the spring. So how did he get in the closet last night?

I opened the closet and pulled out the first brown paper bag. The underwear was soon stacked on the floor, no lanyard. I pulled out the second brown paper bag. Under the layer of socks on top of her jeans was Karen's lanyard.

"Richard, you told me to call if I found any new evidence."

"Did you touch it?"

"No, it is still on the bed where my cat dropped it."

"Good, remove the cat, close the door and wait for me. I will be there in half an hour."

What to do for while waiting for Richard? Maybe I should reward the one who made the discovery? Out came a can of kitty treats. Sam was soon eagerly chasing treats I tossed around the living room and kitchen. Sam much enjoyed this unexpected bonus and eagerly sought out every treat. After ten minutes of search and consume, Sam was ready to retire to the back of the couch for his well-deserved mid-morning nap.

I ground some beans for some fresh coffee and waited for Richard. Richard pulled up in his truck as the last drops were falling into the carafe. I met him at the door, holding it for him since he was carrying the video camera and a backpack.

He dropped the equipment on the kitchen table and he motioned me to sit.

"Justin, tell me what happened."

"Sam is quite a hunter. He brings me his prey, which he usually drops on the floor. Occasionally he leaves his prey on top of the bed, usually on the pillow where Karen used to sleep. This morning after our call I saw the lanyard draped over the pillow. Sam must have brought it in last night or early this morning."

"What makes you think this is evidence?"

"Karen's lanyard was in the closet."

"I am not following you Justin."

I took a deep breath "VAA issues all employees ID badges. Employees who work at airports are required to have their badges with them at all times and usually must have them visible, either clipped on the uniform or attached to a lanyard. The lanyards issued by VAA have the company logo woven into the material."

"So? Most people who work at airports wear lanyards."

"Karen never wore her lanyard. She told me that the ID badges had RFID chips that tracked their location. The TSA only required that they openly wear their badges in certain parts of the airport. When she had to, Karen clipped her badge to her uniform. She complained that they didn't need to display badges all the time if they were being tracked."

"Justin, RFID is not a tracking device like you see on TV. Actually, most Radio Frequency Identification chips are passive devices. They can only generate a signal by receiving the interrogation broadcast from the reader."

"Like a reflection?"

"Yes the signal sent by the reader provides enough energy to cause the chip to respond with its canned message."

"So the reader asks, "Is anyone out there?" And the RFID chip says, "It's just me."

"Exactly, the only tracking that occurs is when the chip passes within signal distance of the reader."

"That explains why the TSA agents demand to see ID badges."

"Yes. Justin, what's this about your cat? Are you are telling me that your cat found a VAA lanyard not owned by Karen?

"Yes."

"And you think this is somehow connected to Karen's murder."

"Yes."

Chapter 33   Bridge of the Gods

I sat alone at the table thinking. We now had a video explaining the circumstances surrounding the discovery of the lanyard. I videoed as Richard donned blue gloves and used a new pair of chopsticks to drop the lanyard into a new zippered plastic bag, which he sealed with tape. Richard explained that the chopsticks are cheap, sterile, and could be included with the other evidence for purposes of excluding contamination. He answered that the laboratory would take a week or so to complete the preliminary analysis. Then he was gone.

I wondered what Richard had been thinking behind his poker face as he listened to my theory that the killer had dropped the lanyard the night Karen was murdered.

"If that is true Justin, we should also find their ID badge nearby. Say the killer attacked Karen and she grabbed the lanyard. The safety latch releases with a tug and now the lanyard and the ID badge are in Karen's hand, at which point the killer strangles Karen with the garden hose. The killer unclips his ID badge and leaves the lanyard behind. Then your cat, a raccoon or a coyote grabs the lanyard and hides it from the police investigators."

"I am sorry Justin, but those are not the actions of a crazed killer or a methodical murderer. It is most likely that this is just a spare lanyard that Karen brought home and your cat stole. Companies buy these things by the case and hand them out like candy to employees."

Richard did offer as consolation that he would stop by with his RFID reader to see if he could find the ID badge.

I didn't care what Richard said, I believed that the lanyard belonged to the killer. The killer was probably her lover too. What would be easier than to have an affair with someone you worked with? It happens all the time.

I stiffened my resolve and set out to trim the Arborvitae hedge behind the shed. As usual, I underestimate the time it takes to do things. It was three hours later when the last of the branches joined the compost pile. I turned the pile, gave it a good soaking then checked to see if Ed was out in his garden. I felt the need for companionship and listening to his fish stories would benefit both of us. He only fishes during the week when everyone else is working. He was not in his garden and his truck was gone. That left me with no one to talk to except Sam.

It was dawning on me how isolated I was out on bail. Most

everyone I could turn to was probably a witness and Anne told me to have no contact with anyone who might possibly be involved in my case. I had the urge to escape the confines of my yard.

The rental car entered SR 14 heading east up the Columbia Gorge. Initially the drive on SR 14 is not nearly as spectacular as that on the Oregon side. The Columbia River is actually etching into the rock as it moves north into Washington. The rock formation into which the Columbia is channeling tilts down. This allows the Columbia River to attack the Washington side a little harder, encouraging the river to move north on a million year trip to Seattle. The result of this trip we see today is in the form of flood deposits and landslides. The alluvial deposits provide relatively flat areas for Vancouver and Portland residents. Ancient landslides attempted to fill the Columbia Gorge a bit to the east of Washougal, which marks the end of the metropolitan area and converts the viewing obstructions from buildings to trees. Without driving off the road, I try to catch glimpses of the sheer 400' high cliffs by Crown Point on the Oregon side. The gorge walls steepen on both sides as I proceed up river. It is not hard to imagine the steep walls as belonging to the toes of giants meeting at the Columbia River, Mt. Adams fifty miles to the north and Mr. Hood thirty miles to the south.

Driving east, I enjoy the wind rushing in through the open windows. That is until I reach the intersection for the "Bridge of the Gods." The Native Americans gave this name to a three- mile wide landslide that temporarily dammed the Columbia River about a thousand years ago.

Legend tells of a great chief who assigned one son to live on the south bank and the other son to the north bank of the river. Then the chief built a great bridge so the families could travel to meet together. Families being what they are, the two brothers argued over a girl. The chief crashed the bridge into the river and then transformed the two brothers and the girl into volcanoes. Their English names are Mt. Adams, Mt. Hood and Mt. St. Helens. The three still fight from time to time.

I felt like fighting too. An urge swelled in me to drive onto the modern "Bridge of the Gods" and cross into Oregon. Just because I knew I was not supposed to do it.

Reason overrides desire and I continue a couple of miles up the road to Stevenson. SR 14 is now a surface street named Second Street as far as the town was concerned. I decide it's time to end my escape and hang a left onto Russell Avenue thinking I would take

106

a couple more left turns back to SR 14. Instead, I entered a minor residential maze, only finding a path to SR 14 by choosing turns taking me toward the river.

My 35 mile trip accomplished nothing except getting me out of my house. I felt a sense of urgency and wasted opportunity by taking this trip. I kept thinking about what Richard said, this is a marathon not a sprint. He may be right, but it conflicted with another comment I have heard, the police solve most murders in the first seventy-two hours, or they are not solved. The police think they met this seventy-two hour window. I had better look at the evidence again if I hoped to prove them wrong.

Chapter 34   Reviews Reports Resume

About three o'clock in the morning I woke up in bed with my light on. The pages of discovery were in piles on the bed and scattered on the floor where I had dropped them as I fell asleep. My plan had been to focus on those areas where I might have better insight than Richard or the police.

Karen's personnel file from VAA seemed the place to start. Included in the files were the usual documents: employment application, resume, periodic reviews etc. I examined the forms and documents, attempting to read between the lines and decipher notations.

The recruiters at VAA were impressed with Karen. US military training is the best pilot training in the world, at least according to what I learned from Tom Cruise. The recruiters liked ex-military because of the extensiveness of the training and the large number of simulator and flight hours devoted to each pilot. Granted, there was not a lot of call for air combat training or in-flight refueling capability in civil aviation. However, a pilot who could master in-flight refueling would probably be able to handle any situation in a civil aircraft. A good pilot in the military would likely make a good pilot in the civilian world.

In reality there is a lot of crossover between the civil and military worlds. Many of the aircraft used by the US Air Force are civil aircraft or modifications of civilian airframes. United States Representatives and Senators want to fly in a Gulfstream corporate jet, not a C-130 troop transport, on their official fact finding trips. I remembered hearing that a Speaker of the House commandeered an Air Force Boeing 757 for weekend flights between Washington DC and California. Experience gained while flying military aircraft, whether ferrying congressmen or bussing bombs, was in many ways transferrable to the civilian world.

I was forced to research pilot requirements to better understand what I was reading in Karen's personnel file. She earned her private pilot license at 17 just before graduating high school. According to her resume, she worked at a Fixed Base Operator, the gas station for airplanes, in exchange for flight time and instruction. In the world of pilots, the private pilot license is the starting point for everyone.

Karen extended her experience as a pilot in college by enrolling in Air Force ROTC. She advanced quickly in part because she already had her private pilot license, which meant she did not have to repeat that training as part of her Air Force ROTC. She pursued a degree in electrical engineering and was a Cadet Colonel by the time she had finished her bachelor's and was commissioned as an Air Force Second Lieutenant. Karen made a big point in her resume that she was instrument flight rated before starting her junior year in college.

Evidently, an instrument rating is a big deal for pilots. Given a choice, I only want to fly or drive when I can see everything I need to see. Instrument rated pilots have the ability to safely operate an aircraft in poor visibility using devices that tell them where they are and where they are going, and seem to take great pride in their ability to do so. Intellectually I understand why it is better if aircraft can operate in a wider range of weather conditions and why pilots who can fly using only instruments are of more value to the military or the airline. Personally, I have difficulty putting my faith in a 'black box' and trusting what it tells me.

Karen also included a long paragraph in her resume about her military flight experience. She was assigned to an air refueling squadron and flew refueling missions for most of her tour. The KC-135 tanker is an aircraft that started out as the Boeing 707 and structurally modified into a mid-air re-fueling platform. Karen stressed that navigation skills were key as they had to fly to designated points and meet other aircraft within very limited parameters. Many of the aircraft they served had limited fuel reserves and had to be met on time by the tanker in order have enough fuel to return to their base. Karen also stressed that precision flying was required. They practiced a flying formation, which required a fighter aircraft to fly very close to the tanker right up to the target, in order to deceive radar. She was proud that many of her flight hours were as Pilot in Command. This was supported by a penciled in plus sign "PIC" notation in the margin.

Karen's military file was not part of the discovery package. Evidently, the police did not deem it relevant. There were several documents that involved the Federal Aviation Administration in the file, but little else other than the performance reviews. Over all there was not much useful.

Sam was attempting to sleep next to me. He usually did not start his morning patrol until about an hour before dawn. I guess I made some noise when I opened my eyes or looked his direction, because one eye was partially open watching me. I looked back at to the ceiling hoping to find something there that I was not finding in her personnel file.

Rationally, I could not believe that years-old documents could include anything relevant to Karen's activities today. My gut said something different. There was something there if I could see it. The first annual performance appraisal was very good, as was her second and third. The fourth and fifth performance reviews were good also, but from a different reviewer. I could not quite put my finger on it but there was a change in tone. The first three reviews seemed to be all about Karen's potential. The reviewer was encouraging and went to lengths to point out ways for Karen to advance and complement her performance. The second reviewer seemed not as impressed and pointed out areas in which she could improve.

Karen answered with comments in the employee response section of both the fourth and fifth reviews. In the fourth review she stated that she was proud to be a pilot and took her responsibilities seriously. The fifth review stated:

"As a pilot I recognize and take seriously my responsibility for the aircraft, passengers and crew. As a professional pilot I depend upon, and expect, other professionals to take seriously their responsibilities and perform their tasks professionally, including air traffic control."

What did Karen mean by that comment? First, how many employees ever make comments in their reviews? Usually, an employee who disputes items in their review is not aware that they are in trouble. The contents of a review should not be a surprise to the employee. I got the impression that Karen was fully aware but thought she was treated unfairly. For some reason, neither the reviewer nor Karen was willing to spell out the issue. Maybe the issue was obvious if one were a pilot.

My belief is that the fewer documents one has in one's personnel file the better. Sure, good news generates paper, but not to the same extent as bad news. I sorted through the pages of the personnel file locating the two documents referencing the FAA. The date of one document correlated to her fourth year review and the second to her fifth year. They did not appear very significant. I had only given them passing interest as the documents were not easy to read by a non-pilot, being full of abbreviations and jargon.

What I took to be the most significant document referenced a voluntary submission to the "Aviation Safety Reporting System" and referred to an "ASIAS Brief Report." After re-reading the ASIAS report several times I was able to guess that there was some kind of confusion regarding the takeoff procedures and where the aircraft was headed. The synopsis gave a little information. There was a mistake by the flight crew:

"FLIGHT CREW MISTOOK A CLEARANCE VIA KEMPR. CLEARANCE DELIVERY FAILED TO CATCH THE ERROR ON THE READBACK AND A TRACK DEVIATION, QUICKLY NOTED BY ATC, OCCURRED."

The flight crew felt they followed instructions:

NARRATIVE for Person 1

"WE WERE GIVEN AN AMENDED CLEARANCE ON ACARS. WE REQUESTED A FULL ROUTE VERBAL CONFIRMATION FROM CLEARANCE DELIVERY. THEN AT THE HOLD SHORT FOR RUNWAY 23 WE WERE GIVEN ANOTHER AMENDED ROUTE WITH KEMPR AS A FIX IN THE REROUTE. WE WROTE THE CLEARANCE DOWN AND SPELLED THE FIX AS KEMAR. BOTH FIXES ARE PRONOUNCED THE SAME BUT HAVE ONE DIFFERENT LETTER IN THEM. WE READ THE CLEARANCE BACK TO ATC. THEY DID NOT CATCH THE MISTAKE. AROUND ACY THE AIRCRAFT TURNED EAST. WE WONDERED WHY WE ARE GOING EAST FOR 50 MILES THEN SOUTH. THE CENTER CONTROLLER GAVE US A 270 TO THE RIGHT THEN DIRECT TO ILM. IF THERE IS A SIMILAR SOUNDING FIX PUT IT ON THE OTHER SIDE OF THE COUNTRY OR AT LEAST A FEW HUNDRED MILES AWAY."

Having written a lot of tax protests, I recognized the tone of "Narrative for Person 1." Instead of starting my protest letter with "Dear Incompetent Blood Suckers," "Dear Commissioner" was more appropriate. 'Narrative' was upset that air traffic control did not catch the mistake and the pilots followed directions as requested. 'Narrative' felt the FAA was punishing them for following directions.

I failed to see the significance of the error. If I leave the parking lot and turn the wrong way I just go around the block, no harm no foul. Somebody thought this was important enough to include in Karen's personnel file.

Her subsequent reviews were good but not exceptional. Whatever the official meaning in those documents, the unofficial meaning was that Karen was no longer on the fast track.

I continued to stare at the ceiling looking for more insight why years old employee reviews could have any connection to her murder. Finding nothing in the paint overhead, I checked on Sam. He was back into full sleep mode.

I could think of nothing better than to join him.

Sunday was another beautiful late summer day in the Pacific Northwest. It should be a day for golf or a barbecue. Instead I was reviewing Title 26, Subtitle A, Chapter 1, Subchapter A, Part IV, Subpart D, Section 41, 'Credit for Increasing Research Activities'.

Much earlier this morning I followed Sam's example to go back to sleep so now I was rested. While selecting appropriate clothing for the day, I considered doing something fun on my day off. However, logic prevailed; I elected to continue my new pattern; work in the mornings for Lithium and work on my case in case in the afternoon. There were advantages to this new arrangement. I literally could work whatever hours and days I wanted, as long as I kept Clark and Mary Ellen happy. Today I was reviewing the rules to determine how much tax credit would be available to Lithium.

Credits are the ultimate prize in the world of income tax. A deduction is only worth pennies on the dollar. A credit is a dollar for dollar reduction in tax or an increase in a refund. The 'Credit for Increasing Research Activities,' usually called the R&D Credit, is not easy to get. Congress is afraid that someone might actually benefit too much from obeying the tax laws, so they attached several hoops through which taxpayers must jump. Spending money on research is not enough. To get the credit you have to spend more than the average amount spent in the last four years. Only the amount spent which exceeds the four-year average creates a one-dollar credit for every five dollars above the average base amount. Finally, to ensure that no one benefited to excess, the credit can only reduce your tax due to zero, the IRS will not write a check for the balance. The unused credit is usable next year, which means you have to wait for your money.

Management considers such credits to be free money. It is free money, if you ignore the cost of keeping track of all the information needed to document your credit. The IRS looks at credits the same way as taxpayers: "there's gold in them thar credits." IRS auditors love to examine credits because it produces big benefit, to the government, for the time expended. My job was to determine what expenditures could be included in the calculation and develop the evidence sufficient to support the amount we were going to claim on our tax return. To calculate the credit I must understand the aviation certification process. Understanding the process is the key to separating the separating research and experimentation costs from the regulatory compliance expenses.

Lithium was in a position to claim the R&D credit this year because of what we spent on our new aviation qualified battery. My first surprised was that the aviation industry still depends upon heavy lead acid technology. Our new lightweight battery should create quite a stir.

Batteries are not new technology and they are not that difficult to make. All Lithium employees learn how to build a battery as part of our employee orientation.

Before the American Revolution, scientists knew that certain chemicals react to create electricity. Anyone with metal dental fillings chewing on a piece of aluminum foil has discovered this process. The tingle you feel when the filling contacts the foil is electricity created by the chemical interaction of the metal filing and the aluminum.

This chemical reaction allows us to make batteries. A simple single cell battery consisted of four components: a jar of chemical, a jar of another chemical that will react with the first chemical, a conductor to link the two jars and a conductor to complete the loop. The chemical in the first jar wants to react with the chemical in the second jar. No reaction occurs if the chemicals are physically separate. The next best thing to physical contact is a bridge between the two the chemicals that allows electricity (electrons) to move from one chemical to the other chemical. This only works if there is a way for the electrons to make a round trip back to the original chemical from where they started. Eureka, we have discovered perpetual motion!

Unfortunately, batteries are not perpetual motion machines. The laws of physics ensure that there are no perfect conductors of electricity and energy is lost to heat while the chemicals slowly degrade during the process of moving electrons. All good batteries must end.

At the beginning of employee orientation, Mary Ellen Simmons gave each new employee a kit to build a battery. The assembly took about thirty minutes while one of the engineers explained what we were doing. When everyone was done, Mary Ellen and the engineer placed each finished battery in a contraption that linked each battery to its own small light.

The owner of the battery attached to the last bulb glowing would receive a prize. There was a purpose to the project: We all learned the basics of manufacturing our product and the importance of quality in the process. There was considerable variation in the longevity of the batteries, I finished second out of eight.

Lithium powered batteries should be a natural choice for aviation uses. They produce a high voltage per cell and they hold a lot of energy per pound of battery. Weight is a big selling point when working with aircraft. Karen once told me that it cost four dollars to carry an extra gallon of fuel from Houston to Portland. Any aircraft component that does the same job for less weight pays for itself over time.

A big factor in the dominance of heavy lead acid batteries over the airplane market is safety. Lithium metal has properties that most pilots do not find comforting. Lithium metal reacts with water to form explosive gases and toxic chemicals. Paper has a flashpoint of 451 degrees while lithium metal spontaneously burns at 354 degrees Fahrenheit. Another undesirable characteristic of lithium metal is that most fire extinguishers are ineffective or react chemically with the metal making the fire worse. When a lithium battery does catch fire it can explode, causing additional damage and spreading the fire. All the engineers and chemists had to do was overcome these minor issues and our batteries would soon be in every aircraft. That is, once the FAA approved.

The head of head of the aviation battery project selected FAA publications he felt I needed to understand. These fell into two groups, requirements that the battery needed to meet and supporting documentation we needed to provide to the FAA to secure approval. In a general sense I knew that the FAA exhibits supreme control over all things related to aircraft and flying, just like the IRS is supreme when it comes to taxes. What I did not realize is that the FAA exhibits more control over aircraft than the IRS does over taxpayers.

From what I could gather, if an individual wanted to build an experimental aircraft and die in the process that was OK. The FAA would leave you pretty much alone. However, the second you consider selling aircraft or operating an aircraft in common carriage of the public, then the FAA has strict procedures and rules, which it can and will enforce. Woe to those who violated the FAA rules, for they would find themselves sitting on the ground begging for forgiveness.

Our goal was to receive FAA production approval for a Class III product under FAA Technical Standard Order 179C. To do this we needed meet the TSO 179C criteria to the satisfaction of the FAA and then the FAA would issue Lithium a Parts Manufacturer Approval for our new battery.

If I were the king of aviation, I would start with the smallest part and work my way up to the whole airplane. According to what I was reading, the FAA starts with the whole aircraft. When the manufacturer designs an airplane, the builder has to specify every part and component. The FAA will then issue a "Type Certificate" for that aircraft. When a part breaks or wears out, the operator may always replace the worn part with the exact part specified in the Type Certificate. To legally install a part, other than the one specified in the Type Certificate, an operator must use a part that meets the Technical Standard Order for that aircraft.

Lithium Energy wants to make a family of lightweight batteries for use as replacement batteries on commercial aircraft, starting with Boeing models. We are targeting commercial operators first. The airlines are not as sensitive to high initial cost when there are fuel savings from reduced weight. But, all of this planning and preparation is nothing more than wishful thinking until we have the Part Manufacturer Approval.

Working with the Federal Aviation Administration documents was highly frustrating. The Technical Standard Order for lithium rechargeable batteries is only five pages long. At first glance I thought, what is the big deal? Then, I started reading the Technical Standard Order in detail. The first paragraph, thoughtfully titled "Purpose," told me that this was for manufacturers and designers of lithium rechargeable batteries. They, the FAA, then said they would tell the manufacturer what the minimum performance standards would be for lithium rechargeable batteries.

This was good, straightforward and to the point. The good news started to melt away in the second paragraph titled "Applicability." That paragraph cited Title 14 Section 21.6119(b) of the Code of Federal Regulations. I feared the time wasting tangents embedded in the regulation. That research adventure could wait until later.

At last, the red meat paragraph of the Order, "Requirements." Immediately it laid out that our batteries must meet the Underwriters Laboratory "Standard for Safety for Lithium Batteries," and pass the tests according to the rules in the appendix. Then there were sub-requirements involving functionality, functional qualification, environmental qualification and interestingly "failure condition classification."

If the battery failed it is to be considered a "major" failure condition if, then came circular references to previous paragraphs increasing my confusion. I stumbled upon Advisory Circular

23.1309-1E which happened to define "failure conditions." The five stages levels of failure are: first, no effect; second, minor; third, major; fourth, hazardous; and fifth, catastrophic. Level three major failures create problems for the crew and aircraft but can be handled unless there are other problems. Level four hazardous failures mean things are getting bad and if anything else goes wrong worse things will happen. Level five catastrophic failures indicate you had better land the aircraft as soon as possible, if you could. It was nice to know that if one of our batteries did fail the aircraft would not immediately crash.

I plowed forward through the labeling requirement and then got to the important stuff, the information we had to send to the FAA. Almost half the document was all about what to provide to the FAA.

To me the most interesting page was the appendix: "Minimum Performance Standard (MPS) for Lithium Multi-cell Batteries." The "Requirements" paragraph stated that these tests must be performed and that you were to "Protect personnel from flying fragments, explosive force, sudden release of heat and noise, and harmful fumes or gases." Then Table 1 set forth the tests, which seemed designed by an adolescent male.

First, the spark test, officially the "External Short Circuit" test, required attaching a wire directly between the terminals of a fully charged battery. Once having almost welded a crescent wrench between the car fender and the car battery terminal, it seemed like this TSO test would assure a good show of sparks.

Second, David Letterman must have approved the "Crush" test: Dropping a twenty-pound iron ball two feet onto a fully charged battery. The test did not seem that stringent until I compared it to dropping a bowling ball on my foot. Then again, this test was likely for ensuring safety in normal operations and not crash safety.

The third test was the suck the life out of the battery test, or officially the "Over Discharge" test. I believe the goal of this test was to test the battery under a heavy workload for an hour, "or to the maximum discharge time for the battery operation." This test was probably the least exciting test for our adolescent male tester.

Fourth, the "Overheat" test required the baking of a fully charged battery at 239 degrees Fahrenheit. It was comforting to know that if the airplane made an emergency landing in a boiling hot spring, the battery would not fail.

All four tests shared the same criteria to achieve a passing grade. During the test, the battery shall not vent any gases or vapors. Is there a difference? Also, during the test there was to be no smoking and certainly no flames, and most comforting to me, no explosion.

I was running the possibilities in my mind. Could there be an explosion without smoke, vapor or flames? Maybe these FAA guys knew what they were doing. I could almost picture one of our sales team arguing that our batteries were superior because they did not emit vapors before exploding, unlike our competitor's product.

The first time I read the fifth and last test, I thought it was redundant and impossible to pass "Fire." The first four tests failed a battery for catching fire during use. After rereading the procedures for the fire test, I realized that the test required that the battery be set on fire. Passing this final test allowed for an explosion, as long as the "fragments or debris" were retained inside the battery. However, smoke and vapors were allowed to escape as long as the fire "self extinguished" or could be extinguished by an external fire suppression system.

Feeling I had sufficient grasp on the basic product Technical Standard Order I turned my attention to several PDF files provided by my boss Clark: FAA Order 8110.42C, Order 8120.2F and several FAA Advisory Circulars: AC 21-32A 'Control of Products and Parts Shipped Prior to Type Certificate Issuance,' AC43-213 'Parts Marking Identification,' and AC20-162 'Airworthiness Approval and Operational Allowance of RFID Systems'. Clark attached a note that the engineer leading the battery project had FAA experience and suggested I skim the documents. I pulled up the Orders on screen for a quick survey. I decided not to print the documents as the short one was 67 pages and the other 183 pages. Not surprisingly, the short document, Order 8110.42C, was the guide for FAA employees who would rule on the Product Manufacture Approval. The long document was the guide for manufacturers wishing to receive Product Manufacture Approval. Not being in the mood to read 250 pages of FAA guidelines, I turned my attention to the FAA Advisory Circulars.

The Circulars were much shorter. The five page Circular AC21-32A said you had better have a good reason for shipping aircraft parts prior to FAA approval, and do your paperwork to prove it. Circular AC43-213 was all about putting labels on your airplane part. Ten pages of guidance which "is neither mandatory nor regulatory" but with which you had better comply. I guess, "12

Volt Battery" would not be sufficient to satisfy the FAA. To round off the trio, Circular AC20-162 gave eight pages of advice on RFID tags. In addition, this Circular was not a regulation but, "if you use the means in this AC, you must follow it in all important aspects."

I found the discussion of Radio Frequency Identification tags included in the AC20-162 interesting. I knew that RFID have been in use a long time, but according to this Advisory Circular, the FAA only recognized this technology for use in aircraft a few years ago. Lithium Energy puts RFID devices on both the product and the pallet for shipment. When you can load a hundred thousand dollars worth of button batteries on a single pallet, it is worth a buck more to be able to track it electronically. What I learned from the FAA Circular was that there were active and passive RFID devices. The passive RFID devices consisted of a chip and an antenna. This RFID device uses the energy from a radio signal to send a message back to the interrogator.

I found the use of the term 'interrogator' instead of 'signal reader' amusing. Did readers have ways of making chips talk if they did not want to? The interrogator did not have to be in 'line of sight' to generate a response, but the range of the RFID tag was dependent upon the signal strength of the reader. Passive RFID devices could only respond with a canned message.

Active RFID chips include a battery that allows them more range and more information in response to the interrogator. This feature increases the cost but makes the chips more useful. Not only could the chip respond with name rank and serial number, the chip could relate things about the environment. Such as, 'I am hot or cold or wet'. The Advisory Circular then drifted off into Battery Assisted Passive devices and then airworthiness concerns. It seemed to me I had I mined as much information as I could from the easy reading. That left the FAA Orders. I was not very excited about getting into these FAA Orders. Something was nagging at the back of my mind. I needed a snack break.

The snack was not for me, but for Sam. It was mid-day and Sam hopped on the desk to say hello and cheek the monitor while I guarded the keyboard from unintentional paw strikes. My hand reaching for the desk drawer that stored the kitty treats was enough to distract Sam from the keyboard.

Sam expertly and efficiently tracked down and consumed every treat. I was not having a good day, as my tosses were not providing much of a challenge for Sam. I was trying to deposit one on top of the bookcase. My toss overshot the top and took a bad bounce upon hitting the floor. The treat came to rest under the closed closet door, in sight but out of reach. The gap between floor and door was too narrow to allow Sam to pull the treat free. Sam thrust his paw under the door in an attempt to grab the treat. The result was to push the prize further away. Sam was fixated on the snack nodule and he would not give up.

I expected Sam to concede defeat and appeal to me for a replacement. Instead, he surprised me by managing to hook a claw in the treat and drag it from under the closet door. Sam audibly crunched the treat then licked his upper lip. Content he sat on his hindquarters in front of the closet licking his paw and rubbing it across his face. As I watched him wash his face, it hit me: the closet, Karen's papers were in the closet.

The brown paper bags I had filled with Karen's papers were on the floor just where I had placed them that first night. I spread the items across the floor in a single layer. Then I grouped them according to class: Periodicals, FAA Advisory Circulars, FAA Orders, FAA Air Worthiness Directives, Code of Federal Regulations, FAA Technical Standard Orders and miscellaneous items.

The periodicals were mainly 'Airline Pilot' and 'Aircraft Owners and Pilot Association' magazines. I paged through some, not noting anything of significance, no notes, no earmarked pages and no missing pages. I assumed the police had checked for documents, money or anything else that they might have considered evidence. Nothing listed in the discovery log indicated items hidden in books or magazines. I did not find anything either.

The five volumes of the 'Code of Federal Regulations' was several years old and well used. There were enough old ear marks and highlighted text spread through the volumes to prevent identifying a pattern. Finding nothing, I slammed the regulation closed and threw it the floor. There was no evidence here; the police would have found it if there was.

I almost gave up and went back to my desk. The police found everything that looked like evidence of a murder. Therefore, nothing that could help me would look like evidence. Flawed logic, tortured rationale, maybe, I had to open my mind to the fact that crucial information may be spread across the floor. I moved on to the Technical Standard Orders stack.

There were a variety of FAA Technical Standard Orders. As an engineer, Karen would have an interest in how things worked. That knowledge would be a benefit in the event of an instrument failure. Therefore, I guess it made sense for her to have TSO C34e 'ILS GLIDE SLOPE RECEIVING EQUIPMENT OPERATING WITHIN THE RADIO FREQUENCY RANGE OF 328.6-335.4' in her personal papers. The only pattern I could detect was that there seemed to be a lot of TSOs related to instrumentation and not many related to the airframe or other components. I guess that made sense, the pilot knows about what is going on with the components of the aircraft through what the instruments tell her.

Seeing no smoking gun in the pile of TSO's I moved on to the Air Worthiness Directives. From talking with Karen, I had a general idea of the purpose of an FAA Air Worthiness Directive. The FAA constantly monitors aircraft and issues orders to do maintenance or make fixes when they discover problems.

I picked one and started reading. It was a final directive issued in 2006, which implied that there were preliminary or proposed directives too. The summary stated that "a control wheel damper assembly at the first officer's drum bracket assembly and aileron quadrant" should be installed. Obviously, this is for an informed audience who knows what a control wheel is and why it needs damping. Like other FAA documents I have read, the author seemed intent on inserting acronyms and abbreviations wherever they would most impede readability. The most interesting part was the argument between the Airline Pilots Association and the Air Transport Association. Both agreed that the fix should happen. What they did not agree upon was how fast to make the change. The FAA stepped in saying we already worked this out with the manufacturer so live with the date we set. I flipped through the rest of the document, nothing. Flipping through the other directives was also a waste of time. This was getting discouraging.

The FAA Orders did not seem to be of any help either. These orders all seemed to be about dealing with the FAA bureaucracy. I flipped through Order 8120.11 'Disposition of Scrap or Salvageable Aircraft Parts and Materials.' A brief 8-page document discussed the proper way of disposing worn out parts. The order stressed the need to make sure that worn out parts did not return to use in aircraft. Grinding and mutilation were preferred methods of making sure the broken parts stayed broke. Grinding and smashing stuff sounded like a fun job, right up there with being a crash test engineer. I turned my attention to the last big stack, the Advisory Circulars.

There were about a dozen FAA Advisory Circulars on various topics related to flying an aircraft. Such as AC91-79, 'Runway Overrun Prevention', or AC120-100, 'Basics of Aviation Fatigue,' and AC120-103, 'Fatigue Risk Management Systems for Aviation Safety.' Evidently, sleeping on the job was a concern. Flipping through the other advisements, I came across a Circular I had seen before: Advisory Circular AC43-213, 'Parts Marking Identification.' Having just read that document today, it did not seem like something that would interest a pilot. I flipped though the Circulars again and this time noted AC21-29, 'Detecting and Reporting Suspected Unapproved Parts.' I could see where this would be of interests to the maintenance technicians but pilots? Beyond the personal safety issue, why would this interest a pilot? Probably this was a required reading assignment from management for all pilots. My level of disappointment increased with every page.

Sam seemed to have a better idea about dealing with these documents than I did. He watched for a long time. Somewhere between the Air Worthiness Directives and the Technical Service Orders, he decided a nap was in order. How cats select their sleeping locations will always be a mystery to me. Today for some feline reason, Sam selected the stack of miscellaneous documents. For the last hour, Sam had been motionless in the Sphinx position atop an inch stack of papers. I compared Sam's stack to the piles of paper I spent the last three hours reviewing. Who had accomplished more, Sam or me?

I retrieved a bag from the desk where I had folded it flat. Sam opened an eye as I opened the grocery bag to repackage the documents. I decided I was finished with this pointless exercise. I stacked the orders, advisories and circulars relatively neatly in the bag. Sam watched sphinxlike from his pedestal as I transferred the papers into the bag. Finally, the only pile left to put back was the stack of papers upon which Sam rested. "It's time to move Sam."

Sam closed his eyes.

OK, it is time for the dominant species to assert his authority and have a little entertainment at Sam's expense. Grabbing the half-inch lip of Sam's paper pedestal, I lifted slowly.

Sam demonstrated no intent to move.

I continued to increase the elevation of the papers, increasing Sam's list. Victory was at hand. You can ignore me, but you cannot ignore gravity. Finally, just before reaching the tipping point, Sam abandoned ship.

Reveling in my victory and ignoring Sam's annoyed expression, I transferred half an inch of papers into the bag with the rest and returned to the remaining pedestal. The headline 'New Technology Could Protect Against Parts Counterfeiting' was on the top paper on the stack. It was a printout of an article from 'Aviation Today,' written by Jim Clark, for an on-line publication. A short one-page article started with a statistic: "the FAA estimated that unapproved parts played a role in 174 airplane crashes or accidents" over a 23-year period. The rest of the article reported on the increasing sophistication of the parts counterfeiters. The article concluded with an appeal that the industry adopt RFID chips to catch fake parts. Interesting if you were concerned about airline safety, but to me another dead end.

I flipped through the other remaining documents. It was more of the same. Such as the article about a repair shop closed by the FAA for improper record keeping. And I did not bother to read "SAE AS 5678A 'Passive FRID Tags Intended for Aircraft Use' 2006" I already knew the ending of that story.

I had just spent most of the afternoon scanning several thousand pages of documents and had nothing to show for it except another vague feeling that I was missing something.

Chapter 37   Houston

Waking, I had to think seriously. What day is this?

My new work schedule was convenient and fit well with the task at hand. Although an unintended consequence was that I was disconnecting from the normal flow of society. Not having to be at specific places at specific times was disorienting to someone used to working a regular job during normal business hours for the last 20 years.

The first order of business was to draft an email to Clark providing a status update. I spent more time on the update than I would have had I been in the office. First, it was important to document that I was still a valuable member of the tax team. Second, not being able to walk down the hall and discuss things was a limitation that could create misunderstandings. Keeping Clark happy and informed was worth the time and effort. Whether it is a tax appeal or an internal memorandum, good writing takes time: first writing, then re-writing, and then the proofing, especially proofing when using spell check. It all takes time.

It was after well after eight AM when I finished and got around to checking my emails. None of the non-work emails appeared to be urgent or contain words demanding immediate action, so I reluctantly put them aside. Time to return to the state apportionment project, it made a nice break from the R&D credits and all the FAA documentation. Sometimes it is best to let your mind digest information, or even let it ferment for a day or two before taking another bite.

A corporate income tax return is only four pages. The supporting schedules attached to the return can run into thousands of pages. Apportionment calculations share the same environment, a huge amount of data to support the production of a small piece of information. I spent the morning tracking down all of Lithium's personal and real property so I could determine how much was owned and rented in each state, county and if needed, city.

Sam was certainly enjoying the new work schedule. Long naps interspersed with petting or occasional seek and consume events involving kitty treats. He had departed several hours previously, to take advantage of the prime solar exposure. Unlike Sam, I had worked almost a full day on the apportionment schedule.

I returned to the emails I had wanted to read this morning. One was from Anne's secretary with an attachment, the police report from the City of Houston. The other email was from Richard

Cushing. Richard said he would stop by this afternoon with the RFID reader to look for the ID badge I hoped was lost in the weeds.

The email containing the police report began with the reports from the officers involved in the search of the apartment and continued with the interviews of neighbors. I have to give the Houston police credit, they did a better job of investigating than I expected. They dusted for fingerprints in an apartment that was almost clean of prints. The police did not make much of that fact as they noted that Karen had a cleaning service. The police contacted the cleaning agency and the cleaner. The current cleaner had only been to the apartment twice, the last time a week before her death. The previous cleaner left without providing a forward address. The police report noted that the cleaning company confronted her with the fact that her Social Security Number belonged to another woman. It would be unlikely the police could locate this cleaning woman.

The current cleaner worked as an independent contractor for the agency. Her client list included 19 weekly customers and about 24 semi-monthly or monthly customers. Karen was her newest customer. She had not been there enough to have a clear impression whether anything was wrong or out of place at Karen's apartment. She always returned objects exactly where the originated after cleaning and dusting. One thing she did remember was the chess table. It was annoying to wipe and replace each individual piece, so as not to disturb the board. Every visit she cleaned all the common dirty surfaces, such as the appliance handles, knobs, countertops and the bath. If she had spare time, she did laundry or other special requests. Since this was only her second visit, she did a thorough job in the baths. She could not be sure but she did not think there was any evidence of a man living in the apartment. "What the owners do in their apartments is not my concern. I try to respect their privacy."

The police report continued with interviews of the neighbors. None of them knew Karen other than in passing. They guessed she worked for an airline because of her uniform, but other than that, they knew little. The apartment manager had no reason to contact Karen. She was quiet and the rent was always early. Karen never contacted him in the three years he had been managing the complex. Neither the manager nor the other neighbors could identify the man occasionally seen entering or leaving the apartment.

I was figuring out the report was not in chronological order.

The next pages discussed the search of the apartment. The police "tagged and bagged" several small items into evidence and took fabric samples of a variety of items. The finger print report noted Karen's prints and a variety of partial prints and two unidentified full latent prints: a left thumb and a right middle finger.

Attached was a separate report that cited an AFIS report indicating that TWIC system identified the owner of the prints as one Carlos Juanro Torres.

At last, real evidence! Elation turned to dejection with confirmation of an obvious truth: Karen and I were done, she had moved on to someone else. The strong suspicion from days ago now was confirmed fact.

I had only started to sink into the morass of feeling like a used tissue when I heard someone pull into driveway.

The doorbell rang as I approached. Of course, it was Richard.

Immediately I started talking. "Richard, did you see the Houston Police report? Is this great news or what? How do we go about finding this Carlos guy?"

"Slow down Justin. Yes, I have seen the report. It arrived late Friday afternoon from the DA."

"What, how come you didn't tell me Friday?"

"So you wouldn't do anything stupid."

That comment brought me up short. "What do you mean?"

"Let's take a look and see if we can find an ID card out back. We can talk while we walk."

It was then that I noticed that Richard was holding an electronic device larger than a cordless phone and smaller than Mr. Spock's Tricorder.

"Justin, before we searched I needed to confirm the type of chip that Value America uses in its company ID badges. Some chips have very short operational ranges."

We headed out to his truck in the driveway. Richard explained: "We need to be within about three feet of the card to get a reading. This creates a problem. Waving the reader around like a tricorder on 'Star Trek' is useless. Holding the reader chest high places it more than three feet away from the ID card and the maximum range of the chip."

To solve this Richard created an extension handle from what looked like an old weed beater. The engine and rotating head were gone leaving a long aluminum tube. Bolted on to the tube was a piece of 2 by 2 supporting a plywood platform. Richard strapped the reader to the platform with Velcro strips.

"It's a seventeen hundred dollar reader, I don't want it falling off," he said, securing the reader.

"I use wood because it does not interfere with the interrogation signal or the reply. Also, the handle allows me to sweep the reader in a larger arc, covering more area."

With that explanation, we walked out of the carport to the shed. Richard covered all the walls then the arborvitae.

"Richard?"

"Yes"

"Could you answer some questions while we search?"

"Sure."

"You saw the police report, what did you think?"

Richard stopped and looked at me. "First, tell me what you think."

"It is now obvious that Karen had a lover in Houston. It is not a surprise. It is just a relief to know that it was not just my imagination."

Richard continued to swing the reader. It was not taking long to scan the yard.

"That is correct Justin. I have seen the same scenario play out a hundred times. It is easy for the spouse to miss, especially if they don't want to see."

"Why did you think I would do something stupid?"

"Learning the truth about infidelity is not something anyone likes to face. Given the chance, many people will lash out in anger, some with violence. I have given up trying to predict who will do what."

"So, how does that apply to me? Whom am I going to get mad at, Carlos? Am I going to fly down to Houston and pick him out of the million Hispanics living there?"

"You don't have to go to Houston."

"What do you mean?"

"In the police report there was an AFIS report. The Automated Fingerprint Identification System can access millions of criminal and civil fingerprint files. Carlos Juanro Torres fingerprints are on file with the TWIC system, just like your wife."

"So?"

"The Transportation Worker Identification Credential is a Transportation Security Administration ID card required for all people who have access to restricted areas at US ports. That includes airports. Carlos has a TWIC ID because he is an avionics technician for Value America Airlines. There is more Justin."

"It's OK, I won't do anything stupid."

"If you attempt to contact him, that's witness tampering."

"OK, I won't try to call him, and I certainly will not go to Houston."

"You don't have to, he lives in Portland."

"Justin! Take a deep breath. Do it again."

"I am OK Richard. It is just such a shock."

"We figured it would be. That is why Anne and I thought it best that I talk to Carlos first."

"You talked to him? What did he say?"

"I got him this morning when he got home from work. He rents an apartment off Sandy Boulevard in NE Portland a few minutes from the airport. He tried to brush me off. Said he had already talked to the police. I tried a bit of good cop routine and invited him out to breakfast or dinner to get him to open up. Carlos agreed to come because "I have no wife to cook for me. But you waste your money, I know nothing.""

"Yes he knew Karen. He knew a lot of the pilots who flew through Portland. No, it was not unusual for pilots to complain to the technicians and mechanics about problems with 'their' planes."

"I asked him about traveling to Houston. Carlos said he traveled though there regularly to visit family in Cancun, Mexico."

"What about meeting Karen in Houston?"

"Carlos said he knew she had an apartment in Houston. It was possible that he might have been there once after they ran into each other in the airport when Karen was between flights."

"Carlos was almost boastful: She was a good looking woman yes? If a man cannot take care of his woman she will find someone who can."

"Sorry Justin, but that is how he came across. He was macho to the point of arrogance."

"What else is there Richard? Let's get it all out."

"I asked where he was on the night Karen was murdered. Carlos said he had the 2200 to 0630 shift and worked on several aircraft. He repeated that he had already been through this with the police."

"Justin, you cannot get onto the airport ramp without a TSA ID card. The TSA and airport records can tell exactly when he came and went through the locked doors. He was on the ramp working on planes all night."

"That looks like a pretty good alibi Justin."

130

Chapter 40   Trust

We walked in silence, me looking for anything that might be evidence and Richard swinging the RFID reader. We covered the large portions of the swale that were accessible. Since we were looking for something that was lost and not hidden, it was likely the ID tag would be more or less out in the open. The brush, blackberry and poison oak made the search more challenging. Richard and I covered both sides of the swale following the worn faint animal trails on each side of the watercourse.

I was hoping but not expecting to find anything. I assumed Richard expected less. I am sure he had been on many wild goose chases and this would not be his last.

We returned to the house with nothing but seeds and other plant materials stuck to our clothes.

As Richard was disassembling his gear, I contemplated speaking. I needed to vent and Richard was one of the few people that possessed the two qualities I needed: We could legally talk about my case and he might possibly believe I was not crazy.

"Richard, if you have a couple of minutes I wanted to discuss my case?"

"Sure, what's up?"

"Does Anne think I am innocent?"

Richard locked down the pick-up's diamond plate tool chest and turned to face me. "Justin, I have worked with Anne a long time. First, I worked for the prosecution as a cop, then for the last six years for her as a PI. I have never seen her give less than 100 per cent for any of her clients."

"That's not what I am asking. It's important for me to know, does she think I am innocent?"

"Justin, in my time I have honestly thought that everyone I arrested had committed a crime. Usually the evidence was so overwhelming there was no room for doubt that they were guilty of something. As a police officer, I left it up to the jury figure out exactly of what they were guilty. Sometimes the jury got it wrong. Sometimes facts come to light long after the fact that prove guilt or innocence. I can sleep at night knowing that I always acted in the way I believed was right at the time."

"Justin, with that said: If you were the murderer, you are the most inept one I have ever met. You could have dumped her weighted body in the Columbia River and been in Mexico with the cash before she popped up."

"You are still here and I know that you are not stupid. Does that make you the most brilliant killer ever? I don't think so. Where is your alibi?"

"I wish I knew."

"I don't mean to offend, but if you did kill your wife, you did a great job of framing yourself. That's why I think you are innocent."

"That means a lot to me Richard."

"Justin, I think that's what Anne thinks too."

"Richard. I want to believe that. When everyone thinks you're guilty, it becomes overwhelming and it takes a lot of effort to keep fighting."

"We're a long ways from giving up, Justin."

"I'm not giving up, though some days I wish I could. Don't look at me like that Richard. I am far too practical to do something stupid like flee the state."

"Good."

"Actually I am working on a theory about why Karen was killed."

"Really? Let's hear it."

"It's just speculation. I have been going through Karen's personal effects. Something's not right and I can't tie down what. She was an avid pilot and a professional but she had interests in areas that seem unusual. Now I am trying to figure out what it means."

"Are you going to tell me?"

"Not yet, I want to work through this in my head first."

"Don't leave me hanging Justin."

"OK, I have an idea: I want you expand your investigation of Carlos? I think there is more to him than meets the eye."

"In what way?"

"I'm betting that his lifestyle and spending are more than can be supported by his income from the airline."

"So you think Karen and Carlos had some kind of smuggling operation? The two big money items are drugs and people."

"I don't think so. People are bulky and have comfort requirements. I don't think she would try to smuggle people into a highly controlled area like an airport."

"What about drugs?"

"I don't think so, too obvious. Every law enforcement agency is looking for drugs and there are lots of measures in place to catch shipments. Karen was too smart to be involved with something as obvious as drugs."

"What do you mean?"

"Karen is used to being in control. If she could not be in command, she would not get involved. I cannot picture her carrying drugs for someone else. And as strange as it sounds, she would view most drug dealers as unprofessional and unreliable."

"For Karen to be in control, she would have to understand the product, the supply chain and work with people she trusted. Once we figure out what she was doing, it will be obvious for to all to see."

"Do you mean like smuggling wheel barrows Justin?"

"What?"

"It's an old joke: A border patrol agent sees the same person week after week crossing into Mexico. The Agent knows the man has to be smuggling something. Every time the man crosses, the agent stops the man and searches the wheelbarrow he is pushing. The Agent unloads the sand from the wheelbarrow, sifts it and even tests it for illegal substances. Sometimes the agent even removes the tire, and still he finds nothing. The routine continues for years, until one day the Agent realizes he has not seen the wheelbarrow man in some time. The next day the Agent gets a postcard.

"You were always gracious in the way that you treated me even though you thought I was smuggling. It must be driving you crazy wanting to know if you were correct."

"Now that I am retired I can tell the truth."

"Yes, I was a smuggler. I was smuggling wheelbarrows."

Chapter 41   Point of Sale

Tuesday morning continued the clear cool fall weather that makes putting up with four or five months of grey overcast worthwhile. The sky was dark and the brighter stars visible from the shadows as I walked towards the Columbia River on 164th avenue. I navigated the underpass of the Lewis and Clark Hwy and negotiated the switchback from the Evergreen Hwy. Fisher Road was transformed into 164th Avenue somewhere in the course of residential development in the 70's and 80's. The result was a small section of the road orphaned from the rest of the avenue by various street improvements. Now this section served more as a common driveway for several of the nicer homes along the Columbia River. This city owned driveway continued the descent from the elevated residential lands on the high bank above the river. The urban forest permitted occasional views of the river, Government Island, the I-205 Bridge, and northeast Portland. The occasional distant rumble of the large aircraft completing their landing approach into Portland International airport disturbed the quiet early morning. It was always interesting to watch the planes on final descent over the Columbia River as I walked. Almost to the river's edge, 164th terminated onto an unnamed park, which provided river access to the locals on foot. I took a last glimpse through the foliage toward NE Portland and reversed my route. The hike up the slope to regain the 100 feet of lost elevation warmed me. The cool morning air reminded me that in another month this brisk walk would be much cooler. In a month after that, the trip would be wet as well, with rain blown by winds coming out of the gorge. I could not help but wonder if this were the last cycle of the season I would experience.

The sky showed a hint of light beyond the Cascade Mountains as I concluded my exercise for the day. The fall equinox was fast approaching and morning dark was reaching toward the workday. Sam was still out on his morning hunt when I returned to the kitchen for my post shower coffee. My bowl of Grape Pits cereal was softening slowly to a chewable state as I made my way into the office to my computer. Shrugging off my earlier gloom, I maintained discipline and checked work emails first. I was a little pleased but not too surprised to have no communication from Clark. Clark's leadership style at Lithium was not to manage to excess. If there was nothing wrong, he generally left me alone to my own projects. The same appeared to be true in my off-site location. As an additional distraction, Clark was probably deep into the calculation of the second quarter estimated income tax payments, due 9-15. That project would ensure few communications in the coming days.

After deleting unwanted emails, I turned to my primary interest. Anne's secretary asked if I could come in sometime this week to sign a form. In another email, she wanted me to come in to review the new batch of discovery provided by the District Attorney's office. This was curious; the other discovery came as an email attachment. I filed it away under mysterious things attorneys do and replied I would try to come in today.

Email triage completed, I was officially on the clock by 6:30AM. By 2:00 PM, I was done for the day with Lithium and reopening the email from the Anne's office. I probably should have called for an appointment when I read the email, but the office phones did not answer until 8:00 AM, and I elected not to leave a voicemail. By 8:01 AM, I was deep into plugging salary data into the apportionment model and forgot about setting an appointment. When I did call about 2:00 pm, the receptionist answered the phone and transferred me to Kari, Anne's paralegal. Anne expected to present the closing argument for her case this afternoon. She would be in as soon as the jury was sequestered. Because of the trial, there were no scheduled appointments. Also, there was no guarantee that Anne would be back at all.

After deciding to risk it, I agreed to come in about four. I killed some time mowing the few green patches of grass near the flowerbeds. The grass closest to the flowerbeds benefited from overspray to the extent that some was turning from brown to green. Mowing allowed me to assess the effectiveness of the watering program. A couple of the flowering shrubs suffered in my absence. I needed to call upon Ed's expertise to see if he could save them.

Yard work completed, I headed for the shower in preparation of the trip to Anne's office. Not a fan of blow dryers, I allowed my damp hair dry in the breeze from the partially open car windows on my way to Anne's office.

Kari the paralegal met me in the reception area. She informed me that Anne had just finished and would be arriving from the courthouse in a few minutes. Kari escorted me to a conference room while offering a beverage.

In addition to the bottled water, Kari supplied a small stack of photocopies.

"Justin, these are Karen's credit card purchases for the last thirty days. Anne would like you to look at the transactions for anything unusual or out of character."

My expectation was that there would be a list of stores and amounts by date. Instead, the pages contained exact details. Each page was one transaction, listing the store and date as well as the description of each item, the quantity and the price.

"Kari, I am surprised the police were able to get so much detail. Was this a special request?"

"No, all this information is easily available from many stores. The POS terminals gather all of that information on every transaction."

"POS terminal?"

"POS stands for Point of Sale. That's the device that reads and approves your credit card as well as recording the details of each transaction. In addition to the printed receipt, the merchant retains an electronic file of all the detail printed on the receipt. Most people do not give a thought to the information gathered about them through their card transactions. The stores use this information to record the accounting and inventory information as well as process the sale. This data is also used for marketing analysis. Of course, all this information is available to the police who search purchase detail history for evidence."

"It is quite useful. Not so long ago Anne lost a DUI case. Her client lied to her, claiming he was not a drinker. At the last minute the police submitted credit card records of his daily alcohol purchases."

Unless you use cash, there is probably a record of your purchase."

I was sitting there feeling foolish. As an accountant, I should have known all that. I tried to justify my ignorance. As tax accountant, my world was big numbers, not the individual details like this produced by POS devices. Lithium was a manufacturer not a retailer. Stores had to have the information from the point of sale devices to capture accounting information. Still, I had been in meetings where we discussed capturing electronic data for tax and inventory purposes, I should have known. The opening of the conference room door interrupted my introspection.

"Hello Justin."

I rose to greet Anne with a handshake. "Kari and I were just going over the details of Karen's purchases."

"Find anything interesting?"

"No Anne."

"We didn't either. However, these are only the most recent purchases. There could have been something purchased months ago. I am trying to determine how far back to go when I subpoena purchase records. Can you think of anything unusual in her spending behavior in the past six months or more?"

"That's just it. She did not spend money when she was around me. From what I see on the credit card detail, she was only spending on work related needs and day-to-day necessities. I am betting a lot of the money she did not spend ended up in the trunk of her car. That ancient worn out RX-7 was about the only thing on which she spent money. Wait a minute, this is strange."

"What did you see Justin?"

"It's not here."

I sorted the stack of papers again.

"These are all the receipts for the credit card and the debit card?"

"Yes, every transaction that the police subpoenaed for the thirty days before her death."

"I do not see a receipt for Rafael's Metro Motors."

"Is that important?"

"I don't know. She got that car detailed or serviced at least once month. There should be a receipt."

"What if she paid cash?"

"It's possible, but not probable. I know this sounds strange, based on what they found in her car, but she did not like to carry cash. Even a cheap auto detail is a hundred bucks. I think she would have used her card to pay."

"I guess it would not hurt to have Richard visit the shop and see if they remembered Karen."

Anne looked like she was thinking. She did not speak for too long a time.

"Justin, there is some more discovery. These discs hold the contents of Karen's and your computers. If all they had to do was copy the files they could have included the DVDs in the first batch of files."

"However, there was more to it than that. It took time to arrange for my expert to be present when they searched the computer. People are finding new and better ways to hide files on their hard drives. We wanted to make sure we recovered all the files. Also, some of Karen's files were password protected."

"Really? Why would she do that? Although I should not be surprised, she kept a lot of things from me." My voice physically and mentally weakened as I uttered the rest: "And I let her."

"We were hoping you could tell us why she needed protection. When they subpoenaed the password they did not find anything that seemed worth protecting."

"You never looked at her files on your home computer?"

"No, I learned my lesson. When we were first married, I opened some of her mail looking for bills. She hit the roof, told me never look at her mail again. I knew she had files on our computer but I never tried to look. Not even by accident. They were in a folder several layers away from the main thread so accidentally opening files was not easy."

"You said there was a document you wanted me to sign."

"Yes, Kari, do you have the general power of attorney?"

"It's on my desk, I will be right back."

"Justin, I don't lie to my clients and I do not sugar coat the truth. I was hoping there was going to be something in this batch of discovery. Did you see anything in Karen's buying habits that would help you?"

"No."

"Anne, have you spoken with Richard Cushing?"

Anne looked a bit surprised as she adjusted to my abrupt change in subject.

"Yes, he told me about the search for the ID tag and not finding anything at your house. Richard also, you asked him to check on Carlos. Why is that?"

"I think Karen and Carlos were involved in some illegal activity."

"I am not unsympathetic, Justin. But is your judgment clouded by the fact he has admitted to having an affair with Karen?"

"Anne, don't you think that is strange? How many people ever admit to having an affair without being compelled to do so, especially, when one partner is murdered? Wouldn't you try to keep a low profile and hope that the investigation never touched you? Why admit to having a relationship with the victim, unless you are trying to distract the police from a bigger issue."

"That is a long reach Justin. You never know how someone will react to police questioning even if they are innocent. Carlos may be smart enough to realize that the police would see that he was one of the last people to speak with her. It would be better for him to get all his dirt out up front. That is especially true if the only person who would be interested in his dirt, was you."

"Oh my God, I didn't think of that. The DA will see Carlos'

testimony as motive for me killing Karen!"

"That's probably how a jury will see it too."

Chapter 42   Channel Your Anger

I was still stewing about juries and what they would think when Kari returned.

She placed the form in front of me and took her seat two chairs down in front of a paper pad and pen.

Anne explained, "Justin, this is a general power of attorney. This allows me to act on your behalf if you are not available."

"Like if I am in jail?"

"Anne, that's where I am going to be if we don't come up with something. As of now, we have no defense. What are we going to do?"

Kari sat silently taking notes of our conversation.

"I agree Justin, if we go to court now the DA will roll over us."

I met Anne's gaze trying to see beyond her poker face for some guidance. "Have you seen lots of innocent clients rolled over by the DA?"

Anne did not flinch at my angry comment.

"Justin, we can only go to trial with what we have in hand, not what we wish we had."

"Right now we have nothing in hand."

I realized I was lashing out at the wrong person. "I'm sorry Anne." I picked up the pen. "You're not the one I should be mad at."

"Justin, you are not the first client to vent his frustrations on me and you won't be the last."

"I'm sorry Anne, I feel so impotent and so angry at the system. I want to hurt them."

"Channel that anger. Focus on what we need to do now. Who knows more about Karen than anyone else?"

"The murderer."

"Justin, keep this up and I will put you in jail myself, that's not what I meant. You know more about this case than anyone else except the killer."

"Sorry, it just seems kind of pointless."

"Listen to me Justin. I am not giving up. If you want to give up, I'll call the DA right now. That will give you about forty years to feel sorry for yourself."

I looked up from the spot on the table that had held my focus.

Anne touched my shoulder. "If you give up, who's going to

140

take care of Sam?"

Anne knew what she was doing. She knew it was easier to fight if I was fighting for someone else. I almost lost Sam once. I was not willing to lose him forever. "I am not giving up. I've signed the power of attorney. What else do you want me to do?"

"If there was something obvious to find in Karen's effects the police or Richard would have found it by now. If there is something they missed, you will be the one to find it."

"I'll try, but it's not something I am trained to do."

"Think of it as your way to hit back. Seeing the DA lose this case will please both of us."

"And speaking of the DA, this means more to me than you but, the rumor in the courthouse is the DA is planning to try your case himself."

"Doesn't the DA try cases all the time?"

"The DA's job is to manage the prosecutorial function for the entire county. He makes policy and oversees the assistant DAs. It is typical for the DA to pick cases that will make him look good. I know Bill Armitage; he is all about looking good for the next election. A juicy murder trial is just the sort of resume enhancement he needs. Winning a 'tough on crime' case like this could provide the good press he needs to be the next State's Attorney General, or maybe even Governor."

"Time is not our friend and the trial will be on us before we know it. We need something soon Justin. I feel that if this drags into next year, the DA will see your trial as too good to pass up."

"I understand Anne. I'll go through the files and see if I can find something."

"Good."

"And maybe Richard will turn up something on Carlos?" Anne said nothing.

I departed the office with the discs and many questions. The Vancouver rush hour traffic was not much of a distraction. I thought about the discs as I drove east. What would I find in Karen's personal files, love letters to Carlos?

Probably not, most likely there would be lots of the practical and professional documents, and all the obsolete stuff that everyone keeps on their computer. I am sure she kept everything needed for her pilot's license. But what else, her Swiss bank account number, pictures, poetry? Nothing would surprise me at this point.

It seems ironic that my task was to look for evidence on my

own computer about my wife's death. Not just my computer, Karen traveled with a small laptop and had a work area in her Houston apartment. The files from that computer were also included in the discs. These files were the key to learning who Karen was. I wanted to find out about the real person I married, while at the same time I feared what I would find.

The discs lying in a small pile on the car seat did not seem like enough to tell the story of Karen's life. Anne assured me that all the files were there. She emphasized how she demanded that the DA give them mirror images of the hard drives in the seized computers.

Anne's expert copied all the data files and reviewed the software for hidden data. He was confident there was "nothing which was not supposed to be there." The stack of discs held all the data files and none of the program software.

I slammed the car door harder than necessary, holding onto my discs and my anger. Anne wanted me to channel that anger, but the only channel I could see was the one heading straight to the state penitentiary in Walla Walla.

Instead of going to my office, I headed to the kitchen. The discs skidded to a stop on the kitchen counter. Being in no mood to open my computer, I opened a beer instead, moving to a chair in the back yard to catch the sinking sun. If I was going to sulk why not do it in a pleasant setting?

I drained and replenished the beverage volume, enjoying the warmth of the sinking sun. Beverage renewed I settled heavily into the chair to watch the final descent for the day. Sam appeared on my lap. His fur soft and smooth under my petting hand as he settled onto my lap to enjoy the evening.

The chill woke me. The North Star was visible and the Big Dipper high in the sky. I wondered about the time, theoretically, it is possible to tell the time from the stars. Once on an evening like this a long time ago, Karen tried to teach me how to tell time using the North Star and the Big Dipper. The process was complex: After compensating for the orientation of the stars from a date in March and positioning an imaginary clock face over the North Star the Big Dipper should tell the time. Tonight the stars were telling me three things: it was night, the temperature was getting colder, and it was time for bed.

Sam sensed my alert status. He jumped down, heading for the food bowl with a confident strut that presumed I was following. Sam crunched kitty kibble as I opened the refrigerator to a large selection of unappealing consumables. Unable to tackle anything solid I settled for milk.

Sam's sharp meow made me realize I was standing and staring at an empty glass. Moving toward the sink, I realized that I had as much chance of finding something useful in Karen's files as in this glass. Anne's advice was to do all I could do to make sense of the information we had. I knew how the police viewed the evidence, it all pointed to my conviction.

If I continued to interpret the evidence in the same way as the police, I was going to jail. As much as I hated the phrase, "think outside the box," that was what I needed to do now. But how? Was there something in my training I could use? A couple of years back the management fad was innovation and process improvement. The program theme stressed the dangers of 'self-imposed limits'. Maybe now was the time to apply those concepts to Karen's evidence.

I twisted the clouded clear glass in my hand. The glass was not in fact empty. First, it was filled with air and second there were the remnants of milk that coated the sides and pooled in the bottom of the glass. It was not much, but it was something. We did not know much about Karen, we had her computer files, and that was something.

"Meow" said Sam. His wise voice called me to join him in the bedroom. Sam was correct again. Sleep was the best choice.

Sam accepted my thanks for the advice as well as the good night belly rub before we headed off to sleep.

Staring into the night sky it was impossible to tell the time by watching the Big Dipper. The constellation was rotating like the second hand on a watch. The stars never ceasing their movement across the aurora borealis clock face long enough for me to make the calculation. I was desperate to know the time, so I could get to the courthouse for my trial on March seventh.

The feeling of someone applying sandpaper to my forearm saved me from this dilemma. I opened my eyes to find Sam licking the salt off my skin. I scratched his ears and rubbed his cheeks as a good morning welcome.

It was light enough for me to see a little, so I knew that dawn was only a few minutes away. I rolled to the edge of the bed and made my way to the bath. While I watched me brush my teeth, I made a decision. Today was my day. I was taking a day off from Lithium. Today I would read Karen.

My impulse to start immediately was strong. The opening images flashed on the monitor as the computer powered up. As I was about to jump in feet first into the files, I remembered the advice of an engineer friend: "If you have five minutes to solve a problem, take three minutes to plan and two minutes to implement the solution."

This was a big job; I could afford a couple of minutes for planning, but where to start my search in this haystack?

Sam landed softly on the desk. I checked his mouth then the floor to see if he had brought any gifts. He stood over the drawer containing the kitty treats pawing the handle, hoping I would take his hint. Not having any clue how to start, or even how to plan to start, I retrieved the treats.

The bottle held only half a dozen treats so I invoked plan B, increase the level of difficulty. I taped paper over a third of the large mouth jar before rolling it to the middle of the floor. Sam chased the bottle then assumed a prone position. Sam had a plan, what about me?

"Sam, what's the best way to go through Karen's files?"

The paw fishing around inside the jar was not hooking any treats.

"When I was a baby auditor, my senior told me that if I was going to make my hour budget I should handle a document once. Get everything I needed the first time and get out."

Sam stuck his paw back inside, trying again to drag a treat

past the neck of the bottle.

"The obvious thing to do is dump all the files in a folder. Pick a file and review it. If there is nothing there, flag it and move on. If I don't know what I am looking at, send it to Richard."

The victorious crunching of the crispy treat echoed though the quiet office. At least someone was making progress.

"Sam, how do I stay focused? Most of the files are sure to be dull and unimportant."

He did not have an answer. He was too engrossed in retrieving another treat.

I faced the task of auditing what my dead wife left behind to learn who she was. The emotional part of me despaired at what I might discover. The intellectual part of me argued it must be done. Self-flagellation over the fact that I had married a stranger was a waste of time. The rational me said get on with it, Karen is no longer a person, she is now an object of study.

"Sam, unless you can come up with a better plan, I think I am ready to start."

Sam licked the remnants of the last treat off his paw and started washing his face.

Now that I had spent my 'three minutes' planning, I was eager to get going. The files uploaded quickly into the raw data folder. The discs were not full and all the files would have fit on a single DVD, had they been trying to minimize the number to discs. As I finished uploading the files, an unexpected situation confronted me: there were non-standard file formats. Along with the usual image, document and spreadsheet file extensions there were application files and some strange file extensions. This development would require a little more thought. I wanted to get started, and it already seemed like I had spent too much time thinking about what I was going to do, rather than doing it. I sent off an email to Richard asking if he had noticed the unusual files. Then I mentally put it aside and proceeded with those files which I understood.

"Sam I need to reconsider my plan. My first run though the files will be to determine the sample I want to examine in detail. Just like an audit, I cannot examine every transaction in detail. What I can do is view each file, and determine which ones need more review or which ones get dumped in the low risk pile."

Enthralled, Sam finished licking his toes and left for parts unknown.

Regrouped and refocused, I was eager to get going. My

own files would be the easiest to triage. All I needed to do was open the file and confirm that it was my file. Even though it did not matter, I started with the file names beginning with A. The 'Addition' file was a plan to add a solar room and convert the carport into a full garage. This spreadsheet had several tabs related to various parts of the project. I moved it to the reviewed folder and onto the next document.

Half a dozen files and several memories later I misclicked and opened an unnamed worksheet tab in my 'Amended Return' file. The tab should have been empty. Instead, it contained some notes and various calculations, kind of a scratch paper I created while working on my tax return. These notes were not of enough importance or value to warrant taking the time to add a title to the tab or to delete the data. I paused with this thought in mind. Here there was data where there should have been none. This information would have stayed hidden had I not clicked in error. Can I assume that Karen was not hiding data?

Did Karen have reason to conceal information? Did she have reason to be scared before her death? Was her argumentative nature because she was tired of me or was she under a lot of stress?

If Karen was under pressure, I had been oblivious. Was there anything in her behavior not attributable to her being in an unhappy relationship?

If I was a disinterested observer, I might be able to answer those questions. As a participant, I was involved in this experiment, my emotions distorting my observations. An objective appraisal of her actions made more difficult by my never outgrowing my childish belief that an action by someone in my presence must have something to do with me. What I did know was that Karen was responding to something before she died. What I could not determine was the source of the influence. Was it her job, her killer or me? This was definitely something to keep in mind but for now, I needed to get back on the files.

This side trip into Karen's emotional state made me reconsider my plan. I had to assume that she deliberately hid data.

Sam interrupted my speculation by jumping on the desk and walking in front of the monitor. He paused to sniff the screen and attempted to touch the blinking cursor. Failing to evoke a response from the cursor, he turned his attention to me. We cheeked each other and I stroked his back as he arched to meet my hand. After several minutes of petting, I was tiring and switched from petting to the bilateral neck scratch. This technique required me to scratch with at least three fingers of each hand. The extension and clenching movements of the fingers on both sides of his neck delivered a gentle scratch from his front shoulder blades all the way onto his lower jaw. Sam's purr response indicator let me know that he was thoroughly enjoying this attention. I however had work to do. I prepared Sam for petting disengagement by initiating bilateral anterior aural attention.

Sam loved it when I rubbed the patches of fur on the top of his head at the front of his ears. Using my thumbs in conjunction with my fingers created a state of bliss for Sam. Two minutes later, he looked only mildly annoyed as I stroked his fur smooth to signal termination of treatment. Sam could have tolerated another hour of this treatment but he recognized that I had reached my limit. Sam shook his head to reboot his ears, oriented on his environment and walked a few inches across the desk. Using his feline analytical skills, Sam determined the perfect spot for this morning's nap, on top of the data discs I got from Kari yesterday. Having finalized his choice of location, Sam commenced his pre-nap grooming procedures and initiated his sleep routine. Sam closed his eyes, slowed his breathing and he seemed to be asleep within seconds. I was wide-awake with a bunch of files and no clear idea what I was looking for. This begged the question: "If I were hiding data, how would I do it?"

Lots of commercial software comes with password protection. That would be the easiest but the most obvious. Does password-protecting files, make them easier to identify as important? What was Karen's purpose in hiding the data? Was she looking to create an insurance policy? Was the data for blackmail? Was this search a dead end? To me the likely answer was that Carlos killed her in a fit of passion. My ego wanted to believe it was in an argument over me. My rational brain discarded that notion.

Then again if Carlos did kill her during an argument, why did he risk coming to the house? Why not lure Karen into his car and dump her body off the side of a logging road? There were many easily accessible seldom-traveled roads in the forest only a few minutes away. Karen's confrontation with her killer seemed more like a business meeting than a romantic rendezvous.

It was now obvious to me I needed to change how I thought about the search process. This was not like a search for a missing or misplaced data file. If Karen wanted the file found, she would have labeled it, 'In the event of my death,' and the police would have it already. The evidence so far told me that Karen was more afraid of the police than of dying. If there were anything in these files, it would not be easy to find.

It was time to spend another minute planning and rethink the search process. I needed to start from a new perspective. What would I do if I wanted to hide data? The data had to be safe. It had to be accessible. Moreover, it must be disguised in case someone caught sight of the data. Based on those conditions where and what was I looking for?

Was the data even in one of our computers? Did she have a safe deposit box in Houston or Portland or Cancun? That seemed like a more secure way to store data, but much less accessible. Maybe this was an item for Richard to pursue. I sent a quick email to Richard and re-focused on the task at hand.

I needed to start over from the beginning, without the assumption that my files were my own. For each of my files I had to do two things: First, confirm that the data in my files was my data. Second, verify that there was no parasitic data. I smiled to myself at the phrase I invented. A parasite lives off a live host. Did Karen attach little data organisms that lived as long as my files lived? If there were, any bogus data living within my files it would be stored in hidden places, like empty tabs in a worksheet or in an added last page of a letter or document.

There would be trade-offs in any data hiding scheme. If Karen was using my files for storage there was always the chance I would discover the unrelated data. If she used older inactive files, it was likely I would never look. How often would I look at the supporting detail for a three-year-old tax return? Unless I got an audit notice, I may never open those files again. There was a chance those files would be deleted in some house cleaning operation. That meant that redundancy would be important. Accidental discovery or unexpected cleaning could result in loss of data or unwanted questions.

These considerations made me doubt that Karen attached parasitic data to my files, but I could not ignore the possibility either. This also meant that the search would be a lot slower than I thought.

There was also the possibility that Karen had faith in password protection. The Information Technology group from Lithium told us that popular office software was good enough to stop the vast majority of hackers. Strong passwords not easily guessed stop all but very motivated hackers. If the hacker was determined, had the resources, and the time, passwords will not protect your data. It comes down to a matter of time and computing power.

What if Karen was not hiding information from a hacker? Was she worried about the police? Did she know that the police routinely subpoena software companies for passwords? Had she decided that password protecting incriminating data is an invitation to conviction?

I was starting to get mentally dizzy wandering this analytical maze. I felt like a character in a spy novel. You know the story, the agent suddenly finds himself on the wrong side of the law and at a loss as to why the agency has turned against him. I was better off than the spy was; I knew why they were after me. I was worse off in that I did not have the tools or the training to figure out why.

A spy's tool chest includes codes. What if Karen were using a code or a cipher to hide important data? My heart sank. I found three letter anagrams difficult. If Karen were using some kind of code, I would never figure it out. The only thing I knew about codes was from the movies and that we won World War II by breaking the Japanese code. Some people devote their lives to making and breaking codes. What chance did I have of finding, much less breaking, a code?

The implications and considerations were multiplying. Each method of storing information had weaknesses: Codes leave patterns and trails, hidden data destroyed or lost, passwords hacked or subpoenaed. Was Karen paranoid enough to use all three methods at once? I had to believe that Karen would use at least two methods to mitigate the weaknesses of each.

Was I just wasting my time in speculation about data that did not exist? Who would go to such lengths in real life? Only someone who had information worth killing for would take these precautions.

I faced the realization that if there was hidden data, all files were important. I must evaluate every document or risk missing evidence. The size of the task intimidated me.

Sam opened an eye when I stood and he watched me walk around the room looking for inspiration in the ceiling. I paused, bending to stretch my knotted back muscles, breathing deep to cleanse my mind.

"Sam, the fact is, Karen was murdered for a purpose and not as a random act of violence. That proves she had something of value the killer wanted. Did the killer not know about the money in her car? If he did, was it more important to use as evidence to frame me?"

Sam now watched me with both eyes. "In the alternative, did he get what he wanted and kill Karen to keep her quiet? Did he leave the money because he did not care, or did he panic and leave it by mistake?"

"Am I making assumptions based on evidence, or what I want to believe? Am I naming Carlos the killer based on logic or emotion? I am making too much speculation on too little fact?"

Sam was now resting his chin on a foreleg watching me pace the room.

"What do we know? Karen was murdered, she had illegal money in her car, and the man I want to name as her killer has a perfect alibi."

Sam yawned. "What do I know about Karen that impacts how she would protect herself? I know she is methodical and prepares for emergencies. She would never fly without a fuel reserve or a contingency plan. The cash in her car, was it for an emergency or was she planning to leave? Did she have something that she thought would protect her?"

Enough speculation, it was time to hit the files. Sam returned to sleep atop the discs as I completed my mental gymnastics. He flicked an ear, which I took that as a signal to charge headlong into the files. That is, if progressing at a snail's pace is considered charging.

This process reminded me of walking in the snow in Minnesota. A couple of inches of the light fluffy crystals make walking fun. Each step forward compresses the flakes into an impression of your shoe. Bringing the trailing foot forward creates an exclamation mark shaped trough in the snow. It is a joy to marvel at the beauty of the pristine white sparkling blanket.

It is an altogether a different matter when the snow is a foot deep. Now each step is the equivalent of climbing stairs. Forward movement requires lifting your foot to clear the powder. The soft fluffy snow assumes the suction power of mud if you try to slide your foot though the snow. It only takes a couple of steps to capitulate to the resistance and adopt a high stepping slog. If not dressed properly the toes and then your feet loose feeling inside the shoes and socks made soggy from melting snow. However, proper clothes increase the workout through the added weight and the resistance of heavy boots and thick clothing. No matter how you are dressed, your pleasant stroll in a couple of inches of snow becomes a major aerobic workout when the snow is knee deep.

Any trip longer than a few hundred yards produces a weary traveler with head down and eyes vainly searching for an easier route though the endless white bog.

My journey though the files was beginning to feel like walking through deep snow. The endless column of files was not getting noticeably smaller, the search was not any easier, and it took more mental effort to open each new file.

My resolve weakened as noon approached. Sam had not stirred since mid-morning. I glanced in his direction. Sam stretched all four legs, all ten toes, yawned powerfully then opened his eyes to look directly at me. Sam seemed to take my measure. He got to a sitting position, yawned again, and then lay down on his other side in the same spot on the desk. I vowed that if Sam could stick this out, I would too.

Fortified with a fresh cup of coffee I returned to select a new file. I reviewed and discarded most documents as being nothing more than my files. To treat myself I opened a 'PDF' image file from Karen's stash. This was her life in certificate form. She had copies of every acknowledgment or promotion or letter of recognition ever received. This certificate and photo history cataloged everything from her Civil Air Patrol Cadet Airman, General J. F. Curry Achievement award, through her military commission. Each image reinforced my belief that Karen first and always was a pilot.

I spent more time on the PDF file than was warranted. I could not believe that Karen would have defaced an award to hide something. That would be like defacing her body. I moved on to another document file and another after that.

Was the very old letter to the utility company complaining of a billing error for real? On the other hand, was the complaint a clever coded record? From what I could tell, I do not think Karen ever threw anything away. Karen converted everything on paper to images. The computer age was a great boon for Karen. She could keep everything and not haul around boxes of paper.

Wading through these records was like crossing a snow-covered lake. The distant shore never seemed to get any closer and the white expanse never any smaller. I had to prompt myself to step high and move the next foot forward, only to repeat the process without any sign of accomplishment. I picked out another file, a word processing document.

In a million years, I would have never expected to find what I found, a file named 'History II.' My first thought was that it would be a reference to great moments in aviation, either Karen's personal life or some hero in the story of flight. Instead, what I found was horoscope entries.

The file appeared to be a chronological listing of daily horoscope readings for each zodiac sign for about the last five years. What's more, she updated the file just before her death. Karen was the last person I would associate with something as illogical as predictions from the stars. She was nothing if not practical and precise in all she did. She believed she controlled her destiny and she alone could guide it. Was this a habit carried forward from youth? Could this be part of some practical research project, such as a correlation of aircraft accidents and horoscopes? Whatever the case, I read some entries for amusement and moved on to the next file.

Sometime later Sam stirred and departed in the direction of the kitchen. It was getting along in the day and I considered stopping for lunch. I contemplated renewing my attack on the big box barbeque chicken I grabbed on my way home from the Anne's office yesterday. I really was not that hungry. The lack of hunger was a result of an unanticipated reality of working from home: unrestricted access to food stocks not generally offered in most offices, and without the need to make offerings to the vending machine gods. Instead of a full lunch, I indulged in my weakness for toasted bagel with butter and cream cheese washed down with fresh coffee. I was brushing bagel crumbs off my tee shirt onto the grass when Sam started rubbing my legs. His fur was soft against my bare legs as he rubbed and then cheeked my shins for good measure. Sam then turned toward the house, pausing to look over his shoulder and meowed at me.

"OK, I'm coming."

Sam was on the desk performing pre-nap grooming as I sat down. The optimal napping spot was again the small pile of discs and sleep overcame his defenses in a few seconds. I returned to my list of files. I opened and discarding many junk files, trying to treat each new file as it were the one that would prove my innocence. The file named 'Supplemental Log' would not open without a password. I cursed silently, started to panic then remembered one of the discs was hand labeled. Sam opened one eye in protest as I slid discs from under his belly. The file opened upon my entry of the requested password. After a few minutes of reading I understood why this was password protected. If I were writing such comments about my fellow workers, I would probably use a password too.

Karen's log seemed more like a personal journal than an official flight log. The record began just after Karen separated from the military. She was surprisingly cryptic about her departure with references to learning from her mistakes and keeping records to support her position. The new entries were positive in that she liked using the GI Bill to complete her commercial training and was excited about getting a civilian job.

The entries continued in a positive vein during her early years at VAA. Her supervisor was an ex-navy pilot and they got along well. The situation changed when he took an early retirement buyout. Her new supervisor boasted aeronautical university training and no military experience.

In Karen's opinion, her new boss was macho asshole who could not get over the fact that she was a better pilot than he was. According to Karen's version of events, he looked for any possible breech in protocol or perceived flight rule violation in an attempt to make her look bad.

The employee comments Karen made in her fourth and fifth reviews were taking on new meaning. The fourth employee review had directed Karen work closely with Flight Operations to optimize flight performance and minimize weather hazards to the aircraft and passengers. Karen's version was that "Jerald" had no balls and would divert to avoid cumulus clouds. So what if some weak-kneed civilian passenger complained about a few bumps. The aircraft and passengers arrived safe and on time. What is the issue? In spite of Karen's complaining, she took additional weather course work and complained in her log about doing so.

As time wore on Karen added additional adjectives to Jerald's name. Some of the nicer terms employed by Karen were, pompous, arrogant and political animal. In year five, the traffic controller incident brought matters came to head. She was of the opinion that the controllers were trying to throw her to the FAA wolves. The air traffic controllers gave her bad directions, which she followed. Jerald did not think that Karen went far enough in questioning the ATC directives.

Karen had no respect for Jerald by this time. "That is what I get for having a boss who flies a desk. He never has to deal with the incompetence of the controllers because he never flies. When an ATC tells me to fly south and I want to fly north, I fly south. So does any other pilot who cares about keeping her wings. If he spent more time at the controls and less time at his desk, maybe he would appreciate what we have to work with out on the routes. What an out of the loop idiot."

Jerald's good fortune was Karen's salvation; he got a promotion to company HQ. However, Karen's career was never the same. There was enough bad material in the two reviews to slow her progress through the ranks. Seniority and union rules protected her job, but her career stalled.

It was not hard to understand that Karen felt she was wronged and held to account for things beyond her control. I was beginning to see a pattern in her writings. A bright person with a lot of promise falls to live up to expectations. Was her failure due to a personality flaw, such as not being able to accept criticism and to correct her behavior? Alternatively, was she lacking the big picture decision-making skills needed by one who would ascend to the top ranks? Whatever the weakness, both the military and the civilian world relegated her to the middle ranks. From her entries, I gathered that Karen recognized that management viewed her as an adequate worker, but not one worthy of promotion.

Was this a classic case of 'The Peter Principle'? In college, an instructor assigned the book in a management class. One of the better books I read in college. Humorous and made a simple point: People are promoted one level beyond their level of competency.

This seemed to fit Karen's career. She would quickly rise through the ranks and then stall. Karen may have been a great individual pilot but not fit to command others in the eyes of her superiors. My guess was that Karen's faith in her piloting skills created problems. Her confidence exacerbated her lack of empathy for her passengers' in-flight concerns and provided unwelcome visibility of Karen by management due to passenger complaints.

If my impression was correct, how would this help me understand her? I thought about what I observed of Karen over the years. The first game of chess we played stood out. Karen knew after six moves that she would win. She was just toying with me. Did that mentality apply to her work? Was Karen too sure of her skill and too dismissive of others that she felt did not live up to her standards? Was Karen the ball player who never passed the ball because she knew she was the best player on the team? Was Karen unable to admit some of the fault lay with her?

This was fascinating to ponder but getting me nowhere. I continued reading.

Gradually there was a change in her writing. Maybe it was acceptance of her lot or maybe she concluded that lesser people would never understand.

I sensed the anger at others for not appreciating her talents. In death, Karen provided more personal information than I had ever received from her when she was alive. I considered myself to be a bit of a recluse. Karen was even more withdrawn than I was. Karen appeared to have no social attachments at all. There were no references to men or dating from her time before me. There had to have been physical encounters, but there was no mention of love or affection. Maybe there were personal letters that she tossed as being too painful to keep. Maybe there were letters still undiscovered. So far, the closest she came to documenting a personal involvement was that she was planning some sort of business deal.

In regards to the business venture, Karen referenced some rejection letters. She stated what she thought of these companies with comments like: "There is so much 'Not Invented Here' bias at Rockferhd Avionics I bet they still design on paper." The comment about Rockferhd got me thinking. Where were the rejection letters? Maybe they were in another file, but I have a feeling that Karen did not keep bad news. Which in a way made sense: Rejection letters would not fit within her ever-growing pile of accomplishment.

Karen's frustration with her stagnant status at VAA seemed to provide motivation for the business ventures. If she could not find recognition as a pilot, she would find it as an engineer. That was failing too, based upon the tone of the comments in her supplemental log.

Then there was a spark of hope. There was a man who had connections. There was talk of foreign suppliers licensing her designs. Then, that dream failed too, as the discussion died after a couple of more vague entries.

It took me a bit to realize that Karen's attitude toward her coworkers had softened. She was not quite as harsh with the observations of her superiors or crewmembers.

Added to this improvement in attitude was a new hobby. Karen had taken a new interest in astronomy. She began making comments and observations regarding the stars and constellations. These small reports documented the location via longitude and latitude and/or time.

Karen's desire to comment on her fellow employees diminished but the astronomical references continued. I scanned every entry hoping that something would jump out at me, but there was nothing. I had too much time invested in this one single file. I had too many more to review. At this rate, I would not finish before year-end.

After reading several more useless files, I found a rejection letter. More appropriately, it was a letter responding to her request for more information about her rejection. It seemed that Karen had submitted a proposal for a design and the engineer responded with an analysis why it would not work. I was quickly lost in the terminology, but the author wrote the summary paragraph mostly in English so I was able to get the gist of what they were discussing.

Integrated circuits generate a lot of heat. Designs using SMT (surface mount technology) were more difficult to cool. Failure of the components was of concern because "their long term reliability characteristics show a reduction by half in the mean time between failure for every 10 degree increase in junction temperature above 90 degrees Centigrade." Alternatively, as I understood it: when chips get too hot too often they failed.

For some reason Karen kept this rejection letter but not others. Maybe it was a line in the sand challenge, or a motivational reminder or some other reason altogether. However, Karen thought this particular letter worth keeping for more than 10 years. Without enthusiasm, I returned to the list of untouched files.

For a break, I opened some of the image files. As I suspected, there was no one I recognized. Two other points stuck out: I was not in any of her pictures and Karen was in all of hers. When I and I believe most people, take photographs it is to remember people and places. What is the point of keeping photos only if they include you? I could see no reason to spend additional time on the file and transferred all the images to Richard's folder. I then returned to the documents I might understand.

Sam yawned and opened his eyes. Even for him, he had spent a lot of time in one place. He slowly got to his feet then stretched his forelegs out and pulled his shoulders back causing this butt to claim the high ground. Sam yawned again before walking over to me to cheek my chin and then lick my lower jaw. I wondered what I had done to be worthy of a grooming award. It usually takes more action on my part to gain Sam's praise.

The sound of my phone ringing startled me. With my 'murderer out on bail' status, I received virtually no calls. Clark and Mary Ellen communicated by email. I could not remember the last time I had received a call here at the house.

"Justin, Richard here. I am on my way back from White Salmon. I saw your email and thought I would stop in to talk about it, if that is OK?

Chapter 44   Engineer

Richard was a half an hour away so I reviewed files while I waited. Karen's expense reports added little of use, other than to show that she was generally frugal with her money when traveling. Her employer operated an accountable expense reimbursement plan, which paid her on per diem rates. Karen kept great records even though the IRS did not require them. Per Diem programs simplify everyone's life: the businesses, the employee's and the IRS'. Karen got a fixed amount per day to cover food and incidental expenses. The employer gets to deduct the expenses and the employee does not have to keep receipts. The upside was if the employee under spent they keep the money. The downside was they probably would qualify for little or no deduction if they spent more than allowed.

Without matching trips to her expense reports to the records of VAA, I had no way of knowing whether these were legitimate reports or a clever record of her illegal activities. I would ask Richard if he thought we should get VAA's reimbursement records.

Richard entered. "Hi Justin, how is the review of Karen's files coming along?"

Richard was kind. He let me ramble on about my theories about parasitic files and codes. Then I finally got around to the email message I had sent that morning.

"The unrecognized files were CAD: Computer Aided Design. Karen used, for that time, a sophisticated software package to design aircraft electronics. The interesting part is that we did not find anything in the files relating to patent applications. I got in touch with my pilot friend, Harry, who knows some avionics engineers in Seattle. I forwarded Karen's designs and the engineers said they were an early adaptation of FPGA avionics."

"What's FPGA avionics?"

"Harry tried to explain under the qualification that he is not an engineer either. In the beginning, aircraft instrumentation was all mechanical. Everything from airspeed to direction used mechanical movement. The problem with mechanical devices is they expand and contract with temperature. In addition, they physically move which results in stretching, wearing and warping. Last but not least, mechanical devices are heavy and they need cleaning and lubrication.

Over time, avionics substituted individual electronic

components for mechanical devices. Instead of reading a dial physically linked to a pitot diaphragm, electronics allowed the replacement of everything except the diaphragm."

"What's a Pea Toe diaphragm?" I interrupted.

"It's the device that measures air speed in an aircraft. Drill a hole all the way through a piece of pipe. Cut the pipe in half lengthwise. Place a rubber sheet (a diaphragm) between the two pieces of pipe and bolt the halves back together. Hold the pipe in a fast stream of air. Orient the pipe so that one of the holes is facing directly into the wind. Obviously, this means the other hole is facing away from the wind. Some French guy named Pitot, that's spelled "P I T O T," discovered that the air coming into the forward hole applies more pressure against the rubber than the air entering the backward facing hole. The rubber diaphragm bulges from the added pressure. The air speed of the aircraft correlates to the diaphragm bulge. Electronics that can measure the bulge in a Pitot tube diaphragm are more accurate, more reliable and weigh a lot less.

"But what does that have to do with FAGP?"

"That's F-P-G-A. The field programmable gate array is essentially a device you can program for multiple tasks."

"Like a computer?"

"Justin, I am neither a pilot nor an engineer, but this is how it was explained to me. FPGA is the next generation in electronics. The previous generation of avionics replaced tubes and transistors in individual instruments with silicon chips. The FPGA generation will replace individual instruments with FPGA platforms that take the place of many instruments. Sensors will plug into one or more FPGA units that process and then display the information on one or many screens set in the instrument panel. The major benefits of FPGA avionics being; weight, cost and reliability.

My pilot friend told me that basic avionics runs to 1/5th of the cost of the entire aircraft. The FPGA itself is cheap but the initial programming expensive. Still, the cost is competitive with stand-alone components and then keeps dropping. Pilots and companies like the idea of being able to upgrade their avionics by installing new software. Maintenance is less expensive as most of the time you replace a sensor rather than overhaul an entire box. Over the life of the aircraft FPGA looks to be a lot less expensive."

"That is all very interesting but what does this have to do with Karen?"

"It looks like she was a pretty good engineer. However, she

was not good enough for anyone to buy her designs. In addition, it could have been that she was an outsider trying to break into the old boys club. Whatever the case, should could not sell her ideas."

"That explains some of the letters in her file and her comments in the log about industry not accepting her ideas. That fills in some gaps about who she was but that is no motive for murder."

"Justin, I don't think that Karen was worried about being murdered. She was a smart woman and if she were concerned about really hiding something, she would have bought encryption software. Instead, she used the standard password protection using simple passwords. Also if she was concerned about her safety she would have had an insurance policy in place with which she could threaten her attacker."

"Justin, the more I think about this the more I believe that Karen was surprised that her attacker was capable of hurting her. Obviously, the killer was invited, or wheedled his way, to the house. Maybe Karen thought she was safe or the killer was afraid to act knowing you were nearby? Maybe the killer planned this out and intended to make you the fall guy. Either way, somebody believed that Karen was important enough to kill. I keep hoping that the reason will turn up in these files."

"It's been a long hard slog through these files Richard. I have found nothing out of the ordinary in my personal data files. That leaves Karen's files as the only likely place we might find something."

"I think Karen believed that she was capable of hiding something so that nobody else could find it. It would be a slap to her ego to have to use a third party, like encryption software, to hide her data."

"And, I agree with you that Karen was not afraid. Maybe she was worried at the end, but not paranoid enough to invest in quality encryption software, or set up some type of insurance policy for protection."

"What I am not finding is anything out of the ordinary. There are some documents, which are a little quirky, or eclectic but nothing suggesting illegal activity or any other motive for murder. Karen took the phrase "a place for everything and everything in its place" to the extreme. All the files are ordered and arranged properly, with each document containing exactly what it should. If it were not for her supplemental log and the horoscopes I would think she was not human."

160

"What about the horoscopes Justin? Many people have unusual hobbies and collect the strangest things. I remember there used to be a museum for Slide Rules in Oregon, what is so unusual about Karen's hobby?"

"Richard, this seems excessive and contrary to her nature. Karen kept a daily record of horoscope readings for all the astrological signs going back about ten years. She is the last person I would have believed would followed horoscopes. Karen wanted to be in control. I cannot picture her ceding authority to some mystical power."

"How much did you read?"

"I read enough to get bored, the first few pages and then skimmed random entries just to see if anything stuck out. It is a huge file. Actually, it is two files; the first volume is 8 megabytes covering six years. The second volume is 6 megabytes."

"Justin, expand on that. Was this a habit? Was she compelled to continue once started? Such as keeping a continuous record of some periodic activity in order not to break the string of entries? Something like collecting scrap aluminum foil or string. The curiosity of how big a ball you can create causes the continuation of a useless task."

"Maybe it's nothing Richard. Like the astronomical observations she was making in her supplemental log. It just seems so out of character for a person as rational and practical as Karen to be interested in horoscopes."

"What does your gut tell you Justin? Is there something there? I scanned every file, and reviewed some in detail. I hate to say it, but I don't see anything in her records. If you think there is something there, you need to find it. Or, at least educate me on your thought process so I can help."

I checked Richard's face for some sign of hope or encouragement and found none. We were both silent, thinking. I was trying to decide what my gut was telling me. Was I on to something or had I had one too many cups of coffee. Sam calling from the office broke the silence. The third time Sam bellowed.

"Justin, is something was wrong with your cat?"

"Let's go see. Sam probably just wants me to give him some kitty treats or some attention."

Sam was still on the top of the desk, mostly on top of the discs, three quarters on his back fully extended to expose the belly fur for scratching. I gave a few short strokes to his stomach and he responded by curling into a ball surrounding my hand. He was licking my skin as I smoothed the belly fur with backhand finger strokes.

"Justin, what did you think about Karen's supplemental log?"

"She certainly was not impressed with most of her co-workers. I see now what I mistook for self-confidence was actually a sense of superiority."

"Justin, let's take another look at her log. I want to hear what you think about some of her entries."

As we scrolled through the log, I related my theory that Karen had some personality flaw that sidetracked her career. Her intolerance for lesser aviation professionals was even more apparent the second time through. We continued reading the log entries together. Richard noted that the file creation dates for Karen's design drawings corresponded to the time of the rejection letter from the engineering firm. The corroboration that the designs matched the rejection letters was interesting but I believed to be of little or no value.

We continued through the chronological record exchanging comments about Karen's view of her fellow aviation professionals. Well into the log entries, we noted the first astronomical observation. Richard had just finished the page and I was about to advance to the next when I realized something was not right.

The last entry on the page was for January sixth stating: "Capricornus observed in the vicinity of Sirius at 17:53:20"

"Richard, there is something very wrong with this entry."

"What do you mean Justin?"

"I know almost nothing about astronomy, and maybe only a little more than nothing about Astrology. What I do know is that I was almost a Christmas baby and my zodiac sign is Capricorn. The constellation related to Capricorn is Capricornus. That constellation raises low in the sky and is no longer visible by January in the northern hemisphere. How could Karen have seen Capricornus in January?"

"Let's check it out Justin. There has to be a star chart on the internet that will tell us conclusively."

Richard, took over the controls of my computer and quickly found a free site called 'Stargazing.net' that provided maps for all constellations. The site generated maps by date and time indicating constellations viewable under perfect conditions.

"According to this, it is just barely possible that Karen could see Capricornus from Mexico, but not Portland. Was Karen in town?"

"Yes, here is a reference to a mechanical issue she raised with the techs in Portland. Let's check out some more entries."

The astrological entries were not regular. The next entry was several days later. This log entry sighted Scorpios 19:26:40. A check of the sky chart disclosed that Scorpios appeared in spring and was no longer visible by September. The entries continued to include improbable or impossible observations. Whatever Karen was tracking, it was not the stars.

"Justin, what is that number reference Karen is using?"

"Isn't that the twenty-four hour clock? Wait a minute. A time of 17:53:20 is just before six in the afternoon. How could Karen see any stars that late in the afternoon?"

"Justin, according to this sunset time site, Karen could not have seen that constellation in the twilight. Let alone that she could see the sky though the clouds in Portland in January."

"Could it be the longitude or latitude?"

"Yes, one or the other, but two values are needed to locate a position. In addition, to make a specific location there must be a method of distinguishing north from south and east from west. Whatever it is I don't think it's time or location."

A quick trip to an internet map site disclosed that the west longitude line traversed Western Europe and Africa. The east longitudinal line also central Europe and central Africa. My first thought was that the line should have circumnavigated the globe.

"Justin," noted Richard, "the zero point for longitude is Greenwich, England and everything is measured as being east or west of that base point. The two possible lines of latitude were equally unhelpful. They ringed the earth a few hundred miles north or south of the equator. Using the same value for all for longitude and latitude combinations produced a cluster of four points in the middle of Africa.

We sat contemplating what we had found. Richard consulted his watch: "Justin, we have something. I don't know what, but it's something."

"I have to go, but you've made a good start. Now tell me what it means."

My neck stiff, shoulders tight, eyes blurry and thought process turning to mush. I did not realize how late in the day it was until I saw that the long shadows. The work was slow and tedious, typical for a data recovery problem. Pulling discrete kernels of information out of a disorganized mess is time consuming at best, impossible at worst.

Word processing documents are free-form unformatted data. Anyone who has written a term paper knows how time consuming it is to pull information from data in book format. Karen's supplemental log had no formatting other than the fact it was in chronological order. If I wanted to make any sense of the data, I needed to add organization.

Sam listened as I talked through options. "The way I see it Sam we need to do three things: One, break the big chunks into bite size pieces. Two, put the small pieces into groups. Third, separate the wheat from the chaff."

He was unimpressed with my biblical reference.

"Sam, Karen's 'Supplemental Log' contained information that she wanted kept secret. The fake star sightings have to be cover for the real data. Since she did not have a problem naming coworkers, there was no reason to use stars or constellations in their place. All we really know is that Karen didn't want to openly identify the person, place or thing. Which brings us full circle back to the question of what Karen was tracking: drug deals, bribes, luggage theft, or aircraft?"

"I've heard of people in Great Britain who watch train engines just like some people watch birds. Somehow I don't think Karen was spotting aircraft and keeping secret records."

Sam thought enough of that conclusion to almost open one eye.

"What is the best way to break big chunks of data in to meaningful pieces? What's important Sam? How should I break her entries into data elements?"

Sam's tail gave a twitch at the tip.

"Good point, obviously we need to group the mystery coordinates, the constellations and stars and aircraft. But, what about all the other junk she wrote. Is her note to track down the technician who left a screwdriver in her cockpit real or code? Is a complaint one item, or is each issue a separate data point?"

I stared at the data filled screen for long seconds. "Sam,

enough of this paralysis from analysis, it's time to get started. Other data groups will just have to be added as they become apparent."

Three hours of work delivered 118 entries into my database. I was able to make such good progress only after I changed tactics. Working with text data in a word processing document is a pain. Initially I tried copying an individual log entry into the spreadsheet program I was using to build the database. Copying an entry into a worksheet cell then carving out chunks for placement in a data table took too long. Even short entries took three to four minutes to parse.

Copying the entries into a table in the word processing document was just about as slow as using the spreadsheet. The thought of hiring a secretary to perform the data entry was increasing in appeal by the minute. If only these were delineated files. If Karen has separated important data with commas this would be easy. I could drop the data in my spreadsheet and parse the records in seconds. Still that would not help random order of the elements in each entry.

Then I realized I was living by a self-imposed limitation. "Sam is there any reason I can't add a character to make these entries easier to break into pieces?"

No, there was not any reason, and at the same time, I could add a number to each segment. The number would allow me to sort and group segment types so I could move chunks of data into appropriate data fields, rather than pull one piece at a time.

The method was far from perfect but it was a vast improvement. My log entry conversion time dropped to about a minute per entry. The result was that I entered about four months of log entries.

About half of the entries included mystery coordinates. Other than entries involving complaints, the rest of the records did not seem to have a discernible pattern.

Being an accountant, I noticed the numbers on the screen first. It was now clear that the mystery coordinates were not time values. Many of the coordinate values exceeded twenty-four, making them unfit as a time unit. I sorted the file to group all the mystery coordinates, then sorted them by smallest to largest value. If there was anything significant, it did not jump out at me. For the most part the entries were unique although there were a fair number of duplications. The log entries in my data set all contained one mystery coordinate, with three exceptions. These dual coordinates were of lesser value than the others were, but otherwise unremarkable.

I copied, sorted the data again, so that the mystery coordinates were in date order. The entries began in January spanning three additional months. The three dual coordinate entries all occurred about the end of each month. Was that significant? Not that I could see.

The only other entry that stood out was the largest mystery coordinate in my list. It was the ninth log entry. Had I been looking at a ledger page I would have assumed it was a month end total. These were not dollar amounts. These numbers were some other type of entry.

"Sam, what am I missing?" Sam opened one eye, stared at me for a moment, opened the other eye and then yawned. Next, he engaged the process that only cats seem to be able to do. Starting from lying on his side, Sam managed to stretch and reach a standing position in one smooth continuous motion. Then somehow Sam walked in a stiff legged cat goose-step over to the monitor. He appraised the situation, reached out with his left paw, stroked the screen several times then turned to face me.

"I know Sam. It's all on the screen. It's right in front of my face."

I think Sherlock Holmes said: "after eliminating all other options, whatever remains is the answer, no matter how improbable." If Sherlock did not say it, he should have. Could these entries be a transactions record?

I had added the eight mystery coordinates just as they were written, only omitting the colons that separated the "Degrees:Minutes:Seconds." The total was 1,615,040 or 161:50:40, which did not match the ninth log entry, a dead end.

Every rookie accountant learns this hard lesson, just because numbers are close does not mean they are related. It is very easy to spin your wheels chasing false leads. Just like this one. I started to push my chair back from the desk, but stopped.

Sam sat watching me intently. He seemed disappointed in my reaction, giving me a look I could only describe as disapproval. I felt like a kitten botching an easy hunt.

"I am not giving up Sam. It's just that I'm stumped."

Sam broke his stare first, choosing to wash his face.

"OK Sam, let's try Sherlock's method. What can we eliminate? The coordinates are not for navigation or time. The entries do not sum to a meaningful total. What else can we eliminate?"

166

With chin on hands at the apex of my forearm bipod, I stared at the monitor. Sam licked his fur. "What else do we know Sam?" He looked up, and then resumed licking once realized it was a rhetorical question.

"From my sample I see that there are no coordinates that repeat further on in the sequence, other than the paired coordinates. The pairs usually share the same date. No pair repeats. What does that tell me?"

Either Sam was not listening or he was bored. He got comfortable and closed his eyes.

Did the pattern in my sample continue in the rest of the data? I eyeballed the next six months of entries. Three or four times a month there were pairs and two other coordinates around a common date. At or near month end, there was a singular entry. Usually a coordinate pair bore no obvious relationship to any of the other entries. Just looking at the dates and numbers they had all the characteristics of a monthly transaction record, other than the fact that it didn't foot.

"Sam, is Karen was using a number code to keep track of transactions? What kind of code is it? All the numbers zero through nine are in use, so it is not a substitution of a different number system such as base eight. None of the entries I scanned includes any non-number characters, so it is not base eleven or larger. On its face, it is base ten, but the numbers don't add up."

"Sam, what if it's not numbers, what if its words?" Sam did not even twitch an ear.

It was time to seek help but I hesitated. The internet is the atom bomb of information, powerful but lacking in precision. There is a reason that accountants and attorneys pay dearly for research software. The tax research software is packed with tools to make your search rational, effective and efficient. The raw internet is an incredible tool that is capable of leading a researcher down blind alleys, false trails and unproductive tangents. I must use it with caution.

Three minutes of planning completed, the search begins. The search term "number code breaking" only generated 138 million hits, not as bad as I expected.

Nearing the end of my time limit, I conceded a couple of weaknesses in my planning. The word "code" has far too many legitimate uses: from engine parts to area codes to social security numbers. Second, everyone was interested in coding language. Numbers were not as important.

There were all kinds of tips on making and breaking coded text, no so for numbers. At least from what I could tell from my research. Richard, or someone he knew, would be a better person to determine if the mystery coordinates were actually coded words.

My attention returned to the coordinates and my assumption that they formed a transaction record. From what I had read about codes, they should be easy to translate but impossible to break. That seemed to me an impossible conflict. Looking at what Karen had done, I was hoping she elected to disguise the numbers and left it simple to break.

"Sam, whatever Karen did it is not simple addition. She only uses base 10 digits, could she have been working in another number set? If she is, it's not in a number format I have seen before. The examples of higher base number sets use the alphabet for additional digits. You know, the way that base 12 uses 0, 1, 2, 3, 4, 5, 6, 7, 8, 9, A, B: A = 10, B=11, 10=12. Can you imagine what it would have been like for the first accountants in Babylon? They used a number system based on 60."

Somehow, Sam was able to sleep through this fascinating history lesson. "My accounting professor told us about the Babylonians using the sexagesimal number system invented by the Sumerians. What started out as clay tokens representing quantities, evolved into cuneiform writing. He also claimed that accountants invented writing out of the need for permanent inventory records of grain, livestock and other things. I know what you are thinking, sixty is unwieldy. Actually sixty is an easy number to work with. It is evenly divisible by 2, 3, 4, 5, 6, 10, 12, 15, 20, and 30, which makes calculations simple. It works so well it was used in commerce and astronomy for a long time. We still use systems based upon sixty for navigation, angles and time. That's why there are 360 degrees in a circle, 60 seconds in a minute and 60 minutes in an hour."

"Wait a minute Sam. Are Karen's coordinates actually a variation of base 60 mathematics?"

I scanned the column containing the mystery coordinates. None of the numbers in the minute or second column exceeded 60. I already knew the hour column exceeded 100. Therefore, I knew this was not a pure base sixty system.

Maybe Karen's system was as simple as it appeared. By using a DEGREE:MINUTE:SECOND format the "Seconds" space would be units of 1, ranging from 0 to 59; and the "Minutes" space had to be units of sixty. Written out, it should look like, 000:00:59 = 59 and 000:01:00 = 60 and extending the progression 000:01:01 =

61 in everyday numbers.

"Let's see if this works Sam. The first eight numbers are 20:13:20 twice, 17:53:20, 19:26:40, 21:11:10, 19:29:28, and 22:02:01 twice. The second's total 140, which means I have to subtract 2 units of 60 to arrive at a number 59 or less. Then 140 less 120 leaves 20, which now I have to add 2 units of sixty to the minute's total of 149. Now the minutes total is 151, which is reduced by 2 units of 60, leaving 31. Finally, add 2 units to the 160 degree's total.

The final result is 162:31:20:

	Degrees	Minutes	Seconds
Entry 1	20	13	20
Entry 2	20	13	20
Entry 3	17	53	20
Entry 4	19	26	40
Entry 5	21	11	10
Entry 6	19	29	28
Entry 7	22	02	01
Entry 8	22	02	01
Subtotal	160	149	140
Units of Sixty to Add (Subtract)		2	(-120)
Subtotal		151	
Units of Sixty to Add (Subtract)	2	(-120)	
Total	162	31	20

"Sam is this is the proof? Does this match Karen's total?"
"Yes!"
I don't know if I woke the neighbors but I woke Sam.

"Richard, you won't believe what I found. Those coordinates in Karen's log were accounting entries. I figured out her method. It is a code based upon the Sumerian number system, the one passed on to the Babylonians. I cracked her code I know how she kept track."

"JUSTIN!"

I came up short realizing that this was not the first time I have heard my name.

"Justin, that's great. Do you know what time it is?"

"Well it's been dark for a while."

"Quite a while, can we discuss this tomorrow? Correction, can we talk about this later this morning?"

"Sorry Richard, I lost track of time. I am real sorry to have woken you."

"That's OK Justin. I will be out in east Portland tomorrow. I will swing by when I am done. Say around noon?"

"I'll talk to you then, Richard. Sorry."

Richard was right. I needed some sleep too, but how could I when I was this pumped up from my discovery.

Sam followed me with one eye to ensure I was really coming to bed. He had lost interest in my activities after I woke him with my discovery yell. My mind was still active, thinking about the meaning of the amounts Karen had been tracking. My presumption was that I was dealing with dollars. There was no hard evidence to confirm that conclusion other than the fact that I was dealing with amounts that accumulated into totals.

Was there any legitimate reason that Karen would keep track of any other unit than money? Maybe Karen gambled. No, Karen would not be a gambler, maybe a bookie who ran the show, but never just a player.

If anyone was a player, it was I. I did not know the rules or the game but I knew the stakes. Karen dragged me into this game and I had a sense that this was at the end of the mid-game. All the pieces were in position waiting orders for the final assault. How would the little information I had be enough to turn back the attack from the District Attorney?

I awoke coming out of a dream about chess. I gathered my wits, concluding it must be Thursday and I needed to get some work done for Lithium. I should not have, but I felt guilty about taking yesterday off to work on my stuff. I was working on the R&D

calculation when Richard called.

Meeting him at the door, I apologized: "Sorry to wake you last night."

"That's alright, what did you find?"

"Karen was keeping track of something and my guess is it is money."

"I got a lucky break in that the first sets of coordinates were small values. If they had been larger, I may not have figured it out. Karen was using the longitudinal coordinate format of 180 Degrees: 60 Minutes: 60 Seconds to convert ordinary decimal numbers into a code. Let me show you an example."

We ran though some simple examples and then I turned to Karen's data.

"What bothered me was that the numbers were too large for dollars. The first month's activity was over five hundred thousand. I was not having any luck getting the amounts from subsequent months to total."

"Then it dawned on me. She was keeping track of dollars and cents. Karen was not using the decimal point. The largest amount that can be written using one coordinate in her code is 179:59:59, or $6,479.99. By including a second coordinate she could reach an amount over four billion dollars. Let me show you."

Richard followed along as I added the individual coordinates for the following months. I converted each coordinate to its dollar equivalent. After completing the individual item conversions for the month, I summed the total and converted it to a coordinate value, which matched the coordinates in Karen's log.

Richard congratulated me on my work then added, "Justin, there is something strange about the individual amounts. It looks like there are regular pairings, far too many pairs to be a coincidence."

"You're right, and there is more. The transactions happened almost once a week. Every transaction uses four coordinates, and the proportions are consistent between transactions. This is the record of dividing up the shares."

"OK, shares of what?"

"The money they got from selling smuggled aircraft parts."

"That's crazy Justin."

"Maybe, maybe not Richard, let's look at the facts we know: Karen had access to a lot of money, she was keeping track of regular transactions, she was obsessed with FAA rules involving parts, she traveled routinely between Mexico and the US, and her partner is the chief avionics technician at PDX."

"Now her boyfriend is a conspirator too? That is a huge leap Justin, I don't buy it. How did she get them into the US, in her flight bag?"

"No, she used her wheelbarrow."

"You're not making any sense. What are you talking about?"

"You told me the joke about the guy who smuggled wheelbarrows. Instead of a wheelbarrow, Karen used her airplane. Who is going to check an aircraft? I can't believe customs agents know how to tell whether a part on an airplane is a fake. Besides, transportation equipment is not considered to be imported if it only operates on international routes. Customs is only interested in items imported and exported.

"How do you know that?"

"A couple of years back Lithium explored using its trucks to deliver batteries to Canada. There was concern that the trucks might be subject to Canadian customs duties and taxes. If transportation equipment likes trains, planes and trucks only delivers or picks up items for import and export there is no issue. There is no reason for customs to inspect the aircraft itself because it is not being imported. Customs looks for drugs, people, exotic animals and anything else of value that someone may stow on the plane. However, nobody cares about the plane itself."

"So how was Karen using her plane to smuggle parts?"

"The more I learn about Karen the more this makes sense. Karen was all about control. When she flew to Mexico, she had her partner pull an instrument and replace it with a counterfeit part. As pilot in command, she controlled the log entries so even if the copilot noted something unusual it never was reported. Then when the plane got to Portland, the bogus part was swapped out for a real part."

"You don't even know if there was anyone in Mexico."

"What about Carlos's family?"

"Pure speculation Justin, where is your evidence?"

"Karen had over four hundred thousand dollars in her car. Give me a better scenario and I'll consider it."

"Justin, we have to be realistic. I know you are upset that Karen was seeing Carlos."

"That has nothing to do with this! Karen was running an illegal operation. I have proof of that in her supplemental log. People don't keep secret coded records for legal activities."

"OK, maybe you have something. It's just that I can't believe it's that easy. Doesn't the FAA have systems and paperwork in place to catch things like this?"

"In theory yes, at least that's what I thought. That is why I hesitated to bring it up, because it seems too fantastic. From what I have learned I'm betting the FAA systems suffer from the same problem that plagues accounting: internal controls."

"What does accounting have to do with this?"

"Richard, accountants learned long ago that anything of value that can be stolen will be stolen. A corollary to that is that most people are honest, as long as someone is watching. The best defense against theft or bad behavior, is a set of overlapping procedures that don't allow any one person too much access or opportunity to misappropriate assets. The person who signs the checks should not be the person who balances the checking account. The person who initiates a check should not be the person who approves the check. Protocols like that create an environment that makes fraudulent transactions difficult to pull off.

"I don't see what that has to do with the FAA."

"The regulators at the FAA are not stupid. They know people will bend rules and take shortcuts if they think nobody is watching. The FAA tries to insure quality by licensing, training and procedures to promote good behavior. However, they suffer the same big weakness as many businesses."

"What do you mean?"

"What I am trying to say Richard, is that there is a big weakness in any protocol: collusion. The FAA counts on individuals to follow the rules because other people are watching. Nevertheless, two or more people working together can get around almost any rule. That is what I think is happening. Based upon the way the shares are divided, I think there are four partners."

"Justin, maybe you are on to something, but your theory is based upon a lot of assumptions and very few facts. And another thing, I don't see how you make any money with your scheme."

"I put a lot of thought into this Richard. In many ways, this is similar to counterfeiting currency. Whether I was counterfeiting currency or counterfeiting parts I face similar problems."

"First I need the counterfeit product. Second, there has to be a way to get the product into circulation. Third, I want to get paid."

"The counterfeit product is probably the easiest step. Bogus products are a big problem for everybody. For example, there was a guy at work talking about selling his coin collection. China has severe penalties for counterfeiting Chinese money, but not foreign coins or currency. The numismatic community is in a panic because perfectly reproduced coins are appearing on the market. Coins so good they can only be distinguished by an analysis of the trace impurities in the silver. I have also heard stories about the problems electronics manufacturers have when they build foreign production facilities. The local work rules allow the factory to run two shifts a day. In reality, there is a third "ghost" shift run by the locals that continues to produce the same product. The ghost product ends up in the black market. To add insult to injury, the best production goes to the black market. The rejects go to the official manufacturer. I have no doubt counterfeit aircraft electronics are available."

"I've heard those stories too, but that doesn't make your theory any stronger."

"I understand your skepticism. I find the thought of fake aircraft parts hard to accept too."

"Let me continue. Second, now that I have my product, how do I get it into circulation? Unless I work for a parts manufacturer, I have to use another entry point. The next best distributor would be a company with high standards and a strong reputation, like an airline. People buying a part from an airline are more willing to accept the parts and the paperwork based on their standards and the high level of FAA scrutiny."

"Third, I want to get paid for my counterfeits. If I am dealing in money, I get paid when I exchange counterfeit money for real money. For parts it is more complicated. It was your joke about wheelbarrows that helped me see how the process works. Start with a counterfeit part. Install the fake part on an aircraft. Take the real part from the aircraft and sell it in the secondary market of used parts."

"You are telling me that Karen bought fake parts and then installed them on her own aircraft?"

"Karen did not install the parts, Carlos Torres and the other partner did."

"Justin is that wishful thinking that Carlos is involved or do you have proof?"

"Proof, no. Is there circumstantial evidence? Yes."

"Carlos and Karen spoke regularly according to the phone records. Carlos is the lead avionics technician in Portland. That position gives him access to the aircraft and no supervisor to catch him. Carlos admits to having an affair with Karen. And Carlos had access to Karen in Houston."

"That is pretty flimsy evidence."

"Richard, I think that it is obvious from the information in Karen's 'Supplemental Log' that there were at least two other people involved. I am guessing someone to buy the parts and someone to sell the parts."

"What have you been able to find out about Carlos?"

"Carlos is a legal US Resident. Originally, he is from Mexico and still has family in Cancun. He got most of his training in the US Air Force. He received a general discharge from the service. Before you ask, as far as we can tell Carlos and Karen did not serve in the military together."

"Carlos has been with VAA two years longer than Karen. He transferred to Portland from Denver about ten years ago. He had some short term assignments in LA and Phoenix, but always returned to Portland."

"Carlos rents a house in northeast Portland a couple of miles from PDX. His main hobby seems to be gambling. He has "VIP Player" privilege cards at all the Indian Casinos in Western Washington and half way down the Oregon Coast. I have not followed up on Reno and Vegas, though it's likely he flew jump-seats to both places also."

"It sounds like he spends a lot of money."

"Justin, we have a few facts but little proof. It is a fatal flaw for an investigator to fit the facts into a preconceived theory. Lots of people gamble and are not involved in any illegal activity."

"I know that Richard. But I think I see several badges of fraud."

"What do you mean? I've never heard of that."

"When the IRS audits taxpayers, the agents are always alert for tax fraud. IRS Agents do not look of a single action or item to tip them off to fraud, they look for a pattern. The IRS has a long list of actions that individually are innocent, but when combined are a strong indication of fraud."

"Like what?"

"Say I live in a nice house, don't use credit cards, have a small business and keep poor records: am I committing tax fraud?"

"You can't tell from that much information."

"Right, here are two equally plausible scenarios. On the one hand, it could be that: grandma gave me the house, I don't trust banks, I like running my own business and I hate keeping books. Or conversely it could be: I am hiding income by dumping it into my house, avoiding a paper trail by using cash, skimming cash off my business to avoid reporting to it the IRS, and hiding my actions by not keeping records."

"Any single action may be innocent but in combination they may build a case for fraud. Even with all the badges in place, all the facts have to be brought forward to know the truth."

"I agree Justin. All the facts need to be taken into account."

"But Richard, all the cards are starting to fall into place. If Carlos had a gambling problem, he needed money. If someone is threatening that money supply it makes for a stronger argument that Carlos is involved in Karen's death."

"Justin, that's two big ifs. If you are correct about the fake parts, they had a sweet deal in place. What makes you think that someone was making Carlos feel threatened?"

"Now this I admit is speculation. I think Karen had a conscience. You have seen her mementos. She loved to fly and thought of herself as to great pilot. I think she was drawn into the scheme when she was mad at VAA and the FAA system. My thought is she got involved to get back at everyone who did her wrong."

"Her dilemma was that she knew that what she was doing was wrong. I believe this because she did not spend most of her share of the money. There was over four hundred thousand dollars that she hid in her car. That's more than enough for escape money. I totaled the monthly amounts in Karen's log and it comes to just over three million dollars, or about three hundred and fifty thousand dollars a year. I am estimating Karen's share was between seven hundred and nine hundred thousand dollars."

"So Justin, what did Karen do with the other three to four hundred thousand?"

"I don't know, but I don't think she spent it. It is not in her apartment in Houston, and it is not here. You or the police should have found it by now if it is in a financial institution."

"I think she regretted her involvement and could not bring herself to spend the money. Once she was in the gang, she could not quit without exposing herself. Maybe she was getting ready to turn herself in and Carlos killed Karen to keep her quiet?"

"We will need more than that to convince a jury. And there is still that minor problem of how did Carlos leave a secure facility, kill Karen, and return without being missed."

Chapter 48   Feasibility

I was still thinking about Carlos and his airport alibi as Richard got up to leave.

"Justin, I will brief Anne about your smuggling theory."

The tone in Richard's voice did not communicate much confidence. "OK, I will catch up with you tomorrow."

"Make it next Tuesday. I am taking the wife to coast for the Labor Day weekend."

Richard's comment shook me. I had completely missed the fact that it was Labor Day weekend. Somehow, I had managed to treat all the advertisements for sales and such as background noise. Then again, in my new status I rarely watched the news or listened to the radio.

Hearing the announcement from Richard struck a nerve. Normal people were making important decisions about barbeques or taking their last weekend trip of the summer. I was free only at the sufferance of a judge. Suddenly the house felt as confining as a jail cell. I grabbed my sunglasses and headed out the door.

I was full of pent up energy from too many hours sitting at my desk. Instead of entering the quiet maze of residential streets around my house I headed toward people, to 164th Avenue. At five in the morning 164th is quiet, the residents asleep and the stores and businesses closed. At five in the afternoon, all lanes of 164th are full of cars entering and exiting the shops or heading for home. I had to slow my walking pace and pay attention to the actions of cars and drivers. I found myself adjusting my cadence in order to cross driveways when they were free from cars. Even though they did not hear me, I thanked drivers for not running me over when they had the opportunity.

I determined that I was not looking for the company of strangers. I continued south, leaving the last of the businesses behind, then past the residential areas. Ahead Highway 14 presented a final serious obstacle. A challenge mainly due to the drivers not being used to seeing pedestrians this far from the businesses. Safely beyond the Evergreen Highway, I descended to the orphaned end segment of 164th and beyond. The blackberries, trees and other plants were no barrier after I found the trail used by the indigenous population. The transients who accessed the river from 164th had created trails that linked the riverbank to the street. I made my way to the riverbank and located a comfortable rock from which to sit and watch the river.

The water level was about as low as it would get for the year. Kept this high only by the half a hundred dams up stream still releasing runoff from the spring. It was too cool for water skiing but there were a few powerboats using the shipping channel. The seabirds and ducks were doing what birds do, sitting on the water or flying around, landing, then flying back around.

In the distance across the Columbia River, I could see and hear the large aircraft. The winds were such that the landing approach was from the east. I traced the pattern of aircraft back from the airport. At least three aircraft stretched from PDX to somewhere east of Troutdale. A fourth plane was approaching from the south not quite ready to make its turn to the west to join the line of aircraft in final approach. I was sure there were more aircraft to the south but too far away for visual confirmation.

The aircraft were mostly airliners with a few business jets joining the mix. I thought how disappointed Karen would be that I could not distinguish the various types and models. Other than size and the number of engines, I had a hard time telling jets apart.

I watched a 747 lead a much smaller executive jet to the airport. It looked extremely small sandwiched between the first Jumbo and another large airliner following behind. I wondered if Sue Johnson, the Lithium CEO, was on that executive airplane.

Watching this private jet on approach to PDX reminded me about the project my boss and I worked on last year for Lithium. The question was whether we could afford to buy an executive jet. It all started when Sue made friends with one of Lithium's materials suppliers at an industry conference in New York. He was leaving the conference via Teterboro, New Jersey on his way to China. He offered to drop Sue off on the way.

Clark laughed as he told the story. "I thought people got over showing off when they got out of high school. The normal route from New York to China is to fly directly to Anchorage, Alaska. Flying to Portland adds a lot of miles and time to the trip. Sue's friend was looking to impress her and he did."

"The non-stop flight from New Jersey to Portland was just the start. The amenities of the private air terminal at the fixed base operation were impressive. The facility was beautiful and the staff eager to assist with every need. Sue had little time to enjoy the facilities since there was no ticket check-in and best of all no TSA grab and grope lines. Their taxi ride from downtown New York City was a helicopter that dropped them at the private air terminal. There was no wait for luggage as the ground crew moved her bags directly from their helicopter into the aircraft prepping on the ramp. If not for the two planes in line before theirs, they could have boarded directly and left without entering the terminal."

"The trip from New Jersey to Portland was quick, pleasant and productive. Sue's host enjoyed pointing out all the features of the aircraft as they relaxed in the soft wide leather seats configured to facilitate conversation. Not only was the aircraft comfortable, it was a fully functioning office, including communications and computer support. After work, the conference area doubled as the dining area. The host was especially proud of the china and crystal his wife had picked out on a trip to Europe. She expected food better than what the airline sells, what she got exceeded her expectations, in both taste and presentation."

"The flight could not have ended better in Portland. The plane rolled to a stop just a few yards from the door, Sue stepped off the stairs onto a red carpet and walked directly into another beautiful private terminal. She did not stop to admire the facility as she walked the short distance through the building, out the front door and into the waiting limousine. As she settled into the comfortable seat, a member of the ground crew deposited her bags in the trunk."

"I got an email that night from Sue asking me to work with accounting on a feasibility analysis." Clark set up a meeting for the following Monday to discuss options.

"Justin, can you pull all of Sue's travel reports for the last year and schedule out her trips. We need to estimate her flight hours as part of our analysis."

"OK, I am guessing they will be less than a thousand hours."

"I would be amazed if they exceed 500 hours. Most commercial airplane trips are three hours or less. Flights seem longer because of what goes on before you board the plane. I am old enough to remember when you could grab your ticket and be at your gate ten minutes after getting out of the cab. Now I need to arrive two hours early and worry about making it through the TSA searches in time."

"Ah, sure Clark."

"I'm talking about the days before deregulation. Back when they fed us real food. Back then, the flights were barely half-full. If you had to share a row with someone, the flight was crowded. The stewardesses, who were not flight attendants and were not male, were charming and eager to please. People dressed up to fly. Last time I flew, people were wearing tee shirts and flip-flops."

"That's great, but how can a few hundred hours of flying justify buying an airplane?"

"Think of it like this: 150 flight hours is, twenty-five, six hour round trips a year. When's the last time you flew every other week for a year?"

"Well, never."

"For people like Sue and her team, travel consumes a material portion of their work week. If there are options that can make them more efficient and more effective, they need to be considered. Do you want Sue to spend time looking for her luggage or planning the company's future?"

"Maybe if she had the time she could review salaries?"

Clark ignored my wit.

"There are really only three options: charter aircraft, outright ownership or fractional ownership. Flying first class is not really an option. It just makes inefficient travel more comfortable."

"If Sue was traveling a few times a year from Portland to San Francisco, a regular charter might make sense. Charters work best for low frequency travelers. Charter companies vary considerably in capability, service and performance. If you do not work directly with the charter company, you have to use a charter broker. Then there is no assurance you will get the same operator each time, or ever the same type of aircraft."

"Outright ownership gives the most flexibility at the most cost. You own, or share ownership, of an aircraft. An owner has all the flexibility of flying whenever and wherever. An owner also has all the burden of operations, crews, maintenance and insurance."

"What's the deal about insurance?"

"I have a golf buddy who has an aviation insurance brokerage. He pointed out that aviation is its own specialty with lots of unique problems. Most people never take their car to Canada but it's likely you will fly your plane to Europe or Africa. If the local government seizes your plane for running into a giraffe on the runway, is that covered by your insurance? That, and there's lots of international law to consider in addition to all the usual casualty issues."

"My friend's favorite closing pitch is "How would you like to be the last person to work on Donald Trump's airplane?"

"What's that supposed to mean?"

"If you worked on the plane before it crashes do you have enough insurance when you get sued by the estate?"

"Insurance is a big part of owning aircraft. Not only are the airplanes expensive, but the passengers represent high value liabilities and are expensive to compensate. He was involved in a multi-million dollar wrongful death claim resulting from a loose gas cap. The pilot was also an orthopedic surgeon with lots of earning potential."

"What happened?"

"The cap popped off the gas tank on the right wing. If this happens when flying, the air flowing over the wing siphons the fuel out of the fill spout. The gasoline comes out as a visible vapor that looks worse than it is. The Transportation Safety Board theorized he was so worried about running out of gas that he forgot to fly the airplane. He crashed three miles from the airport coming around for an emergency landing. The left wing tank was full."

"Did the company settle?"

"The security video from the FBO viewed by the jury proved that the pilot was the last person to touch the gas cap. His heirs had to settle for his life insurance."

"My point is Justin, owning an aircraft is complicated and requires a team of specialists. If a company buys a plane, they are also buying a flight department to support the aircraft as well as all the tax compliance responsibilities. And, we have not even started the discussion about what kind of aircraft we need."

"Clark, you've ruled out charters, purchasing is too expensive, what's left?"

"Some people might call fractional ownership the best of all worlds. The buyer purchases between 1/32nd and 32/32nd of an aircraft. That gives them the right to use the aircraft between 25 and 800 hours in a year."

"I didn't realize you knew so much about the aviation industry."

"My first tax job after college was with Eastern Air Lines. When deregulation hit the airlines in the late seventies, I went back to school and got a Master of Taxation degree. After that I kept in touch with people who are still in the industry."

I did the math in my head: "There's over 8000 hours in a year, how can 800 hours be considered to be 100% use of an aircraft?"

"The purpose of a business aircraft is not to fly the plane. It's to get people from here to there. The important things happen after you arrive, not while you are in the air. Here's an analogy: Let's say you drive 12,000 miles a year at an average speed of 30 miles an hour. How many hours have you used your car?"

"Four hundred hours."

"Is that enough use to justify owning your own car?"

"But it sits in the parking lot at work, and I don't drive while sleeping."

"Exactly, aircraft are subject to the same use limitations. Most of the time, the plane is sitting at an airport while the passengers are off doing more important things. When I was at Eastern, if we could fly our planes 3000 hours a year we were very pleased. And that was scheduling flights 24 hours a day 7 days a week."

"I see where flight hours are a lot different than calendar hours. The hours we are buying from the fractional company are flight hours?"

"Yes, though most companies add a tenth of an hour to the flight time for aircraft taxi time at departure and arrival. The big benefit is that the owner does not pay for non-flight time and positioning flights. So if owner B flies to LA Monday morning, the plane will return to Portland for Sue's afternoon departure, at no cost to Sue. The aircraft then returns to LA to pick up owner B on Wednesday for his trip to NY."

"Isn't it expensive to move aircraft back and forth?"

"It is that is why the aircraft manager would like as much lead time a possible to match aircraft arrivals to departures. In general, there is a minimum four-hour call out period. That is just enough time to get a crew and plane in position for the owner's departure from just about anywhere in the USA."

"Let me see if I got this straight. If I buy 1/8th of an $ 8,000,000 aircraft I pay $1,000,000 and get to use it for 100 hours a year."

"Well, you also have to pay the hourly operational costs, fuel, and other fees. In addition, there is the monthly maintenance cost for your share of the aircraft. In general, it is a five-year contract. At the end you can renew or sell your share to the manager or a third party."

"It still sounds expensive."

"It's cheaper than owning and there are economies of scale. The management company schedules maintenance and supports you if the aircraft you are using breaks. What would you do if you were sitting on the ground in Fairbanks with mechanical problem?"

"I don't know sounds like it might be fun."

"Seriously, the management company will dispatch another aircraft so you can complete your trip if it's not a quick fix. This kind of support is expensive but well worth the cost."

"Since we are doing the work to justify the purchase, I think we should get to use the plane for a weekend."

"I'll run that past Sue and see how far we get."

Like most companies, Lithium's aircraft use policy restricts use to VP and above so Clark and I will not get to use any of the three eighths of an airplane we ended up buying.

Is the cost of our fractional aircraft a lot more expensive than flying first class? Absolutely, but Sue liked our new plane and the board of directors liked Sue.

I watched the plane that might be carrying Sue disappear behind the trees on Government Island. From my position on the riverbank, I could not actually see PDX. The trees on the island were over my head creating a false horizon blocking my view of the actual airport.

Richard had a good point, how does someone leave and return to a secure facility, like PDX, unnoticed? The control tower tracks and records the movement of planes using the airport. The airplane manifest records passengers and crew. All the people who work at the airport have badges that track them as they come and go.

I pondered the question as the sun dropped low against the Coast Range. The aircraft on approach assumed an orange tone as the sun sank. I wondered how the pilots could fly directly into the blinding setting sun.

Was Richard right? Was I blind to the reality of what was?

I considered Richards question as I watched the waters swirl around an underwater obstruction. I rationalized that I was thinking objectively as I scanned the rocks and riverbank. A gull feather stuck in the rocks gave me incentive to get up. Sam would like this.

The walk back was much little less frantic than the trip to the river, but probably more dangerous. It was now full onset twilight and the eyesight of the drivers had not improved in the declining light. Everything was moving into deeper shadow. I prayed that the same was not true for my case. I needed more light, and more visibility of what Karen and her pals had done.

The answers to Karen's murder were on the other side of the river, a place I could not go.

I fell back on a tactic I had used before in my life when I felt troubled. I hid in my work. For most Americans, Labor Day is a three, possibly four-day weekend. For me it was forty-three hours billable to Lithium. Sam took full advantage of the waning summer to occupy sleeping locations that would soon be uncomfortably damp.

The only relaxation I pursued on these days was answering Richard's unstated question: could someone make enough money selling used aircraft parts to justify a smuggling venture?

Richard's question bothered me. I had avoided researching the economics out of fear that the truth would invalidate my theory. This weekend I had to prove whether my smuggling scheme could generate enough money to make it worth the risk.

I started my analysis with a reasonableness test: Was the value of the avionics in common commercial aircraft enough to make counterfeit parts profitable? Somewhere I remembered hearing that a new Boeing 747 costs over 100 million dollars. A quick trip to the internet proved my memory wrong. The latest model of 747 is well over 300 million dollars per aircraft. My accountant brain engaged. How many passengers would it take to pay for an airplane?

To make it easy I assumed a thousand dollars per passenger and no other expenses for fuel or crews or maintenance or anything else. A thousand passengers at a thousand dollars apiece will yield a million dollars. That meant that just to pay for the aircraft, an airline needs to fly three hundred thousand passengers on that plane. Viewing it another way, if the plane averaged 300 passengers on every flight it would take a thousand flights just to pay for the aircraft. How does any airline ever make any money?

I was tempted to venture into a more detailed analysis by using numbers that are more realistic to provide a better payoff estimate. Reason prevailed and I prompted myself to return to the important question at hand. Could a person make good money selling fake parts?

I returned to my reasonableness test. The internet informed me that a Boeing 737 cost in excess of fifty million dollars. To be conservative, I used 50 million dollars for the airplane cost. Richard's friend said that 20% of the cost of an aircraft related to the avionics, which yielded 10 million dollars as the cost of the avionics. To make this a realistic test, I allocated three quarters of the cost to wiring and installation. The result was that the component cost of avionics in a Boeing 737 was two and a half million dollars.

How many instruments are there in an airline cockpit? I looked at pictures that showed lots of gauges and instruments in arrangements that were hard to count. I had avoided researching aircraft instruments because I am not a pilot and would not understand what I was reading. Now it seemed that I had no choice.

Having seen the movie *Airplane* several times, I knew what an altimeter looked like and believed I understood what it did. Other than that, I was at a loss, and did not really care to know but I had to learn. The internet gave me the basics. There were actually groups of instrument types. The groups related to what the aircraft was doing, what the engines were doing, where the aircraft was going and communicating with others.

Before I started, I assumed the designer configured the instrument layout. Actually, there are standard configurations for certain key instruments. The "T" arrangement requires four instruments in specific order laid out like dots forming a "T." The Altitude, Attitude, and Altimeter from the crossbar and the Heading indicator formed the leg of the "T," According to what I read this was the normal configuration on US built aircraft since the 1950's. All the other instruments in the panel are oriented around this basic "T." The British added a turn indicator (I did not know aircraft had turn signals) and a vertical speed indicator to their "basic six" core cluster.

This was mildly interesting but not what I needed. I should have spent three minutes planning before I jumped into researching avionics. It was interesting to learn that a mechanical gyrocompass was a variation of the kid's toy I was never able to work correctly. What I really needed to know was, were there enough different avionic components to make Karen's fake parts swindle work?

It was a throw away comment in an article that answered my question. There are upwards of a hundred different instruments in a modern commercial aircraft cockpit. Using my two and a half million-dollar value, that meant the average component value when new was $25,000.

It sure looked like Karen's scheme would work. Did the market support my conclusion?

The first web site I happened to enter included a page titled "Why Used Avionics?" Although geared toward the private pilot sector it provided insight to the world of used parts. Money of course was the primary motivation. The web page promised that used avionics are reliable and compatible with your aircraft, just a lot cheaper.

The comment on compatibility was a good reminder of the FAA requirement to install only equipment accepted per the original Type Certificate or a Supplemental Type Certificate. As long as an aircraft was flying, there would be a market for parts that matched the certificate limitations.

The page went on to promote the option of upgrading to last year's top of the line model for a lot less money than the current "state of the art" technology. Finally, the page noted that the component would have a "Yellow Tag" (maintenance release) or a "Form 8130-3" (airworthiness certificate). I was not quite sure of the difference between the Yellow Tag and the Form 8130-3 but they both seemed to indicate that the instrument had been tested and met manufacturer's operational specifications.

The "Yellow Tag" notation jogged my memory. One of the documents in Karen's papers related to the identification of usable parts. A "Yellow Tag" indicated that a technician had deemed the part usable. The "Form 8130-3" indicated it was new from the manufacturer or overhauled to original specifications. A "Red Tag" indicated that the part was beyond repair.

After looking at several web pages, I realized that I had not wasted my time. My diversion into the cockpit and the ways of the basic "T" and the "Basic Six" provided me some benefit after all. At least now, I was able to guess the function of some components. How the sellers arrived at their offering prices made no sense.

Seemingly, identical parts varied wildly in price. Parts with the designation "as removed" implied to me that they were similar to a used car sold "as is where is." You paid your money and you took your chances. The lower prices seemed to support my "as is where is" comparison.

What confused me the most were the subtle variations in the part description that resulted in large variation in part prices. The exact same model could be two or three times as expensive without obvious difference. If there had been an odometer reading or a model year listed, the variations would have made some sense. From what I read, the parts seemed identical but something affected their value in a great way.

Returning to one of the sites, I compared two parts from the same manufacturer having the exact same part number. The only difference between the two was the cryptic notation "h12 m34" and "h3 m44." In a fit of inspiration, or basic reading skills, I scrolled to the top of the auction web site and re-read the column headers. The notation "time left" above the "h12 m34" did not refer to the time available to purchase the part. The numbers had not changed from the last time I was here. This must have something to do with the part. Maybe the FAA could shed some light on this.

The FAA web site is actually quite accessible and huge. The search term "part" is useless because every regulation title included a variant of "Part 91" or "Part 135" which generated thousands of matches. I tried many combinations with "part" such as time, repair, replacement, used, and life. It was 'Part Life' that generated the answer I needed. Unlike our cars, the FAA deems that some parts grow old and die. Moreover, parts may have more than one life. A component may have a repair life, meaning it can be inspected and overhauled in order to live again, or it may have a life limit, meaning it dies when it gets too old.

The age limitation confused me. Units of time I understood but I also saw references to cycles in the FAA guidance. Cycles seemed to be a term so obvious and so well understood by all in the aviation industry that it need not be defined. Fortunately, I found an aviation dictionary on the internet.

This presumed authoritative source defined a "cycle" as a complete functional operation such as a turbine engine starting, operating and shutting down. A cycle for landing gear consisted of a takeoff and subsequent landing.

I translated what I read into terms I understood. Operating a car under FAA guidelines would allow me to drive my car 50,000 miles or 2000 engine cycles. When I reached either, the mileage or cycle limit, the engine is overhauled. Regardless of how well the car was operating. It is easy to imagine a commute on which it was possible to run out of one limit long before the other. Also under FAA 'car' rules, at 3000 cycles I must buy a new transmission, no matter how well the car runs and how few miles on the car. How the airlines stay in business under these regulations I did not know.

This research experience taught me that: parts are expensive, there is a demand for used parts, and the value of the part increases the longer it is has to live.

Karen and her team could make a lot of money counterfeiting parts.

Chapter 50   To the Border

My feet hit the floor and I winced. Not only were my legs stiff but the soles of my feet were tender. Yesterday I was feeling good about my investigation into the value of airplane parts. I had worked hard the whole weekend, but neglected my physical exercise. Late in the afternoon, I headed out for a walk to the river. The last of the Labor Day traffic was rolling on SR 14 as I cautiously crossed under it to reach the Evergreen Highway.

Instead of continuing to the river, I turned right, heading west on the old main route. This is not the best choice for safety. Back when Primary State Highway 8 was a major part of the transportation system between Eastern and Western Washington, sidewalks were not part of the budget. A construction decision that made sense at a time when this was rural farm land.

Today, walking along this road can be exciting. The shoulders of the highway are from an era when road pavement ended at the edge of the traffic lane. The shoulder consisted of packed aggregate that prevented most plants from growing within one to two feet of the traffic lane. Other than the lack of plants, there was not much to identify it as a shoulder. It was unclear where the shoulder ended and the road right of way began. Someone had mowed most of the ground vegetation four to five feet out from the lane. I took that to be the line of demarcation. Along the way, I noted that the lack of official parking along the highway did not prevent the occasional local from parking wherever there was room.

The condition of the roadway struck me as poor until it dawned on me that the concrete used in the Evergreen Highway was the better part of a century old. The road still served well the residential traffic that traversed its cracked slab sections.

The further I walked along the road the more it galled me that I could not drive the couple of miles across a river that thousands of other people crossed every day. After twenty minutes of walking, I had only had glimpses of the river from between the houses that lined the highway. What could have been a pleasant stroll was interrupted by a constant need to watch for inattentive drivers. My trek along the highway seemed no closer to my objective as a weakness in my plan materialized. The trip from my house to the Glen Jackson Bridge is only a few minutes by car. It is a lot longer on foot.

In addition, the quality of the trail did not improve the

journey. The path varied from packed gravel two or three feet wide down to a few inches of hard dirt encroached upon by blackberry or worse. In places trees and brush were closer to the road than I thought prudent. Fortunately, the road was generally straight in this section with only small gentle curves. Therefore, my presence should not surprise any driver as long as I stayed out of the vegetation. I peered ahead to see my objective. The dense foliage along the road limited my visibility to about half a mile. Finally, just as I reached the edge of the Columbia Springs Environmental Center I caught sight of the elevated bridge span.

I walked past the old fish hatchery that made up most of the buildings of the environmental center. The elevated roadway rose thirty feet above as I entered the shadow of the bridge.

Realization that there was no access to the I205 walkway diluted my elation at reaching my destination. Another planning flaw revealed. Now I remembered that bicycles appear and disappear from the bike path along SR14. If I wanted to get to the walkway, I needed to get to SR14.

The options did not look good. The Columbia Springs Environmental Center's forest acreage bordered I205 on the east was infested with what appeared to be lush a growth of impenetrable blackberry. Under the bridge a chest high chain link fence surrounded the pillars supporting I205, indicating that the Washington Department of Transportation did not want people walking under the roadway. Alternately, I knew there was no street or sidewalk that would take me to a restricted access road like SR 14 from my current location. Finally, on the west side was a residential maze that included fences belonging to homeowners predisposed to summon the police.

I considered climbing atop the conveniently located phone company equipment box providing easy entry into, but not exit out of, the fenced area. However, just beyond the box was an open gate. My keen eye then located the well-worn path created by the maintenance vehicles. This must be how others get to and from SR14 and the I205 walkway. The hard beaten path led 200 yards under the freeway until I spied the ramp up.

The long ribbon of blue sky above me widened as I neared the top of the three hundred foot long ramp. Finally, I was on the bridge. I marched purposefully toward the Oregon border somewhere in the middle of the river. I would heed Anne's commandment: "thou shall not leave the State." That did not mean that I could not get as close as possible to Oregon.

Walking south, the riverbank below me receded as the traffic sped past on either side of me. I turned my attention to the airport as I walked between the six lanes of traffic. It was downhill to Oregon from here. Maximum elevation here near the Washington shore allowed river traffic to move up and down the Columbia.

I was disappointed with the view. I thought the height would have given me an unobstructed view of PDX. Unfortunately, the trees of Sand Island were tall enough to hide parts of the airport. I continued on, hoping that when I got to Government Island the view of PDX would be clear. Advancing another hundred yards toward Oregon did not improve the view of PDX. The trees of another island obscured more of my airport view.

I looked ahead to see how far it was to Government Island. Instead, what caught my eye was a previously ignored highway sign, now only a hundred yards head "Welcome to Oregon."

My trek aborted, my mission a failure, I turned for home. Since I had come this far carrying my binoculars, I returned to the spot with the least obstructed view. The 7x50 old-fashioned pre-electronic binoculars are heavy. Resting my elbows on the railing, I gaze at the airport. I hope the people whizzing by will think tourist and not terrorist. The cars are sparse enough that occasionally I can look for a whole second or more before having the image blurred by another vehicle. Unintentionally the 7x50-power binocular is a good choice. The bridge vibrations would have been a real problem with a more powerful set. As it was, the motion was only annoying when the large trucks shook my view.

The view of the airport from just over two miles away was better than I expected. With the naked eye, the control tower and the structures were noticeable but not distinct. Through my binoculars, I could pick out the terminal and many parked planes. It was possible to distinguish the aircraft by size and number of engines, but no minor details. The worst problem was the distortion caused by warm air rising off the buildings and pavement.

I had a good view of the main East/West runway closest to the river. Several planes landed while I watched, including two large airliners. The aircraft taxied to gates out of sight on the far side of the terminal. An executive jet landed and taxied to a spot south of the terminal obscured behind the trees growing on Sand Island.

In a way, I had a better view of airport operations than someone inside the terminal did. A person inside the terminal can only see the events directly in front of their window. I saw large portions of the airport, the take offs and landings, the movement of the planes after landing, the airport vehicles, and the service equipment. After watching several aircraft not park at the terminal airline gates, it dawned on me that there were other operations at the airport. An aircraft for an express package shipper departing to the east reinforced the fact that the passenger terminal was a large part of airport operations, but only a part.

I recalled the businesses that lined Airport Way. Businesses that either support the airlines, like catering, or complementary activities like cargo services. I had assumed that Carlos worked near the airline gates. In reality, Carlos probably worked in several locations both at and away from the passenger terminal. I could see now that an airport is a huge facility that provides access to many different businesses, lots of activity and many people.

Viewing the airport raised the question: What was the security that prevented Carlos from coming and going at will?

I could not see the fence from here but I knew it was there. I assumed security patrolled the fence for breaches and holes at least daily. Unless someone was making a one-time entry, cutting a hole in the fence was not a good plan. The fence was the first line of defense, surrounding the entire airport. The integrity of the fence had to be ensured. Facilities, like the passenger terminal, were access points into the airport. Access points meant control.

I packed my binoculars and started for home in the dimming light. I just knew the airport held the key. I would have stayed longer but the sinking sun was taking away the light I needed to see. The puniness of man's ability to light his environment is demonstrated when the sun goes down. An airport is likely one of the better-lit places. Even so I was having problems seeing into the shadows before the sun set. Now that the sun was down, I was wasting my time.

The trip down the ramp yielded a surprise, which should not have been a surprise. The sidewalk that joined the I205 Bridge walkway extended west to downtown. There was no sidewalk east. Walking along a limited access road, may or may not be legal. I decided not to find out.

From the lighted area at the base of the walkway ramp, I scanned the area under the I205 Bridge. There may have been some indigent persons lurking in the near darkness but I could not tell. I decided that officially I had seen none. Quickly I headed back the two hundred yards to the Evergreen Highway. In reality, the road was likely more dangerous than the dash under the bridge. Dark clothes, poor light and no real shoulders increased my odds of becoming a statistic. Fortunately, the neighborhood traffic was way down.

Sam opened his eyes as I entered the house. He greeted me with a look that said, "Where have you been?" He joined me in the kitchen entwining in my legs as I converted cold meat to warm meat in the microwave.

"You know Sam," I said. Although I knew, Sam did not know and cared less. "I'll bet there are rules and regulations dealing with airport security." Sam did not even bother to respond with a "duh" look at that comment.

"I wonder what the regulations have to say about airport security." Sam stirred from his spot on the table and walked over to inspect the breadcrumbs on my plate. He stopped only long enough to make a confirming sniff that crumbs are not cat comfort food, before stretching up to cheek my jaw. I took that as an affirmation and headed to the internet to do some research.

The Transportation Safety Administration website holds a lot of information. I by-passed the passenger information sections and went onto the regulations.

In general, any airport meeting TSA criteria must have a detailed security plan. Portland International had to have a plan. Airports that do not have scheduled airline service and only serve general aviation such as private pilots and charter operators, have much lower security standards than PDX.

An airport required to have an 'Airport Security Plan,' must have the plan approved by the TSA. Then the plan is held in secret. The TSA spent many pages on making sure that everyone was taking security seriously. The TSA discussed in detail how to comply with the distribution, disclosure, and availability of Sensitive Security Information (SSI). The airports security plan itself was SSI.

Like most government regulation, it went into excruciating detail. Such as the rule requiring that the name and phone number of the Airport Security Coordinator to be listed in the plan. In reality, the plan needed to do several major things: Map the Secure Areas, Map the Sterile Areas, Map the Air Operations Area, and detail the procedures that prevented unauthorized people from entering inappropriate areas.

It seemed like the rest of the rules dealt with implementing the last point. Who were the airport tenants at the airport? Did the tenants' security plans comply with the Airport Security Plan? What was the airport's contingency plan for its airport security plan, which was not to be confused with the Alternative Procedures Plan for use in natural disasters? In addition there were also lots of rules on training, record keeping and record destruction.

After an hour of reading definitions and skimming plan requirements, I decide I have the flavor of what TSA expects from the airport. I wonder what the Portland International Airport has available on its website?

After working my way through the usual passenger information, the first document that caught my attention was "Portland International Airport Rules." I took it to be a good sign that this 135-page document included a 22-page table of contents.

I went first to the Map in the appendix. There was a small red "H" shaped structure identified as the terminal. The map legend indicated "airside" in pastel blue and the "landside" in light green. Everything else not part of the airport was white. What did they mean by landside?

Now it was time to check out the nine pages of definitions. Definitions are the key to a lot of rules and regulations. The Portland International Airport Rules were no exception.

The definitions identified a variety of areas having various states of security. In a way, it resembled an onion. The perimeter fence was the onionskin. The restricted area was the first thick ring of onion. It included everything inside the perimeter fence. The Air Operations Area (AOA) is onion ring inside the Restricted Area. The AOA includes everything involving take off, landing and taxiing of aircraft. The Secure Area is inside the AOA and surrounds the terminal on three sides. This is where all the loading and unloading of aircraft occurs. Innermost is the Sterile Area where the passengers are screened before they board. Combined, all these areas were the Airside.

In reality, the airport more resembled and onion with a wedge cut out. The wedge was where the public interfaced with the airport; that part of the terminal open to all, the parking, businesses and all the access roads. The wedge also represented the Landside.

Our onion was not perfect. There was a blemish called General Aviation. The executive aircraft I observed did not park at the terminal. They had their own parking section. The General Aviation Area was inside the Restricted Area and included the Fixed Base Operation. The FBO was the gas station for all the private aircraft and provided maintenance and other support services for the executive jets.

The airport was very concerned that only authorized people had access to the airport grounds in general (the Restricted area), the area where planes were (the Air Operations Area), and the area where the public boarded the planes (the Secure Area).

The airport controlled the movement of people via the Access Control System. This computerized system requires an Access Device to get through doors or gates. Every one working for or on the airport is issued a badge. Only those with the appropriate Access Device could unlock doors to enter the Secure Areas.

If I remembered correctly, the secure area included the baggage loading and unloading area around the gates. What prevented someone from walking into the Secure Area from another part of the AOA? The answer was the Midfield Secured Area Checkpoint, where the badge of anyone entering the Secure Area was validated.

The entire AOA, Secure and Sterile areas were SIDA: Secure Identification Display Areas. Everyone had to show his or her badge at all times. The only exception was the General Aviation Area.

Like all regulation definitions, there were subtle differences that were important to the administrators but not to me. There was a difference between an Access Device and a Security Key: An Access Device could get you into the Sterile Area. While a Security Key only allowed access to the AOA or the Secure Area. So be it.

I got more out of the definitions than the rest of the document, except for the map. I did find out that PDX owns the security badges and controls the types of badges issued. I learned that pedestrians are not allowed to enter the AOA through vehicle gates. In addition, the airport tenants are responsible for not letting unauthorized people into the AOA. Finally, if you lost your badge it cost $50, $75 then $100 to replace. If you lost it four times, an appeal to the Airport Security Coordinator was required.

I wonder if Carlos had reported any lost badges.

There was much more about the penalties imposed by the port for various infractions. It was clear bad things happen to someone who strays into the Movement Area by crossing the white/red/white line. Nevertheless, none of this was relevant.

After my long walk and long hours of research, I went to bed without having any better idea of how Carlos could leave and return to a facility full of checkpoints and card readers unnoticed.

Moving around the house eased my stiffness and the feet were feeling a bit better. Walking was not included in my exercise plan for today. I figured that I had done about three day's worth of walking on Monday. I took my fresh coffee to my office in preparation for the start of the workday.

The email in my inbox was evidence that the world of tax accounting never seems to change. Every year tax accountants around the globe pledge to have the tax return done early. Every year something happens that results in finishing the return at the last minute. Every quarter we vow to start the estimated payments early, and every quarter we work until the last minute to get them out the door.

This quarter was no exception. Senior management wanted to run some 'what if' tax calculation scenarios involving a possible change in accounting method. Clark sent me an email detailing the calculation he wanted. I was making good progress and projected I would be finished before Thursday's deadline. The phone broke my concentration as I noted it was closer to four than three in the afternoon.

Richard Cushing called on his way back from Washougal. He was only a few minutes away and wanted to catch up on where we left off last Thursday.

Sam noticed Richard, sniffed his foot and rubbed his shin with his cheek. Richard patted Sam on the lower back the way many people pat dogs. Sam tolerated the abuse, then anticipating our destination beating us to the office, settling next to the printer as Richard and I took our seats.

I decided the direct approach was best: "You can make a lot of money selling used aircraft parts."

"OK" said Richard.

For the next minutes, I spoke almost without breathing. There was concern in my mind that if I took a breath Richard would shoot down my theory with a single comment.

I explained that the airline industry embraces used parts. I followed immediately with how the Type Certification process and all the FAA rules encourage the use of used parts. The number of parts manufacturers is suppressed by the high costs of entry for a new manufacturer. I could tell Richard was interested about the concept of limited life of parts. My conclusion stressed that the value of parts varied significantly in regards to the cycle or chronological life of the part.

I took a breath.

"Type Certification, what is that?"

I felt like the kid in the movie 'Home Alone', I wanted to shout "Yes!" and pump my fist. Richard was on board.

I explained in detail how the FAA issues a Type Certificate establishing every acceptable part used in the plane. If XYZ wiper blades are used in the Type certificate then only XYZ blade refills can be used as replacements. That is until another manufacturer proves that their wiper blades met the FAA standards for that aircraft.

"I can see the FAA's point. They don't want wiper blades tearing off at 500 miles an hour. What I am not sure about is the FAA rules for the life of parts. I know there are lots of businesses that do maintenance based upon hours or miles, and companies that overhaul truck engines at specific ages. What is so special about the FAA rules?"

"A lot of the nuances elude me. Some parts have both a calendar life and an operational life. A part may sit on the shelf for years new in the box and the FAA may require the part overhauled or scrapped, if the calendar time exceeds the FAA limit. I have to admit, the policy does make sense. Many parts that include gaskets and seals degrade over time. It's this rule that makes counterfeit parts more valuable."

"A part that is factory fresh, recently overhauled, or removed from an aircraft with substantial life time remaining is worth a large premium, if it has the supporting paperwork. People willing to sell counterfeit parts are probably not concerned about forging the paperwork too."

"Richard, this is what really concerns me. The FAA system still relies on paper documentation and ID tags riveted on parts. I cannot believe that this is a secure system."

Sam washed his face with his paw. Richard sat thinking.

"Justin, it is probably not as easy as you have laid it out. On the other hand, I do not see any obvious flaws. I am going to run this past my pilot friend and see if it holds water."

Richard stood, turned to leave, then turned back to face me. "I don't like this Justin. My kids are flying home from college over the holidays. I don't like this one bit."

Chapter 52   The Same Five

Richard had moved quickly and with purpose. I had a lot more to say but he was out the door before I accepted that he was leaving. He seemed agitated, as if something that he entertained as unpleasant fantasy was now reality.

Up until this point, I felt that Richard was a professional doing his best for a client. Had he now converted into being a believer in my cause?

I pondered this positive development as I decided I was done with Lithium for the day. The computer had consumed too many of my hours of freedom recently. Adult beverage in hand I headed out to my yard. The inevitable change in seasons was proceeding. A cooler air mass had come in overnight. It was still clear but the sun did not warm the day as much as it had a few weeks ago. I moved my lawn chair from out of the shade of into the full sun. Sam emerged from the cat door and started an inspection tour. He was particularly attentive to the flowering shrubs.

Karen had taken charge of the flowering plants in the yard when she moved in. The flowerbed had contained mainly perennials when we bought the house. Karen replaced about half the bed with flowering shrubs. Thus, the ordeal began.

Karen thought herself a gardener, but only with respect to certain duties. She liked the flowerbed but left the garden and the rest of the yard to me. As for the flowerbed, it never thrived. The azaleas Karen preferred never took hold, and Karen refused to try another plant. It seemed like every few months Karen had to replace one or another shrub.

Karen refused my offers to assist. She bristled when I suggested she talk to our neighbor Ed and tap into his years of experience. She would have none of that. She was smart enough to figure this out on her own. If she had lived, maybe she could have saved the plants. She was not alive, and the azaleas were following close behind.

Sam's inspection route included Karen's dying azaleas. The lack of watering while I had been in jail was too much for already stressed plants. Sam scratched both cheeks on various dry branches then decided that this was the ideal spot to take a nap.

"Sam, you know that azalea is not going to make it. What should I replace it with?"

Oops, I had a momentary lapse in thinking. I had no business planning for the future. If I did not figure out how Carlos

198

killed Karen, I would not be here to see anything bloom.

Dejected I headed into the house. The phone rang as I set my glass in the sink.

"Justin, Richard here. Are you still working on Karen's supplemental log?"

"I have not looked at it in days. I have been busy with work for Lithium and checking out the parts issue."

"I am just saying that I think you are on to something. Don't let it drop."

"I was not planning to. It is just that I was working on other things."

"Good, I have some things I want to check out in Portland tomorrow, if I don't make it over to talk with you tomorrow I will come by Thursday."

Wow, Richard was really taking an increased interest in my case.

It was early. Maybe I should still look at Karen's files before bed.

The last time I had worked on this file was after I had parsed the supplemental log document entries. Then I focused on what Karen was doing with the coordinates. Now was time to look at the rest of the entry. I sorted the records by each subject. I was hoping that the 118 records in my data set would provide a large enough sample size to be meaningful.

The data sort by aircraft tail number produced entries that seemed reasonable for a pilot. Most aircraft references were reminders to follow up with specific employees about some chronic problem with an aircraft component. Karen seemed intent in gathering evidence on other employees who were not performing up to her standards. Again maybe I was reading too much into too few entries to spot a pattern. This did not seem to relate to Karen's illegal activities.

Making the analysis more difficult was the fact that the data I was reviewing was a supplement to Karen's other logbooks. The supplemental log referenced both Karen's pilot logbook and the individual aircraft logbooks. I had access to Karen's pilot log but not the aircraft logs. I had to admit that this seemed like a dead end.

The data sort by person was also useless. During the analysis of the Tail Number information, I realized I had already reviewed most of the people in the data set. Those people not tied to an aircraft issue appeared to be engaged in normal employee interactions.

When I finished the analysis of the other data sets, my conclusion was that the only areas of interest were the coordinates and the astronomical notations. The coordinates were significant; she used them to track money or something else of importance. The astronomical observations were significant because they had no reason to be there.

Sam's feet plopped softly onto the desktop. He must have decided that it was time to come inside now that the sun was down. His bed under the dying azalea chilled, by the lack of sun.

Sam looked at the computer monitor, looked at me, then sat on his rear to watch.

"Sorry Sam there is not much to see. I have sliced and diced this data and there does not seem to be any there, there. Karen believed in few words and usually all of her words counted, but not this time."

Sam watched me. I had the feeling he was expecting me to do something, or have a revelation, or formulate a great theory based upon what was on the computer screen.

"I don't know what I am looking at Sam. Karen did not do things without a reason. She always was looking three moves ahead, so this has to have a purpose. Otherwise she would not have taken the time to enter the data."

Sam came over and rubbed my chin with his head. I responded by scratching his exposed jaw. He switched sides of my chin and I switched sides of his jaw.

"Karen made these astronomical entries for a purpose. But there does not seem to be any meaning or relationship to the rest of the supplemental entry."

I sorted the astronomical entries again, leaving them in date order. There was nothing there. The format of the observation always seemed to include a constellation and then maybe a star or a planet. Sometimes the entry was one constellation, sometimes it was two.

If I was going to find some trove of information, it was not going to be from these star sightings. If anything, there was less information as the entries progressed. The last third of my data sort contained only a constellation.

"Sam it does not make sense."

Sam responded with a quizzical look.

"If the constellation is a substitute for something else, what could it be? Maybe there were people that Karen did not want to name. As she had already named many coworkers, were references to people outside of the airline. Were the constellations code names for organizations like the Mafia or drug cartels? If constellations are not code names what are they?"

Sam returned to my chin to give me a good rubbing. At least one of us was getting some benefit out of this exercise.

I returned to the data and sorted again. This time I sorted by entries naming a single constellation without stars or planets. There were four constellations listed several times and one constellation listed twice. Did this pattern continue in the rest of the supplemental log entries?

The raw supplemental log file confirmed the trend. After the first few months of astronomical observations, Karen no longer included stars or planets. In fact, it appeared the Karen was using a limited number of constellations. The same five constellations repeated: Aries, Capricornus, Leo, Gemini and Scorpios.

"Sam, I am just too tired. I will look at this tomorrow when I am rested."

He stared at me then left. Can cats stomp off in a huff? If they can, Sam did. He did not sleep on the bed that night. I wondered what I had done to offend Sam.

I was up early to take a short walk, more to wake myself than to get any real exercise. It was still dark when I returned to the house. Sam was nowhere to be seen.

Clark was counting on me to have the change in accounting computations finished today, so I jumped back into the calculations. I finished in mid-afternoon, about then Sam showed himself. I made a peace offering to Sam by launching a generous portion of kitty treats to points around the office.

Now that the change of accounting calculation information was in an email to Clark, I could return to the supplemental log files. Sam joined me on the desk, confirmed the proper working order of the monitor and curled up for a nap.

There had to be some significance to the fact that Karen used only five constellations. Maybe I should research each constellation to see if there was some meaning or history that would explain their use.

Aries, being the first of the five alphabetically, seemed the logical place to start. My fingers got ahead of my brain resulting in my typing ARIES enter, instead of ARIES CONSTELLATION. As my little finger hit the enter key I realized that this would not provide the results I wanted. The millions of search results started with a page full of offers for Horoscopes, Tarot Cards, and "Real" Psychic readings. I moved the cursor back to the search box, pausing thinking about the offers displayed on the monitor.

The answer was staring me in the face last night. Karen only referenced five constellations, all of which were signs of the Zodiac. She recorded the constellations in the supplemental log file as a code, a cross reference to another data file.

I searched the file list to locate "History" and "History II." Opening History revealed the hundreds of pages of daily Horoscope readings saved by Karen.   Scanning the entries revealed no more information than the last time I looked, there were no patterns and no inconsistencies. These appeared to be real horoscope readings.

Referring back to the Supplemental Log, I located an entry containing a zodiac sign: Aries. Using the date and the sign, I looked up the horoscope for Aries in the *History* file.

"Today you might find yourself feeling a little low, **Aries**, but it doesn't seem as if there's any real reason for it. You may just have had a bad night and need some extra sleep. Some good news from far away could cheer you up in the afternoon. You might receive an invitation to go out to dinner with a close friend. You should be feeling like your old self again by evening. It is a good day for business with Jupiter in conjunction with Betelgeuse."

This astrology reading presented nothing out of the ordinary from what I could tell. I cross-referenced another entry.

"You're apt to speak and act with a great deal of power, **Scorpio**, but be careful that you don't get swept away by emotion. There's a surrealistic quality to the day. It could lead you to believe a mirage is real. You might get so caught up in the drama of your feelings that your power of reason gets watered down to the point where you lose track of your objectivity altogether. Matters of the heart figure prominently with Mercury departing the House of Vita."

As with the other reading, more words that may or may not represent a real horoscope. I highlighted ten referenced entries, reading every horoscope for the date in question. She may have mentioned the planets more frequently in her selections, but only a statistical analysis could confirm that observation and that would require a larger sample. If she did mention planets more often, was it significant?

"Sam, there is something here that I don't see. I think it's time for expert advice."

The Vancouver Yellow pages list 66 Astrologers. Many of these are also psychic. I guess being psychic is helpful when interpreting astrological data. Fortune smiled upon me as Rene Gauquelin had an office on 164th Avenue. Yes, she was in her office and available.

Fifteen minutes later I was in there in her office with a dozen pages of horoscope readings in hand and the subtle scent of incense in the air. I assumed the fragrance emanated from the candles burning around the room. Each candle nestled among one or more large crystal fragments. Motion of someone moving from the shadows into the light caught my eye. The person I assumed to be Madame Rene glided forward in long flowing robes, her eyes capturing my attention. She somehow occupied the whole space in front of me, appearing larger than her five foot four height. Rene moved purposefully to clasp my right hand while her left hand gripped my elbow. Her eyes never left mine, fixing me in position as she stared deeply into me. I do not know what I was feeling but I had no desire to move or look away.

Rene broke the silence. "It is so nice to meet you Mr. Caise. Now I understand why the fates intervened today. This believer has never canceled his appointment. You are very troubled, come, sit."

She pulled me by the arm to an enclave behind the reception area. The windowless three wall bay area contained a small low table, two chairs and a love seat along one wall. A small desk on the wall opposite the loveseat supported burning candles, a crystal ball, tarot cards and other tools of the psychic trade. The black and grey striped cat sleeping on the love seat opened its eyes to watch.

Rene released me to sit and assumed a stance across from me.

Before sitting, I retrieved the printed readings to place them on the corner of the table. Renee reached, taking hold of my left hand before I could retract it, turning it gently but firmly palm up.

"Ms. Gauquelin, I am only here…"

"Hush now, sit," she commanded softly.

We sat in unison, her watching my palm, me watching her.

"In your life you have great turmoil. Forces beyond your control attack without rest. The questions are great, for which you seek answers. Sharp is the knife's edge on which you stand, remain there you cannot. Soon you must choose a side of the knife, be it salvation or doom. Not to choose leaves the power to choose for you. Soon will be the time for the choice you must make."

Renee looked up from my palm and stared deeply into my eyes again.

"That may be true, but that…"

"You are not a believer. One need not be psychic to see that."

"You are adrift in the sea of the practical world and logic is your life raft. Trust that there are forces that cannot be measured that affect your future."

"If they cannot be measured…"

"Trust that I know of these forces. It is God's curse that provides me a window to see some of what will be. It is God's blessing that I am to share my gift with all, the believers and those who choose not to believe. It is my joy that my powers may only be used for good. You are in need of help. I am here to help you."

204

The soft plop of cat feet hitting the tabletop distracted me from Renee's eyes. The cat assumed a seat on the table, his eyes replacing Renee's.

"Samson senses that you are a good man. Your cat too knows this about you. Trust his guidance."

The cat turned and departed.

"Madam Gauqualin, thank you but I did not come here to have my palm read. I was wondering if you could give me your professional opinion."

I sat waiting, the soft tinkling of wind chimes entering my consciousness.

"Of course, Mr. Caise, You have practical questions about horoscopes. I will do my best to answer."

I handed over the printed sheets with an explanation that some of them seemed bogus.

Rene read carefully for several minutes. She spread several sheets across the table to make comparisons.

"You will not find answers to your questions in these horoscope readings. These texts are nothing more than the uninformed gibberish of an astrological imposter. These musings discredit the gifted astrologer. This is drivel. A product for the newspaper syndications and would serve its highest purpose as fish wrapper."

"Oh, so there is nothing unusual about the readings." My heart was sinking there should have been something.

"In the astrological readings no, there is nothing. The answers lay in the fake parts attached to the readings."

Renee laid out a page for me.

"This entry, see. This is typical trash published in newspapers. Look here, this one. See the vague generalities that mean everything and say nothing. That is, except for the last sentence that is clearly false."

"These events are unknown to astrology. Someone has thrown together words without meaning. I sense that there is much unhappiness and deceit in these words."

"More, I cannot tell you."

"Thank you so much. This is exactly what I needed."

"So it would seem, Mr. Caise."

"If you don't mind Ms. Gauquelin, how does one end up as a psychic?" I was desperately trying to put the words back in my mouth, but my foot was in the way.

"It is my honor to be a granddaughter of Michel Gauquelin.

I inherit my talent from him. Like you, he too understood the practical world. Unlike you he believed in the unseen world and accepted the gift which God provided. You may find practical comfort in his statistical analysis of Astrology. Many believers and non-believers discuss his proofs to this day."

"To your question Mr. Caise, I have found that charlatans end up as psychics. I did not choose my role, it was chosen for me. I can deny my role no more than a fish can deny water."

"Ah, thank you again Ms. Gauquelin. Um, what do I owe you for your time?"

"Only you can decide that Mr. Caise," Renee said as she floated off to the back followed by Sampson.

I had eighty-seven dollars in my wallet. I have paid more and gotten less, it seemed right as I dropped it on the reception desk.

Chapter 54   Facility Liaison

"Sam. Was I crazy to ask a psychic for her professional opinion?" He opened one eye almost half way to demonstrate what he thought of the question.

"Yes, Rene could have done a quick search on the internet and read about my problems. And, if she saw cat hair on my shirt, it is your fault she figured out we live together. It's just she seemed to have such a good appreciation for my predicament."

"Anyway we have confirmation that Karen was using a cross reference code to record information. Now we need to figure out what information she was tracking."

Sam curled into a tighter cat ball on top of the bed indicating that it was time for sleep. I had to agree and turned out the light.

The only dream I remembered involved me walking the sharp edge of a knife to be confronted by the down sloping curve of the blade. Unable to go forward or back, the unknown mists on either side gave me no clue of what awaited me if I stepped off the blade.

Richard surprised me by calling at 7:30 AM. There was no problem with him stopping by. I started a fresh pot of coffee in Richard's honor.

"Justin, I have been doing some additional investigation. First, Rafael's Metro Motors is owned by one Rafael Antonio Torres."

Richard anticipated my response: "Yes I thought that was a coincidence too."

"Digging deeper, hidden behind three Limited Liability Companies is another business owned by Rafael: Larch Mountain Aviation Services. Larch Mt. Aviation is an FAA certified repair station for instruments and radios. I did not find the relationship until I did some more digging yesterday.

There's more, the facility liaison listed with the FAA is Carlos Torres. The shop is located at just off the Troutdale Airport, a few miles east of PDX."

"Richard, I am guessing that Rafael and Carlos are related?"

"Yes, they are brothers."

I sat, letting the permutations multiply in my mind.

"Justin, Larch Mt. Aviation has a presence on several internet sites and trades in used avionics. Like you said, getting paid is the third leg of a successful fake part scheme."

It was all coming together. Carlos had access to the aircraft where he could substitute counterfeit components for real components. He had access to the VAA maintenance system, which he could use to generate the physical paperwork to make the fake parts legitimate. He had a legitimate company that he could use to sell the parts on the open market.

What had Karen done that threatened Carlos to the point that he felt she was better off dead?

Richard jarred my thoughts by asking, "Did you find anything of use in the supplemental files?"

"I think so. Don't laugh at me but I went and saw a psychic yesterday about the horoscopes Karen kept in the two files labeled "History." The good news is that there is something there. The bad news is I still don't know what it is. Karen was definitely keeping records of parties involved in the transactions. She used the entry in the Supplemental Log file as a cross reference to the transaction information. The date in the Supplemental Log references an astrological sign corresponding to the horoscope reading for that Zodiac sign. Karen modified the horoscope reading for that day to include coded transaction information. Most of the horoscope readings in the two "History" files are just horoscopes. They are included as filler, or fluff or camouflage for the coded entries."

"To someone like me with no knowledge of horoscopes the entries look legitimate. But when I took them to Madame Renee she was able to point out the phony parts of the entries."

"Madame Renee is still around?"

"You know her, Richard?"

"Justin, you cannot be a cop in this town for over twenty years and not get to know the psychics. Never had any real trouble with her, just the usual buyer's remorse complaints.   She claims to be related to some famous French astrologer. Renee's trademark is she never quotes a price to clients, she just asks the marks to pay her what they think her services are worth."

I squirmed in my chair, time to move on: "Richard, I think we're missing another key. I think that there is a file, an index or a legend that explains what each code word means."

"Like a Rosetta Stone?"

"Yes Richard, something that will translate Karen's code. A set of rules or references that explain what each code entry means."

"OK, I will look again. Maybe knowing a little more about what we are looking for will help?"

"Richard, the more we find the more it looks like Karen did

have an insurance plan. I wonder if Carlos panicked when Karen threatened to tell. On the other hand, maybe she never got the chance to threaten him."

"What do you mean?"

"I don't think Carlos knows about the records or the money. Karen would have planned this out like a chess game. I bet she was so involved in positioning her own pieces that she forgot to watch what Carlos was doing. When she realized she was one move behind, it was too late."

"Justin, I doubt we will ever get the chance to ask Carlos."

"Ask Carlos? Does that mean you are on board with my theory that Carlos killed Karen?"

"Justin, I think someone in the counterfeit ring killed Karen. Whether it was Carlos, or his brother or somebody they hired, the group is responsible. I believe enough that we need to bring Anne up to date."

"Anne asked me to come in and brief her today at 4:00 pm. Usually I don't invite clients to these briefings, but this time I think you should be there."

I should not be nervous. I know everything that Richard knows: Didn't I?

The day dragged on as I tried to work on Lithium projects. Finally, about 3:10 I headed for downtown Vancouver. Of course, I was way early so I stopped at a coffee shop for a cup I really did not need. I was sitting in the law office waiting area with my coffee when Richard arrived right at 4:00.

Anne apologized when she walked in at 4:15. The judge who presided over her 3:15 plea and sentencing hearing held her over for an in chamber meeting on another matter. The legal matter only took five minutes. The real delay was due to the judge showing off her new tablet by running through a long picture montage.

Anne invited us to follow. I was pleased as we moved past Anne's office into the conference room in the back. The conference room's chairs are padded, wheeled and equipped with arms.

Richard started with a summary of where we were on the investigation. I thought it was an excessive compliment when Richard said that he was following my lead on the investigation. He laid out the basic theory about Karen being involved with a bogus part or smuggling scheme that involved Carlos Torres and his brother Rafael, and probably one other person.

Richard wanted confirmation that my theory was not just a bad movie plot. He called in a favor and got his pilot friend to set up a meeting with a retired chief of maintenance for a large helicopter company based in Oregon. At the meeting, Richard's most difficult task was getting the retired chief to believe that someone in aviation would do something like this for money.

This retired chief mechanic, and probably everyone he knows in the business, is dedicated to the profession of flying. It is foreign to his thinking that someone would intentionally put a bad part on an aircraft. The retired maintenance chief exuded a sense of pride and accomplishment that he expected all other aviation professionals to share. An expectation he based upon their common experiences gained from the hard work required to get the certifications they all hold. He kept interrupting Richard with comments like, "But he would risk losing his airman's certificate for doing that."

Once Richard got the point across that money might be a bigger motivation for some than the love of aviation, the chief was able to discuss the merits of scheme objectively. Yes, it was possible to introduce bad parts into the system. Yes, the FAA still relied on system that depended on paper and the integrity of the people repairing the parts.

The chief even cited examples of problem parts in the industry. He related how when he was running his shop he had a policy of not buying parts out of South America. He was even suspicious of parts coming out of Florida because so many originated in South America. Without conducting "a full paperwork audit of the part from birth", you were taking a risk buying from dealers in Florida. Yes, there were definitely bad parts on the market.

Richard then followed up with a quick summary of my research showing that there was money to be made selling used parts. Then he turned the floor over to me to explain the system of accounting based upon fake coordinates.

I ran through an example converting dollars to coordinates and back in just enough detail that Anne's eyes did not completely glaze over. A good attorney relies on the accountant to tie out the numbers. Anne was a good attorney.

The discussion of the money record segued to the horoscope code. I believe Anne enjoyed my account of the trip to the psychic and thought my eighty-seven dollars well spent. However, it was hard to tell. Is there some rule of the Washington State Bar that requires attorneys to always be serious?

Sitting there listening to the rehash of the evidence had me feeling better than I had felt in days. We were making progress.

Anne took over the discussion.

"OK, now we have a good idea where we are at with the evidence, this is where I see your case."

"If we walk into the DA's office and present this information, the DA will balk. First, there may, or may not, have been a crime committed. Second, if there was a crime, we do not know if it involved Karen, Carlos or Rafael. Third, the crime may have gone on for years. Fourth, there may or may not be a record of transactions recorded in code. Fifth, if there is a record of the transaction in code, we do not have the codebook. And finally, the biggest issue for the DA is that the crime I described is not the one of interest to the DA as it does not impact his case against you."

"The DA has no interest in Carlos or Rafael or anyone else if they are not considered part of Karen's murder case. So how do we get the DA interested? I don't see anything that we have that ties

Carlos et al. to Karen's death."

Despite Anne's dour summary, I smiled to myself. Do attorneys notice when they drop words into conversations like et al.? Anne had asked a good question: Did we have anything that tied Carlos to the murder?

"What about the lanyard that my cat found?"

Anne almost looked surprised at the mention of the lanyard recovered by Sam.

"Didn't you send it for DNA testing?"

"Yes, of course. I had just forgotten about it. It is pretty much a long shot."

Anne activated the speakerphone and dialed an extension.

"Hello, this is Kari."

"Hi, Kari, we sent some samples to the lab for DNA testing for client Justin Caise. Have those test results come in?"

"I know we got some results in today but I have not had a chance to put them in the client files. Let me check."

"Anne, I thought it took weeks if not months to get DNA test results?"

"It does Justin, if you have to use the State Crime Lab. Private labs turn around results in a lot less time."

We were waiting for Kari to return to the phone when she walked into the conference room.

Anne accepted the report from Kari and began reading silently. After finishing, she looked at Richard with a strange expression.

"The report describes that they accepted samples from my office and that the tests were conducted in accordance with state forensic laboratory protocol and internal protocols. This is all documentation required to prove chain of custody and that the lab followed state rules of evidence. Things like retaining samples so that the State can conduct its own test to verify the labs results."

"Here is the meat of the matter: First, they found non-human DNA for a 'Neotoma Cinerea', commonly known as a packrat, and DNA for a 'Felis Silvestris Catus', a house cat. If need be we can get a sample from your cat?"

"Sure," I nodded my head in agreement, not sure, if Anne was serious or not.

"Also on the VAA lanyard they found sufficient human hair and skin cells to perform DNA analysis. There were two individuals identified: one male and one female. Subsequent comparison of the female DNA sample to Karen Elaine Winslow--Caise was a positive match."

"Wow," was the only thing I could think of saying.

Richard seemed ready to burst.

"The second set of sample items provided sufficient

epithelial cells and mucus for DNA testing. Results of the test indicated a single male individual. Per the request of the submitting attorney, the second sample was compared to the results of the first sample. The male DNA produced from the first sample was a positive match for the DNA of the second sample."

Anne stopped reading. Her attention was full on Richard. I did not know it was possible for person to grin that much.

"OK, Richard do you want to explain that smile?"

"Sometimes you have to play a hunch," Richard laughed as he spoke.

"It was Saturday when Justin's cat found that lanyard. He was convinced that this was the murder weapon, dropped by the killer in the confusion, and lost in the rush to leave the scene. Since we could not send the lanyard to the lab until Monday, I decided to take advantage of an opportunity. I had already planned to contact Carlos as he was getting off work early Monday morning. I turned on the good cop routine and offered to buy him breakfast, or dinner, since it was the end of his workday. He surprised me by accepting the offer."

"We met at an all-night sit down restaurant off 102nd Avenue. I asked my questions while he ate his hamburger and fries. I was a bit concerned because he was not using his utensils much nor was he drinking his water. Fortunately, he sneezed into his napkin. Carlos was not in a mood to talk to me and was eager to leave. I made an excuse to stay behind. I gave the waitress $50 to remember that Carlos and I were there. The manager got $100 for the place setting and the napkin. Kari included the dishes and the napkin as the second sample."

Chapter 57   Secure Facility

Anne did not let us bask too long in our success.

"Justin, this is some very good news. I do not want to minimize its importance but we still have a long way to go."

"The DA will view this as a distraction, or something thrown out by us to muddy the waters. Just because we have the evidence, does not mean that we can use it at trial. The DA will put up every objection he can think of to keep any of this from ever being included as an exhibit the jury will see. I will fight tooth and nail to get it included, but it will be a fight."

"Also, just because we have a nylon strap with Karen's DNA on it does not automatically mean it is the murder weapon or will be accepted as such. The DA will provide many reasons why the lanyard should be ignored, even if it is admitted."

Richard injected, "I thought the coroner excluded the garden hose a weapon. Doesn't that open the door to entering the lanyard as the weapon?"

Anne explained. "The coroner hedged his bets. His statement about the ligature marks approximating the dimensions of the hose offset his admission, that the skin abrasion was not entirely consistent with plastic hose. Even if I can get the coroner to concede the hose was not the murder weapon, it does not automatically open the door to enter the lanyard as the weapon."

"If those hurdles were not enough there are two major issues without answers: the code and the alibi."

"Richard and Justin, getting as far as you have in deciphering the codes is important. However, unless we can present a complete translation of the code it is just a theory. Theories do not go far in convincing a jury. I have seen firsthand how sneaky and conniving people can be. Lawyers read hundreds of cases that demonstrate just how creative criminals can be in their illegal activities. People sitting on the jury don't have that experience."

Anne summarized. "Therein lays the problem. Can we explain to a jury: first, that the information we are presenting actually is a code; second, why Karen would go to such great lengths to hide her actions; and third, that four hundred thousand dollars is not Justin's motive for murder."

"But I didn't find the money Anne. How can the District Attorney say it was my motive if I didn't know the money was in the spare tire? And I called 911. Doesn't that prove I am not the

215

killer?"

Anne continued. "Justin, I am just laying out the District Attorney's plan of attack. Criminals have been known to call in the crime to establish an alibi, and that's the idea the DA will plant in the jury's mind. The District Attorney can present that idea to the jury a couple of ways. He can tell a story of how you panicked and called 911 when you could not find the money. Or the District Attorney can flip it and paint you as a master criminal intentionally letting the police find the money just to support your phony alibi."

"At this time disproving motive is not our main concern. The big problem we face is getting the judge to allow the code into evidence. We really have no admissible proof that this fake aircraft parts scheme is real. Without being able to link the code to an example of a counterfeit part installed or removed from an aircraft I do not see that the judge will let this in as evidence."

"Without tangible examples, the code is nothing more than an eclectic collection of unknown purpose and meaning. The DA will move to exclude this from the trial as being irrelevant. I can guess at one or two psychiatrists who would get on the stand and explain that Karen's codes were meaningless, or due to stress or some other reason besides fake parts."

"The second major hurdle is the alibi of Carlos Torres. How does a person leave and return to a secure facility without being noticed?" Anne said.

"Richard, what do you want to tackle first?"

"Unless Justin digs up the 'Rosetta Stone' we are at an impasse with that code. Let me check out the airport to see what I can find."

"Anne, if I knew what a Rosetta Stone was I would dig one up today."

Richard came to my rescue: "The Rosetta Stone was a decree recorded on a stone tablet by an Egyptian king, written in three languages. Scalars used the Greek and other language to translate the Egyptian Hieroglyphics version of the decree. The Rosetta Stone was the key to breaking the code of hieroglyphics."

Anne interrupted the history lesson. "Richard you are going to PDX to check on airport security?

"Yes but I am not quite sure where to start."

"How about starting with the Airport Security Coordinator, Richard?"

"Huh, why not start with the Port of Portland Police Department Justin."

"Labor Day I was feeling house bound and really wanted to get a look at PDX."

"You know what I said about leaving the state, Justin."

"Anne, I did not leave Washington. I turned around on the Glenn Jackson Bridge before reaching the Welcome to Oregon sign."

"You drove the wrong way on Interstate 205?"

"No, let me explain. There is a sidewalk and bicycle path running the length of the bridge. I walked out as far as I could and turned back. I did not realize that the State border was in the Washington channel of the Columbia River."

"Why" was all Anne had to say?

"I wanted to look at the airport. It was important for me to see where Carlos worked."

"But it has to be more tha-never mind, I'll keep quiet."

"Anne, I discovered several flaws in my plan after the fact. Walking from my house to the bridge seemed like a good idea when I left the house. It did not seem so smart over four hours later when I got back. I wanted to get out of the house and taking my binoculars to look at airport operations was a good excuse for some exercise."

"I did not plan the trip well and my assumption that I could get much closer to the airport was incorrect."

"Can you see anything from two miles away?" asked Richard.

"Actually I was surprised about what I could see. People were not visible but I could watch the movement of aircraft: landing, take-off, taxiing and I could see the service equipment functioning by the aircraft."

"The biggest benefit I got out of the excursion was a sense of the size of the airport. I wanted to appreciate the physical aspects of the airport so I could understand the security systems."

"It's too bad you could not see anything of importance from the bridge." Richard said.

"Yes, that is why I researched the FAA security regulations. If I could not inspect the airport facilities at least I could read about them."

"The FAA regulations told me that PDX had to have a security plan. Although the PDX plan is a confidential document I figured that at least part of the plan had to be published so that individuals and vendors can comply."

"The Port of Portland rules give quite a bit of information about various security areas on the airport. If I had my computer I could show you the published security zone map."

"How about using a computer here?" Anne turned to the credenza, opened a door and removed a wireless keyboard and mouse.

"Richard, could you power up the monitor, please?"

Richard hit the power button on the large TV monitor mounted on the wall at the end of the conference table.

Anne struggled to find the airport rules, finding lots of internet information about the airport itself but not finding a match. Why are things that are supposed to be publicly available so hard to find?

"When I started my search I wanted to know about the Air Operations Area. I think I entered "Portland International Airport AOA" as a search term."

The second item listed was the link to rules.

"There is a map in the back."

I assumed the role of tour guide, explaining the layers of the airport onion as represented by the map on the monitor.

"Richard, please point out any flaws in my understanding of airport security."

"Sounds good so far," Richard said.

"Entering and exiting the airport by jumping the fence is impractical and risky because it is an obvious easy entry point. And, I am guessing that airport security routinely monitors the fences for tampering."

"Entering the restricted area of the airport via public access through the terminal is easy, with a badge and a key. The problem being is that entering and leaving leaves a record in the airport security system."

"There are a several access gates for vehicles, which are not supposed to be used by pedestrians and also require a badge and key. "

"Any person in the restricted, but not secure, area of the airport can enter a secure part of the airport if they scan their badge at a Midfield Security Checkpoint."

"Finally, there are the vendors and businesses which have operations that cross the airport perimeter. The vendor is responsible for employees and customers abiding by airport rules."

"In general, the airport is very concerned about the encroachment of people and equipment into the Movement Area. There is a two color, triple stripe line separating the area where aircraft are in operation and in motion from the parking, loading, maintenance, and fueling areas. Any person or piece of equipment that enters the Movement Area without authorization creates an incursion incident. Such an event is a big deal and requires reports and statements from witnesses. What I take from this is that the Airport Tower monitors the Airport Operations Area at all times for people and equipment straying out of the Non-Movement Area."

"As for people walking around in the Non-Movement Area, it is SIDA. A Security Identification Display Area requires that people wear their badges at all times, but otherwise they are unrestricted in their movements. The only part of the AOA, or Airside, that does not require the display of badges is the general aviation aircraft parking and the Fixed Base Operation."

"Thanks Justin. That was a good summary."

"Anne, I have some ideas I want to check out at the airport." said Richard.

"Is there anything you want me to do Anne?"

"Aside from finding the key to Karen's code, no."

Chapter 58   Testing

All the way home, I was tempted to stop in to see Madame Rene. Rationally I knew it was desperate and irrational. It fit my mood perfectly.

In a way, knowing that we had found solid evidence made my mood worse. We were so close I could almost taste it. There were just a couple of minor issues blocking success.

Sam could sense my discontent. I tried to hide it by tossing a lot of treats for him to find and once he had his fill he came over to console me. Somehow, it is hard not to giggle when a cat is licking your neck.

Sam was right. Moping and self-pity were not going to solve my problems. We headed to bed to attack issues anew in the morning.

I was toweling off my hair while powering up my computer just after 0630. I opened my emails to see an urgent message from Clark that had arrived at seven last night. The tax accountant's nightmare had come true again. Senior management liked the tax effects of the change in accounting method. If we adopted it this year, we could defer several million dollars in taxes and reduce our second quarter estimated payments by almost a million dollars. That was great for Lithium cash flow but it was terrible for the tax department.

Contrary to the perception of senior management, corporate tax software does not do all the hard work. Clark had thought the estimate was blessed and approved on Wednesday. He had set in motion all of the state and federal tax payments via electronic funds transfers on Thursday. Unfortunately late in the day management asked if it was too late to change the estimates. Clark being a team player said he would try.

Now we had to undo or cancel all the electronic payments in the pipeline, modify the estimate calculations and enter the adjustments at the federal and state level, calculate the new tax liability and resubmit all the electronic payments by 11:00 am Pacific Daylight Time, Monday.

If we worked hard and nothing went wrong, we hoped to be done on Saturday. That would allow Clark time to review the estimates on Sunday and submit the electronic payment Monday for settlement by the bank on Tuesday. Contrary to the movies, electronic funds transfers do not happen instantaneously. Each transaction has to be initiated one business day in advance. I got to work.

Sam abandoned me about half way through my first cup of coffee. I assumed he was making the most of the last premium days for sleeping in the sun outside. As for me, the only breaks I took were for lunch and dinner. I did not even consider looking at Karen's code before heading to bed.

Saturday I was back at it again first thing in the morning. By mid-morning, I was cursing myself. Preliminary results were not in line with what I expected. Somewhere along the line, I had entered an amount backwards, dropped a decimal point, or caused some basic accounting error that screwed up the estimate. Fortunately, it only took me three hours to find and fix.

Again, I was in no frame of mind to look at Karen's files after I sent my work papers to Clark early Saturday evening. I needed air and Sam followed me out into the back yard as to look at the sunset. Thin wisps of high clouds formed sun devils around the sinking sun. Sam rubbed my legs as I sat watching and waiting for the shadow to engulf my chair.

"Where do you think I should look Sam? There must be another file holding the key to the code. Maybe if I use the search function in the operating system to look for Zodiac signs or names of stars it will link me to the right file?"

The shadow was up to my lap and Sam jumped off to check out the dead azalea. Sam cheeked the branches and headed into the house.

The sun was finishing its descent into the arborvitae when I decided to follow Sam's lead. Tomorrow I would tackle Karen's files anew.

Sunday morning found me at the computer searching Karen's files. Three hours later and hundreds of searched terms yielded nothing new. I tried searching all the planets, then all eighty-eight constellations, and then I started with the brightest star names and worked my way dimmer. The first 93 second magnitude and brighter stars provided no hits. I was well into the 190 third magnitude stars list and decided this was a dead end.

I was alone in the office staring at the blank screen. It was better than staring at the last failed search results.

The last three days of stressful tax work and today's fruitless file search had me full of pent up energy. I needed some physical release. I struck out for the river at a quick pace, navigating the weekend daytime traffic with care. Reaching the river, I found that it failed to soothe my mind as it usually did. The silent waters moved relentlessly to the sea but there were no answers in the swirls and debris floating by.

Returning home, I headed to the back yard in hope of picking a tomato to eat with lunch. Ed was out in his garden pulling up corn stalks.

"Hi Ed, are you cleaning up the garden?"

"Hi Justin, yes this planting is pretty much done. It's too tough for me and the next planting is ready, so there is no reason to keep the stalks around."

I nodded in agreement. "You're making me feel guilty Ed. Here you are slaving away in your garden every day while I lounge around."

"I imagine you have other things to work on."

"Well, it has been a bit busy at Lithium. Income tax is a never ending cycle."

"I was hoping to pick your brain a bit. What plants do you think I should get to replace the azaleas?"

"Justin, something like the Shasta Daisy should grow good in that spot. I have fondness for Dahlias as you can see from my flowerbed, but there is more work in cutting old blooms than you may like. As for Lupines, they can be a little aggressive but they sure are pretty."

"But the first thing we need to do is get that soil tested. Something in the ground there is hard on plants. It will be easier to work in conditioners and adjust the Ph if the ground is open and tilled."

"Let me know and I will bring over my soil test kit. With proper treatment that soil should produce some good flowers."

"Thanks Ed. Need any help with the corn?"

"Nah, I am pretty much done."

I left the fence and checked out the tomato plants. Somehow, a few small tomatoes survived the deer and the lack of water and were now getting almost ripe.

I walked back to the house. Sam camped out under a dead azalea. No, I decided. It was time to get rid of Karen's plants. I was not sure where or why that thought surfaced in my mind. Now was time to purge my yard of an item belonging to Karen.

The soil worked by Karen earlier in the summer had dried out while I was away. The renewed watering helped but my shovel was not making as much progress as I liked.

The pickax was a much better tool for breaking and loosening the hard clay rich soil. Twenty minutes of vigorous picking and shoveling dirt into a pile got me an eight-foot oval trench around the two dead plants.

I used the pickax to pry the left bush free from the ground. I hoisted the fifty-pound plant and dirt ball and dropped it hard on the ground next to the dirt pile. My intent was to break up the dirt on the root ball before adding the remains to my compost pile.

I looked up to see Ed coming through the fence gate with something in his hand.

"I saw you digging and thought this would be a good time to test the soil."

Ed watched as I hoisted the second plant into the air to let fall next to the first.

"Justin, that plastic in the hole might be part of your problem. You may want to clean that out before putting in a new plant."

I turned from the dirt pile to check on Ed's comment. There in the hole, mostly covered with dirt was the corner of a clear plastic bag. I knelt down to reach into the hole and stopped.

"Ed, this is real important. Can you wait here while I make a quick phone call? Don't touch that bag. Just wait here. I will explain in a minute."

I ran into the house and dialed Richard's number.

"Good afternoon, this is Diane."

"Mrs. Cushing? This is Justin Caise, a client of Richard's, is he available?"

"No, he is sleeping. He was up late last night working. May I take a message?"

"This is very important. Could you please wake him and ask him to talk to me?"

"Well, what should I tell him?"

"Justin found the Rosetta Stone."

Chapter 59   Azaleas

I came out of the house, back to the hole.

Ed was carefully removing dirt with the shovel from around the plastic bag.

"Did you touch it Ed?"

"No Justin, I just scraped dirt off with the shovel. This has something to do with your wife's murder, doesn't it?"

"Yes Ed, I think this is the key to proving my innocence."

"Could I ask you to stay here with me while I wait for my investigator to arrive?"

"Sure thing, what do you think it is?"

It looked like a gallon zipper lock freezer storage bag. Inside was another similar bag folded over to fit inside the outer bag. Inside the inner bag was a rectangular package a little larger than a thick paperback book. The rectangular block wrapped in black plastic was sealed with clear two-inch wide tape.

Ed and I were speculating about the contents when Richard arrived twenty minutes later.

Richard stated by videotaping Ed holding the front page of the Sunday paper and having Ed make a statement about the events leading up to the discovery. I added my statement to the video and Richard handed the camera to me. He narrated how I notified him as to the possible discovery of new evidence. He extracted the package wearing blue evidence gloves and laid it on a strip of white butcher paper.

Richard opened the outer zipper bag, dropping the inner bag on the paper. The inner bag contained a black plastic rectangular brick about ten inches long, six wide and three inches thick. In addition, the bag contained four silicate pouches used to keep items dry when shipping.

Richard slit the bottom of the inner bag.

"I want to preserve any prints around the seal." Richard explained as the black brick slid onto the paper.

He examined the black package as it lay on the paper, then cut a slit exposing enough of the contents to see that the brick was made of money. We were looking at a ten-inch stack of hundred dollar bills.

"This is a good find Justin. But it's not what we needed. Let's see if there is anything else in the holes."

Richard and I took turns filming and sifting the dirt and expanding the holes in search of more evidence. There was nothing more. I was defeated. I picked up a dead plant to toss it on the compost pile.

"Justin, don't move."

Richard picked up the camera and began filming me. He handed off the camera to Ed, explained how to point and shoot then donned a new pair of blue evidence gloves. Carefully Richard extracted from the roots of the plant a six inch long rolled piece of plastic about an inch in diameter.

Unrolled the plastic became a sandwich sized zippered bag. Inside was another sandwich bag containing a small black plastic item about a half an inch wide and two inches long.

"Justin, this is the Rosetta Stone."

Richard wrapped everything in the butcher paper then called Anne's secret cell phone number. We were to be at her office at 7:00 AM tomorrow. He told me not to fill in the holes then left. I was too wound up to do nothing and too agitated to concentrate. I think I fell asleep about 4:00 AM.

Nevertheless, I was up early and beat Kari to the office by three minutes. She let me in so I could pace the floor waiting for Anne, Richard and Walter.

We met in the small conference room where Anne's computer expert Walter accessed the thumb drive "For purposes of ascertaining whether this drive was in fact evidence in an ongoing criminal case."

This data we could use.

Walter made a copy of the drive in Anne's computer; Richard placed the thumb drive in an evidence bag, sealed it with evidence tape and turned to Anne. "What next?"

Richard and I listened as Anne set out our plan.

"...last of all, I need to meet with the DA and convince him that working with us is in his best interest. If there is one thing I know about William James Armitage is that he always acts in his best interest."

"Can both of you be available on short notice this week?"

"Good. Let me see what I wheels I can get in motion."

I got back to the house about 9:30 collapsing into the couch to think. Sam found me and assumed his rightful place in my lap; I petted, he purred, I talked, he slept, I crashed.

The ringing phone woke me from my place on the couch. Could I be at Anne's office at 4:00?

In the next two hours, I reviewed the last few weeks of my life. I looked again at all the hours of planned and unplanned research and relived all the slow and sudden revelations about who Karen really was and what she was doing. I condensed it into a one-page outline then left for downtown.

Kari opened the conference room door: "...and if you had gone to real law school like U of W instead of the Lewis and Clark tree hugger school of law, I could get you a real job as a DDA."

Anne turned to me. The taunting had not appeared to faze her: "Justin, this is William J. Armitage, the Clark County District Attorney."

I did not offer to shake hands, mouthed "Hello," and moved

226

to sit at the far end and far side of the twelve-person conference table.

Anne picked up the slack in the conversation by announcing Richard's arrival.

Armitage grasped an opportunity. "Richard, it's good to see you again. The sheriff lost a good one when he let you retire. How is the PI business treating you? Good? I miss your stoic face in the witness box knocking the defense out of the park. I always counted on you to deliver first rate testimony at trial."

Richard accepted the compliment with a hint of grin and a slight nod of acknowledgement. I watched in awe seeing this political animal in action. His ability to schmooze and glad hand in any situation was amazing.

"Bill, officially this is an off the record hypothetical discussion. If this were an actual discussion of a real situation, it would be of great interest to a district attorney, either locally or in Multnomah County.

"Is that so?" Armitage said.

"Also, it is reasonable to speculate that such a hypothetical situation might well be of federal interest. I would hate to see some headline grabbing DA from Oregon take credit for all the great prosecutorial work done in another state, hypothetically, so to speak."

"My client, Mr. Caise has found himself with some excess time on his hands and has developed a theory." Anne said.

Something compelled me to stand. I did not want to talk to Armitage, so I spoke to Anne: "It all started when I was doing research on investment tax credits. My company is developing a lithium battery suitable for use on aircraft, which led me into the FAA rules for manufacturing aircraft parts. Further, that led to research into the FAA rules regarding the parts identification process that insures the integrity of the parts that go on aircraft."

Armitage interrupted, "That's all very interesting, I had several law school classmates who ended up in aerospace, both industry and government, but where is this going?"

"I am an accountant, Mr. Armitage. I understand the need for good internal controls and the importance of sound systems in maintaining the integrity of the accounting records. In many ways, the FAA has the same need for internal controls and robust systems that ensure the proper conduct by everyone involved in aviation. What I have discovered in my research is that the FAA relies on antiquated procedures that provide opportunity for unscrupulous people to bypass FAA safeguards. I believe that there exists the potential for disaster and even loss of life. Deficiencies that are so severe that I think that substandard and counterfeit aviation parts have entered the system in meaningful numbers."

"Well, I would say that this is a federal matter, best handled by the FAA or possibly the FBI." Armitage said.

Anne interjected: "Bill, I think you want to hear this."

"Imagine a pilot working for an airline. Unhappy, unappreciated, overworked, underpaid, and in a word, disgruntled. Maybe there is a senior technician working for the same airline, always a little short on money. Our technician works every day with expensive avionics. Many of which are small enough to fit in a lunch box."

"What if our unhappy pilot and our technician in need of money see weaknesses in the FAA protocols? Such as the FAA's reliance on handwritten documents to track parts, or their faith in the assurance of technicians that parts are fit for use, and their dependence on people voluntarily reporting irregularities. Such an environment is an irresistible opportunity to someone looking only for financial gain."

"As you said Mr. Caise, this appears to be an internal control issue, one for the airlines and the FAA. It would only be of interest to my department if it involved theft or fraud and it happened in Clark County. As far as I know there are no problems at Pearson Field."

"That you know of. Do you know if anyone is looking?"

I did not wait for an answer or give Armitage a chance to reply.

"As I was saying, an unscrupulous technician could exploit these weaknesses and substitute fake parts for authentic parts?"

"I find it hard to believe the FAA is asleep at the wheel. If this is a problem, I am sure the industry is addressing this and the FAA has all kinds of rules and procedures to prevent that from happening. After all, neither the industry nor the FAA wants their planes falling out of the sky," said Armitage.

I resumed my argument. "You're right the airlines don't want lawsuits nor do they want to scare the public. However, in this case good engineering and safe aircraft design allows them to hide from the issue. Many aircraft parts are important but not critical and the crucial systems are redundant, making a single part failure unlikely to be catastrophic. If an incident does not generate publicity, the airlines have incentive to treat a problem part as a routine failure to avoid fallout from both the FAA and the public. How often have we seen industry or the government take action only as the result of a problem too big to ignore?"

"Whether industry acts or not is not my concern. Why am I here and where is this going Anne?" Said Armitage

"Bill, if you let him speak for a minute you'll find out. However, maybe you're not interested. I could give Sue Ellen a call at Multnomah County; I think she has her eye on the US District Court."

"Regardless, Sue has a great eye for what makes a good news story. Maybe she learned that from that radio talk show host. Bill, you must have heard the guest spot she does on his show about crime in Portland. I wonder what she could do with a story with national implications." Anne said.

Armitage mulled this over giving me a chance to resume. "My training and your experience show that almost any protocol fails in this scenario. When two or more people conspire, they can circumvent most security procedures. Therefore, it is not unreasonable that three people can scheme to conceal the removal and substitution of counterfeit electronics in commercial aircraft?"

"It still sounds like a problem for the FAA. The local DA has no expertise to deal with such a scenario," Armitage said.

I countered. "That may be true. If you bear with me, you will see how it might also be of interest to a local DA. I'm sure this is a scenario that you have seen before, Mr. Armitage."

"Assume there is such a band of counterfeiters. One conspirator likes to gamble. He pushes the others to install more parts more often. Then one partner gets cold feet, such as the pilot who flies planes on which she knows use substandard parts?"

"'Sure I have prosecuted cases like that. There is no honor among thieves, Mr. Caise. One party turns state's evidence on the others, and they all go down. It's just that some go down harder than others." Armitage said.

"So you agree that my scenario is within in the realm of possibility?"

"Of course, and winning the lottery is within the realm of possibility, what's your point Caise?" Armitage said.

"Mr. Armitage, I'll bet you've won convictions with witnesses like this. As you said, there is no honor among thieves. Suspicions mount, the members of the group lose their trust in each other and someone decides to keep records of the transactions. Their motivation may be good bookkeeping, getting their fair share or maybe they think they need an insurance policy. If this person is paranoid, she keeps the records in code." I said.

Armitage glared at Anne. "Conspiracies, codes, this sounds like the plot from a bad movie." Armitage said.

I pushed on. "What do you see Mr. Armitage?"

"Anne, where is this going?" Armitage said.

"Humor him Bill, you might learn something." Anne said.

"It looks like some type of coordinate, a partial compass reference, or a longitude coordinate and a Zodiac sign." Armitage said.

"I see $1828.95 and a cross reference to the transaction detail. Here let me show you." I said.

I used the mouse to open up my spreadsheet.

"See the how the amounts translate and total? Then there is the transaction detail: The planet indicates the physical location of the transaction. The star is a unique transaction identifier. The details are in a separate document linked by the star name. The details include the aircraft tail number, the part installed or removed, and the serial number of the part."

I pressed on: "the zodiac sign serves two purposes, identification of partner and type of transaction. The signs Aries, Leo, Scorpio and Capricorn all indicate people. The sign Gemini is used to indicate a purchase or a sale of a part."

"It's a three part code. All the pieces are required to for anyone to interpret a transaction. Someone seeing one or two of the three documents effectively knows nothing."

"Again Mr. Caise, this is all very interesting, but still a matter for the FAA, not me." Armitage said.

"If it stopped here I would agree. What happens if the person with cold feet makes a mistake? What if she tells one of the others of her concerns, or she makes a suggestion that it's time to quit, or that she says she wants out? What happens then, Mr. Armitage?" I said.

Anne jumped in. "You know what happens, Bill. Someone panics and does something stupid."

I paused to let Anne's comment sink in, almost giving Armitage a chance to speak.

I continued, "Let's suppose our technician works at a local airport, like PDX. While the pilot in our group lives conveniently close to the airport, just off the freeway on the other side of the river. It is so convenient for the pilot that it takes less than ten minutes to drive to PDX to catch those early morning flights."

"Then again, someone working graveyard shift could take lunch, say at three in the morning, leave PDX, visit the victim, and be back at work without being missed." I said.

"Forgive me Mr. Caise but aren't you overlooking one minor detail? Everyone working at PDX wears a badge that is recorded in the Access Control System every time someone enterers a secure area on the airport. I learned all about airport security at a seminar dealing with TSA and Airport police. How did our hypothetical technician leave and return to a secure facility without being noticed?" Armitage said.

"I think Richard can best answer that question." I said.

Richard followed my example and stood.

"I think Justin has done a good job of laying out the players. And to answer your question, the security system plays an important role in our hypothetical scenario."

"The three of us discussed PDX security in this very room. The Port of Portland helpfully provides a map of the airport that indicates the boundaries between the unrestricted civilian side, the land side, and the restricted access of the airside." Richard said.

Anne used the mouse to bring up the display of the map on the large monitor.

"I was sitting about where Mr. Armitage is now when I saw the map. We have all flown out of PDX and driven on Airport Way to get to the terminal. What is not obvious from a car is that all the buildings provide direct access between Airport Way and the physical airport. Literally one can walk in the street side and walk out the airport side of these buildings." Richard said.

"Richard, the airport is well aware of these access points. The Airport Authority makes all vendors file security plans showing compliance. Every airport employee for the port or any vendor is bound by the 'Responsibility to Challenge' protocol. A person not showing ID in the SIDA will be challenged as to their authorization and purpose on the airport. Nobody is going to walk off the street into a warehouse and onto the airport. Anne, I do not see the point of this geography exercise." Armitage said.

"Bill, it's just a hypothetical example. It's not like you have a major case that could fall apart from information like this." It was hard to tell for sure but Anne sure seemed to be enjoying Armitage's agitated state.

Richard resumed. "The point of this geography lesson is to show that there is one area on the airport where the public has physical access to the airport inside the fence that is not covered by the Access Control System."

"Like I said, I was sitting in your chair and got a very good look at the airport map. Please note the location of Columbia Flight Center, just southeast of the terminal."

A red laser dot appeared and circled three small buildings.

"The colors used on the map make it difficult to see. Note that the green landside area includes Columbia Flight Center, the Fixed Base Operator, which is inside the perimeter fence. The public can walk in off the street through the FBO and onto the airport. Once a person is inside the fence they have full access to the entire airport." Richard said.

"So, the FBO is not going to let just anyone walk in off the street and onto the airport. All FBO employees have a 'Responsibility to Challenge' obligation for any unescorted person. It's part of their vendor compliance plan with the Airport Authority." Armitage said.

"I agree completely. The thing is that our hypothetical technician is not 'just anyone.' I looked at the airport rules. The FBO is required to guard against access by unauthorized persons. However, our technician is an authorized person, who carries a badge allowing him access to secure areas of the airport. When properly challenged he can properly respond with an ID badge and authorization." Richard said.

"Just because someone has a badge does not mean that the FBO employees are going to let him wander around at will." Armitage said.

"My sentiments exactly, Columbia Flight Center has a good reputation and has had no issues with the Port Authority regarding security. What if, to settle my hypothetical curiosity, I spent the last few nights talking to people who work at Columbia Flight Center?" Richard said.

"I'd say you have an overactive imagination Richard." Armitage said.

"Maybe our hypothetical technician is a gregarious guy who likes to chat. Periodically, when business is slow, he walks down the ramp and visits with the night crew at Columbia Flight Center. Now, not only is he properly credentialed and authorized, he is a well-known visitor. What if on occasion this hypothetical technician leaves the airport through the FBO to visit his girlfriend? What if the ramp agent thinks he is just helping the technician get one over on the boss? How could the ramp agent do anything wrong by allowing someone holding a higher security clearance than he to enter or leave?" Richard said.

"Assuming your hypothetical scenario, a person could leave the airport for any number of legitimate legal reasons, as well as many illegal reasons which have no bearing on any real or hypothetical case I am working. Even if your person was smoking dope or getting a drink, this is still a matter for the airline and the FAA not me." Armitage said.

Richard was grinning again. "Out of curiosity, did anyone check the Midfield Security Checkpoints for the comings and goings of a hypothetical technician? If I had been investigating a crime, I probably would not have bothered checking the records. After all, what could be proved by the comings and goings of someone on the airport who was already on the airport? It would just show when they returned to one secure area from another secure area." Richard said.

"Anne, are you going to present something of substance or are we going to speculate on increasingly convoluted hypotheticals. Is there any solid evidence that places this hypothetical killer in proximity to the hypothetical victim?" Armitage said.

"Would you consider something the cat dragged in to be solid?" Anne said.

"Anne, I don't have time for wild speculation or jokes at my expense." Armitage said.

Richard saved Anne from having to respond.

"I have investigated a lot of crimes and learned early on to follow the evidence where it leads and not make premature conclusions. Such as, what was the murder weapon? It is easy to believe the most available weapon was the weapon used. After all, things like ligature marks usually point to the murder weapon. Nevertheless, while ligature marks are good for gross classifications, they can mislead when fine details matter. For example, a garden hose textured in a manner similar to a nylon strap of similar width could leave grossly similar ligature marks. It would be easy to conclude that the item found at the crime scene was used."

"Richard, please spare me the 'Basics of Evidence' lecture and get to the point."

Richard ignored Armitage's barb and continued. "What if our technician called for a meeting, a meeting to convince the pilot not to turn on the gang? It is easy to see how such a meeting can go wrong. The pilot has already made the tough choice to quit. The Technician is desperate, his money supply in jeopardy. Upon meeting with the pilot he gets mad or panics or both and pulls off his lanyard and strangles his weaker, smaller partner. As she collapses to the ground, the technician realizes what he has done and flees. Losing or intentionally dropping the lanyard as he flees back to the airport to secure his alibi."

"Richard, I am familiar with the airport. It's a long walk to employee parking and the shuttle busses run infrequently at that time of night. Under the best of scenarios, your killer could not make this trip in anything less than an hour."

"Bill, that's what I was thinking too, if our killer used employee parking."

"Let me guess; now you are going to tell me that you have hypothetical security video of our technician coming and going from short term parking."

"Now Bill, anyone who understands airport security and ID badge tracking will not be tripped up by common security video. That got me thinking, if I needed easy access parking without any records, or at least obvious records an investigator would seek, where could I park?" Richard said.

"I don't know but I am sure you'll tell me."

"Most of the airport vendors have gated entry, excluding Columbia Air Center and the hotels on Airport Way. I wonder if our technician might have slipped a few bucks to the night manager at the hotel next door to the FBO. Just a thought I had."

Richard was grinning more as he added that last jab.

Armitage growled. "Richard, hypothetically you would not layout these details if you had not confirmed them as fact. Nor would you mention the existence of an alternate murder weapon if you were not sitting on it."

"Bill, I am shocked, shocked I say." Anne said in a bad Claude Rains imitation.

"You know I would never withhold evidence, even hypothetical evidence. As soon as I had confirmed that such matter was in fact evidence in a crime under investigation, it is my duty as an officer of the court to turn over such evidence to the proper authorities."

"Right."

Richard resumed control. "As I was saying, what if a lanyard was discovered? Say by a cat. And, this material was provided to a hypothetical qualified laboratory for testing to see if DNA was present. And by coincidence our technician provided a sample for testing at the same time."

"Anne, we need to talk." Armitage said.

Chapter 62   New Normal

Sitting in my office, I was, in theory working on Lithium projects, in reality I was surfing the internet reading about my case. Sam listened intently to my out-loud musings, though he chose to do so with eyes closed in the Sphinx position on the desk.

"Sam, even though I despise him I have to admire his political genius. Do you think Armitage writes his own press releases or does his staff?"

Sam's left ear twitched.

"I agree he makes his staff write them. This is unbelievable. You would think by the news stories that he personally led his crack team of investigators in sifting through the evidence day and night, building the case for months. But we know better, don't we, Sam?"

Sam's right ear twitched in agreement.

"You have to admire how he is milking this for all its worth. Getting good press coverage in both Portland and Vancouver I expected. Making the news San Francisco and Seattle that was brilliant. I wonder if he pulled in some favors in the Washington State Patrol to get such good cooperation with the Oregon State Police. The way he implied that this was a coordinated multi-agency action across state lines spearheaded by him almost made me gag."

Sam shared my indignation listening in stunned silence.

"It was amusing to see the Multnomah County DA tripping all over herself to cooperate with the investigation and expediting Carlos' extradition proceeding."

Sam patiently waited in silence for me to continue.

"William James Armitage has a great sense of timing. I would have arrested both brothers at the same time to prevent the other brother from fleeing. Instead, he gets top billing for two news cycles by waiting a day to arrest Rafael. Although, Anne does not think the accessory to murder charge will stick, I am sure Armitage will be happy to release him into the arms of the FBI after the media moves onto a new story."

"Sam, do you think he overplayed the case by holding that news conference at Boeing Field yesterday? Only a man like Armitage would fly up to Renton, the rest of us would drive a car."

The increased volume in my voice prompted Sam to crack open one eye.

"Armitage had no reason to hand deliver the Form 8120-11, Suspected Unapproved Parts Report, directly to the Northwest Mountain Regional Director of the FAA Security and Hazardous

Materials Division? You would think the FAA had at least one functioning fax machine."

Sam's ears twitched as the Form 8120-11 hit the desk; the form that I prepared from Karen's records; the form that I handed over to Armitage; the form that he was now waving at photo ops and taking all the credit.

Sam twitched his tail.

"I know Sam. Anne warned me. Armitage's first priority is Armitage. I should not be surprised that he is showing all the markings of a political animal. Nevertheless, holding that press conference at Boeing Field with all the aircraft in the background was a bit much, even if it was effective.   Nothing says competency like a politician who provides a good backdrop that proves he knows his subject."

Both of Sam's ears twitched.

"Anyway isn't it nice to know it's safe to fly again, now that Armitage is humbly doing his part to make the system more secure. I'll bet the FAA is overjoyed to know that he will gladly cooperate with the FAA's and meekly offered to assist in the federal prosecution. Thus bringing the parts case to a conclusion."

Sam yawned.

"Best of all Sam, it is over. Armitage joined Anne's request for the judge to dismiss my case with prejudice Monday. Now here I sit with a copy of the dismissal in hand. Should I frame it?"

Sam did nothing.

I checked the time and decided I was ready to go see Anne.

Late Friday afternoon her office was quiet. I imagine any attorney that could, was already gone. Anne came out to meet me personally a couple of minutes before our scheduled 4:30 appointment.

"Justin, it's good to see you. Are you enjoying the fact that you now free and clear?"

"I guess."

"Come, let's talk for a minute."

I settled into the unpadded client chair across from Anne.

"You don't look happy Justin."

"I'm not Anne. I thought there would be this great relief and everything would be wonderful. It was, for a little while, but it didn't last. Now there isn't anything, just emptiness."

"Justin, I am not going to tell you it will all be OK and everything will soon be back to normal. Everything is not OK and the normal you knew before Karen died is never coming back."

"I am not a shrink, but it is my legal advice that you see one."

"You have been under incredible stress for weeks. Now that it's gone, there is nothing to fill the void. I am not saying you are crazy. You're not. What I am saying is that your life has changed forever. You will not, and cannot, look at your life the same way ever again. Most of my clients are guilty and deep down they know they deserve the attention of the justice system."

"You are not one of those clients. You did nothing to deserve the abuse the system heaped upon you. You have a right to be angry."

"I am angry, at Armitage?"

"He is not the issue Justin. The best comparison I can think of is surviving cancer. There is nothing fair about who does or does not get cancer. All a person can do is fight. Nevertheless, it is a fight requiring you to look death square in the face day after day. No one survives a fight with cancer and without being affected."

"No one can be the subject of an investigation like yours and not be affected either. Until someone has experienced the emotional trauma that defendants, and their attorneys, go through, they will not understand how you could be unhappy on what should be a joyous day."

"The advantage cancer survivors have over you is that they have support groups. Unfortunately for you, I have never heard of any 'I just got exonerated' support groups. Getting some professional help as soon as possible is your best route back to a normal life."

"One more piece of advice, then I will shut up."

Anne was silent as she looked at me for several seconds.

"Justin, I am, and I have been treated for clinical depression. After learning how to recognize my depression the best piece of advice I got was this: Never make permanent decisions when you are depressed."

"Justin that emptiness you feel may well be depression fighting to take over your life. If that is correct, now is not the time to make any irrevocable decisions."

"Thank you for sharing that, Anne. I don't want to admit it, but I know you are right. A grown man should not be holding serious conversations with his cat. I'll look into getting some help and support."

"Good, it may not feel like it now, but your life will return to normal. It's just that your new normal will be different from your old normal."

Anne slid an envelope across the desk to me.

"Justin, there are a couple of house cleaning items and then you can say goodbye to me forever."

"The check is for the balance of unexpended funds. I only managed to spend about thirty. Don't let word get out that I didn't burn through your whole retainer. My colleagues might think I am losing my touch." Anne added with a smile.

"That form needs to be presented to the clerk of court along with a copy of your case dismissal."

"OK, what's it for?"

"Oh sorry, it is to recover your bail bond. Unfortunately the county keeps 15% as an administrative service charge, but it's still about $25,000."

"Thanks Anne. I had forgotten about that."

"Any plans for the rest of the money Justin?"

"What money? I thought Armitage got the two hundred thousand we dug up."

"Yes the State and Clark County keep that and the money from the car. Money obtained in illegal activities, whether drugs or counterfeit parts, is seized by the government. Since we have no proof that the funds were obtained legally by you, we have no basis for a civil suit to force their return." Anne said.

"I figured I would not get to keep Karen's money. At least the bail refund will pay off the income taxes due on my IRA withdrawal. That is a big setback for my retirement plan."

Anne was smiling a bit more. "Justin, if there is one thing that separates a good attorney from the rest of the pack it's her ability to make sure she gets paid."

"Even after that interesting start at your bail hearing, I believed that you were innocent. I knew it would be a long, hard, expensive battle costing far more than the retainer you gave me to start. I had a real incentive to clear your name. The life insurance company would only pay off on Karen's policy if you were declared innocent."

"I sent off a copy of your case dismissal to the life insurance company this morning. You should have a check for half a million dollars in a couple of weeks or less." Anne said.

"I don't know what to say Anne."

"Justin, it was one of the things that had me concerned, and why I wanted to talk. A depressed person getting a huge windfall could easily end up as a depressed drunk, or worse."

Anne was right. There were a few too many empty bottles in the recycling bin than were good for me. I changed the subject.

"I have to give it to the DA. He may be able to ride this all the way to Olympia. Do those reporters really believe him? I mean, I thought it was over the top what he told them after my dismissal hearing."

I stuck out my chin and deepened my voice: "As district attorney I am more interested in seeing justice done than racking up convictions."

Anne smiled. "Reporters like a politician who gives them a good quote. It makes their job easier. Bill knows if he makes their job easier, they are more likely to go easier on him."

"One final question, I know that attorney's and DA's make deals to settle cases. Aren't these meetings usually just between the two attorneys? I was surprised that you had Richard and I do the presentation."

"Yes Justin, but this was an unusual case. I have never had a client who was also my expert witness. You lived the investigation and put all the pieces together. I had to show Bill that if I had to put you on the stand you could hold your own. It made him a little more receptive to the obvious. In reality Justin, I do not know if I would have put you on the stand. It is the last thing that any attorney wants to do."

"But we are never going to have to face that dilemma, are we?"

"No, I certainly plan not to."

"One more final question Anne, then I promise I will let you go."

"Do you know why Karen married me?"

"I am sorry Justin, I wish I knew."

I was checking the engine oil when my cell phone rang.

"Justin, Mary Ellen Simmons from Lithium, I have the COBRA health care forms you wanted. Are you sure you won't change your mind?"

"No, this is the right thing for me to do. I talked this through with my therapist and he is comfortable that I am acting rationally. I will still be in the area. Maybe there will be some per diem work in a few months, how about I check in with you when I get back?

"Well then Justin, you take care and drive safely."

I was finishing my departure check on my newly acquired used motor home when Richard Cushing called an hour later.

"Justin, I followed up on the questions you asked. I was able to contact some people with access to the records. You heard that Carlos agreed to plead guilty. The DA threatened him with the death penalty under the 'Aggravated First Degree Murder" statute because he killed her to 'conceal the commission of a crime.' Carlos spilled his guts on everything to avoid capital punishment."

"The night of her murder, he called Karen from a disposable phone saying he had to meet her. They argued about her getting out of the counterfeit ring. Karen threatened to expose him using information stored on a thumb drive. Carlos was in a panic, he fought with her to get the thumb drive and claims he did not mean to kill her. He threw the thumb drive off the Glenn Jackson Bridge while on his way back to the airport." Richard said.

"What about the lanyard Richard?"

"He did not realize he had lost his lanyard until retrieving his badge from his buddy at Columbia Flight Center. To make sure he was not tracked by unknown IFRD readers he always left his badge at the FBO." Richard said.

"I wondered why we never found the ID card and the Port or Portland never issued a replacement."

"Yes, Carlos was thorough in planning but panicked after the attack. He was already inside the airport when he realized that he still had the disposable phone on him. Afraid of getting caught with the phone and he turned it into PDX airport lost and found, saying he found it on a plane. The police did not think to check the lost and found for evidence because they never suspected Carlos."

"What about the apartment?" I asked.

"Carlos caught a jump seat on another airline with a direct

flight from Portland to Houston. A direct flight takes less than five hours so he had time to clean out Karen's apartment before the police knew about it. He caught an afternoon flight back to Portland in time to make it to work. The police had only a casual interest in Carlos so they did not notice he was gone for about 15 hours. Carlos realized his affair with Karen would be discovered. He hoped by cleaning the apartment of his stuff, he could pass off his relationship with Karen as a casual fling rather than a long-term relationship."

"Who was the partner in Mexico?"

"Jose Lopez married Carlos' sister Louisa Torres. Jose is also an avionics technician for VAA. He removed good parts and installed bogus parts for the return flight to Portland. It is believed that Jose Lopez ended up in Columbia with Louisa Torres. Rafael called Louisa the day Carlos was arrested. Jose disappeared before the Cancun police could pick him up. He took a big chunk of money with him."

"What about Karen?"

"Justin, maybe I should come over?"

"Richard, I'll be fine. It's just the final piece in the puzzle that I need to put this all behind me."

"OK, Carlos told the police everything about their parts scheme. Karen was much more constrained about adding parts into the system. Carlos wanted more money faster."

'Why am I not surprised?"

"About three years into the scam, Carlos formed a plan for one really big score. A deal that could make enough money for all of them to retire. The problem was it would take months, maybe years, to set in place and then ripen. Karen was the key to the plan."

"The plan involved helping one of the drug gangs in Mexico. There is a problem being a crime lord. While it is fun and exciting when you are young, what do you do when you want to retire? It may be possible to pass on the crime business to an heir, but the police are not about to forgive and forget."

"Karen's part in the plan was to recruit and marry a man. A man who was not too old, without close family, and who would not be greatly missed if he faded quietly into retirement."

"By that I mean, at the right time your HR manager would get a letter stating you had to quit for personal reasons or some family emergency. Sometime later Justin Caise would reappear as a quiet retiree in some other state."

"The problem being, that in reality, you are now dead. In your place is a retired crime lord reborn as you. He can now continue your life, engage in legitimate activities, and carry on as a typical upstanding citizen."

"It is the ultimate in identity theft. That is why Karen married you."

Richard filled the expanding silence: "I am sorry Justin."

"Don't be sorry Richard. I wanted to know, I had to know, even though I knew that the reason would not be good. Not knowing why she married me was gnawing at my soul. Now I am truly free from Karen."

"Justin, if it's any consolation, she couldn't go through with it. Karen retained enough conscience and felt enough for you that she could not let Carlos kill you. Her refusal was a problem with her and Carlos."

The realization of what Richard was telling me entered my mind, expanding to push out all other thoughts out of my head.

"Justin, talk to me."

"Thanks Richard, that is nice to know."

"Say again, Justin?"

"I mean, thank you. I mean, Richard what I am trying to say is I appreciate that you were able to find out for me. I didn't think I could be shocked by Karen's motives, but it's unnerving knowing that I was just another expendable part." Hold on there is someone at the door."

"Hi Justin, may I come in?"

"Richard, you said you weren't coming over."

"My gut told me I should."

The shock deflated in relationship to my growing appreciation for Richard's gut.

"Well I'm glad you are here."

"Justin, It's bad enough to learn a woman has been using you, but this is in a class of its own. It's not a piece of news to hear when you're alone. I make most people meet me at my office when I have to deliver shocking news. However, I figured that anyone who could go toe to toe with the man trying to put him away for life could handle some surprising news in his own house."

"Thanks for the vote of confidence. Of course, you're right about Karen too. It is a big deal that she would not let Carlos kill me. Of all the things, I didn't know about Karen I guess that was the most important. "

Justin, are you still taking off on your world tour?"

"I would hardly call the southwestern United States a world tour. I am going to take a few months and not spend a winter in the rain and snow for once."

"You are a little young to be a snowbird. What are you planning to do? Did you bring your folding rocking chair to fit in with the RV crowd?

I am not retiring Richard. The income off the life insurance will not support me for the rest of my life if I don't let it grow for a couple of years. But if I am frugal it will provide most of my support so I can write my book."

"Not many people expect accountants to write books, good luck. Let me know when it comes out."

"On the other hand, maybe I will find some temporary work as I travel about, low stress, just enough to cover my expenses. After all, I could just work the tax season and relax the rest of the year. All those RV nomads need their taxes done too."

"To many people only working the tax season would be the perfect job."

I talked it over with my therapist; I am avoiding the traditional path and leaving on an adventure. Many people do it when they graduate college; Sam and I are just starting a few years later."

"I have never heard of someone traveling with a cat. My dogs love to ride in my truck. I have not heard that about cats."

"We have it figured out Richard. I have my pop up screened gazebo for Sam and me and the finest in RV cat furniture. I think Sam will do fine."

"Good luck, Justin. If you get bored doing taxes you can get your private investigator license, you seem to have a knack for the job."

"Richard, no offence, but I have no desire to do high stakes investigation work again. I consider that part of my life, case closed."

Patrick McGinty is a full time tax accountant and a part time writer. Cats George, Nelson and Xena share their house with him in Oregon When not writing he is active in Toastmasters.

Look for other works from *Magnolia Epublishing* on Amazon and Google